Mystery at the Inn

Mystery at the Inn

CAROLYNE AARSEN

Guideposts

New York, New York

Mystery at the Inn

ISBN-13: 978-0-8249-4825-2

Published by Guideposts
16 East 34th Street
New York, New York 10016
www.guideposts.org

Distributed by Ideals Publications, a Guideposts company
2630 Elm Hill Pike, Suite 100
Nashville, TN 37214

Guideposts, Ideals and Tales from Grace Chapel Inn are registered trademarks of Guideposts.

The characters and events in this book are fictional, and any resemblance to actual persons or events is coincidental.

All Scripture quotations are taken from *The Holy Bible, New International Version*. Copyright © 1973, 1978, 1984 International Bible Society. Used by permission of Zondervan Bible Publishers.

Library of Congress Cataloging-in-Publication Data

Aarsen, Carolyne.
    Mystery at the Inn / Carolyne Aarsen.
        p. cm. — (Tales from Grace Chapel Inn)
    ISBN 978-0-8249-4825-2
    1. Bed and breakfast accommodations—Fiction.   2. Pennsylvania—Fiction.   I. Title.
    PR9199.3.A14M97 2010
    813´.54—dc22

                                                                    2010006719

Cover by Deborah Chabrian
Design by Marisa Jackson
Typeset by Aptara

Printed and bound in the United States of America

10 9 8 7 6 5 4 3 2

Acknowledgments

Thank you to Leo Grant, who makes me laugh while making me a better writer.

—Carolyne Aarsen

GRACE CHAPEL INN

A place where one can be
refreshed and encouraged,
a place of hope and healing,
a place where God is at home.

Mystery at the Inn

Chapter One

*J*ane Howard brushed the dirt off her old, worn blue jeans and stretched her arms above her head as she looked over her garden plot. During the past few weeks, the garden's bounty had been gathered, canned, frozen, preserved, jammed and jellied. The remains of orderly rows of vegetables had been turned under. On this Tuesday in early October, except for the pumpkin patch, the garden was an area of dark brown earth waiting for the snow to cover it until spring.

A faint breeze teased strands of Jane's dark hair loose from its ponytail, swirled around her, then leapt up to the trees surrounding the garden, tugging brightly colored leaves from the branches. The first of fall's patches of red, gold and orange spun down, flashing in the sun and scattering over the rich loam of the garden.

"Thank You, Lord, for bounty and harvest, for seasons of planting and growing and taking in," Jane prayed as she set down another pumpkin, still warm from the sun, in her wooden basket. "And please help me figure out what I'm supposed to do with the rest of these pumpkins."

A feeling of dismay settled over Jane as she surveyed the twisting, verdant pumpkin patch with its pumpkins of all sizes and colors, varying from deep green to bright orange.

All of Jane's plantings had grown in abundance, but the pumpkins outgrew all the others, taking over the end of the garden and providing a harvest that would challenge the hardiest of gardeners.

Jane had nurtured these plants from seedlings, visions of pumpkin pies and jack-o'-lanterns spurring her on. She weeded, fertilized, trained and sang to these plants, and now she saw that her efforts were successful. A tiny part of Jane urged her to use what she could and throw away the rest, but Jane was a cook as well as a gardener, and the memory of throwing away produce in the fall, she knew, would haunt her all winter. Come February she would remember these luscious, beautiful pumpkins and wish she had not taken them for granted.

So she picked and cut and baked and preserved, but each morning she felt as if she had barely made a dent in the patch.

A quick glance at her watch showed her that she had to get going, for she had pumpkin muffins baking in the oven. So she picked up her basket and hurried as fast as her burden would allow her to the back door of the inn.

"More pumpkins?" Louise asked from her seat at the kitchen table, looking over her eyeglasses at Jane, who set the basket of pumpkins on the kitchen floor.

"This is only a small part of what is still out there." Jane slipped on a pair of oven mitts, then drew a tray of freshly baked muffins out of the oven just as the timer started its insistent beeping. She set them on the butcher-block counter to cool. The cozy scents of cinnamon and clove filled the kitchen.

"Goodness, you must have enough pumpkins to keep all of Acorn Hill in jack-o'-lanterns and pumpkin pie. How did you end up with so many?" asked Louise, ever the practical sister.

"It all started out so innocently," Jane said, leaning on the counter, slipping the oven mitts off her hands. "A single package of seeds. So tiny. So harmless. This spring they looked so lost and forlorn in the palm of my hand that I almost hated to commit them to the dark, cold ground." Jane held out her hand as if to demonstrate, then pointed at the basket with a dramatic flourish. "And now look. They have taken over my garden and my life."

"Indeed," said Louise with a dry tone. She took off her glasses and let them dangle from their chain around her neck. "So with all this bounty, am I to surmise that pumpkin muffins will be a regular feature on our guests' menu for the duration of the season?"

"Your surmise is correct. Pumpkin muffins and pumpkin pie, pumpkin loaf, pumpkin jam, pumpkin tarts, pumpkin bars, pumpkin pumpkin. I'm going to have to go on the

Internet and search for some interesting and unique recipes to prepare for the freezer." Jane frowned at the challenging fruits as she absently flapped her oven mitts together. "At least I can use up most of the larger ones around Halloween. They will spruce up the front porch."

"Did we decide if we are going to do anything special for our guests who will be staying over the weekend before Halloween?" Louise asked, setting down the music book she held. A piano student was coming after school, and he had asked Louise to find an easier piece to work on.

"I'm not sure. Alice and I exchanged a few ideas, but we didn't come up with anything concrete. It's still three weeks away, so we have time."

"It would be fun to do something special, though I'm not sure either what we could do."

"Not sure you want to wear pancake makeup and dress up as a witch? We could dye that beautiful silver hair of yours and put some black gum on your teeth," Jane said with a twinkle in her eye. Her teasing netted a disapproving look from the proper Louise.

"I can hardly imagine that it would be appropriate," Louise said primly.

"I can hardly imagine you giving up your sweater set and pearls for a raggle-taggle black gown and a pointy hat."

"Whereas I can easily imagine you as a gypsy," Louise replied.

Jane glanced down at the bright purple peasant top she had tucked into her blue jeans. It was decorated with wild, colorful embroidery and silver discs. She had found it at a secondhand store and immediately fell in love with it. Her sisters often teased her about her unconventional clothing, but she didn't care. The artist in her was always looking for ways to express herself. Clothing was one of them. "How about Bohemian Jane, Queen of the Pumpkins?"

"At any rate, it is difficult to find something special to offer our guests in keeping with the season and yet maintain an air of decorum." Louise returned her glasses to her nose and looked at her music book again as if closing that subject.

"Still, it would be fun to offer something. I wish I knew what, beyond decorations," Jane said wistfully.

The back door of the kitchen opened, and their sister Alice stepped in. Her cheeks were flushed, and her brown eyes fairly snapped with energy.

"Did something unexpected come up at the hospital to make you look so flustered?" Louise asked.

"No. Well, maybe." Alice fluffed out her reddish brown hair, then sat in the nearest chair and set down a sheaf of papers clutched in her hand. "I couldn't wait to share this with you."

Jane glanced at the papers. "Let's see. Flushed cheeks, flustered sister. I'm guessing . . . a letter from someone important perhaps? A dashing gentleman who goes by the name of Mark Graves?"

"No, not at all, it's something else," Alice said with a light laugh, dismissing Jane's gentle teasing about her good friend. "I met a fascinating woman today after work." She pointed at the papers with a flourish. "And because of it, I have come up with an idea for Halloween weekend."

"That's interesting. Jane is drawing a blank on that topic," Louise said, angling a smile toward her youngest sister.

Jane wrinkled her nose. "Before you spill what is obviously bubbling inside of you, would you like some tea with some pumpkin-spice muffins? The first of the deluge?"

"Deluge?" Alice asked with a frown.

"Our garden has produced prodigiously, which means I will be finding new and creative ways to use our pumpkin outpouring. This new pumpkin muffin recipe is my first attempt."

"That would be lovely." Alice tapped her fingers on the papers, her restrained excitement intriguing her sisters.

"So? What is the big plan?" Jane asked.

Louise and Jane could count on Alice to be a steadying influence. She was, after all, the middle sister, twelve years older than Jane's fifty and three years younger than Louise, the eldest. Alice had also been the one to stay behind in Acorn Hill to take care of their widowed father, while

Louise went to Philadelphia to study music and Jane went to California to study art and cooking.

When their father died and the sisters came back for the funeral, their shared grief and their happiness at being reunited prompted them to start Grace Chapel Inn in their old family home.

It was a good partnership. Louise and Alice took care of the business, and Jane did the cooking and baking. All three pitched in to make their guests feel welcome and enjoy their stay, both at the inn and in the town of Acorn Hill.

"Remember how you talked about doing a mystery weekend in the wintertime?" Alice asked, turning to Jane. "Where people are given clues to a murder over a buffet supper and then they have to solve it?"

"I recall that at the time I was vetoed." Jane nodded toward Louise. "Though I was glad for the quiet season. It seemed like more work than we would be able to do."

"I found a way we could do it," Alice said, practically giddy. "I met a lady named Barbara Bedreau. She was at the hospital today giving a presentation to the doctors. I caught the final part of it after my last shift. She is such a warm, wonderful person and so full of energy!" Alice shook her head as if still surprised by this amazing woman. "She helps raise money for a charity that helps fund doctors who travel to needy countries and provide their services to impoverished communities. It's called Doctors Without Borders and it's an outstanding service."

"That's true," said Louise. "We are so blessed with such good medical care here that we often take it for granted."

"I should know. The patients I had today were hardly models of patience."

"Bad shift, Alice?" Jane asked, setting a cup of tea and the plate of muffins in front of her sister. She joined Alice and Louise at the kitchen table.

"Bad enough that I am thankful I only work part-time," Alice said, bending over the plate and inhaling appreciatively. "These look marvelous as usual. What did you put on top of them?"

"I drizzled some caramel sauce over them."

"You are amazing," Alice said.

"It's all in the wrist. Now tell us about this Barbara person. Or would you rather talk about cantankerous patients?"

"Barbara would be preferable." Alice took a sip of tea and sighed her pleasure. Then she sorted through the papers. "I got some information from Barbara on the charity as well as on some of the other activities she is involved in." Alice handed Jane some papers and Louise some others. "When I talked to her after her presentation, she told me she wanted to do a murder mystery weekend to raise money for the charity but wasn't sure how to go about it.

She didn't know where she could have it or how it would work out." Alice paused, tapping her finger on the side of her teacup. "I know we've been busy the past few months, but I suggested that she do something here at Grace Chapel Inn.

Louise adjusted her glasses and glanced over the papers Alice had given her. "This proposal looks like a play of sorts."

"Of sorts," Alice said. "That is the general idea of what Barbara wanted to do here. She's hoping that if the trial run works here, she could work on it, expand it and market it as a package deal that she could use to raise money or pass on for the charity to run."

Jane leafed through her papers. "From the looks of things, the host puts on a buffet supper. I'm guessing that would be our responsibility."

"How many people would we have to feed, and would we be expected to do it gratis?" Louise asked.

"No. We could charge a small amount for people to participate, which would cover our expenses and, we hope, raise a bit of money for Barbara's charity," Alice said. "While she would love to raise money the first time she tries this, she would be content to break even to start. I was also thinking that if it worked out for us, it would be something we could offer the community regularly."

"I must confess I'm still somewhat vague on how this would play out." Louise fiddled with the chain around her neck that held her glasses, frowning in uncertainty.

"We would be responsible for food and the use of the inn. Barbara said she would come to Acorn Hill to help us put together the murder mystery part of the evening. We could advertise it as a special event and see if our guests as well as members of the community would be willing to participate. For interested guests, there would be no extra cost. Everyone else would have to pay. They would get a fun evening and a buffet dinner at the same time."

"Would people want to participate?" Louise asked, still frowning.

"It sounds like a lot of fun," Jane said. "In San Francisco one of my coworkers went to a couple of these and told me about them. She had a marvelous time. That's why I wanted to try it here. I thought it could be something different."

Louise still didn't look convinced.

"C'mon, Louie. How often do you get to participate in a murder mystery?" Jane prodded.

"I can't say that it has been a burning desire of mine," Louise said.

"Not even when Charles Matthews butchers a selection from Brahms?" Jane gave Louise a playful nudge. "That parlor may be practically soundproof, but it can't completely hide the noise that boy makes."

"What Charles Matthews lacks in proficiency, he makes up for in enthusiasm," Louise said, gathering up the music books. "At least he comes on time and with a smile on his face."

"He is friendly, that's for sure," Jane said. "Every time he comes I get a big hello and a smile. But oh, the music!"

Louise shook her head. "I'm afraid that the piano is probably not his forte."

"Perhaps he should switch to the pianoforte?" Jane asked with a grin.

Louise glanced over her glasses at Jane and shook her head. "You are incorrigible."

"So what do you think of the mystery weekend?" Alice asked, bringing the two sisters back to the subject at hand.

"I like the idea," Jane said.

"I suppose we could do it," Louise conceded. "Though I am hoping it will not require too much extra work on our part. I don't relish the idea of being so busy that we neglect our guests."

"If Barbara comes, as she said she would, I don't think we will have to worry about that," Alice said. "She could take care of the planning with some input from us, but overall, I don't think we should worry about being overworked."

"I think we should do it," Jane pressed.

Louise looked from one to the other, and it seemed she was still not convinced. "If Barbara is keen on doing this, and you and Jane are so enthusiastic, I guess it will be up to you to get it done."

"That's fine," Alice said, sitting back in her chair. "We can manage. I know that once you meet Barbara, you will be as taken with her as I am."

"Then I'll look forward to meeting her," Louise said. "And now, I have to get ready for dear Charles."

"Have you thought about steering him toward a better expression of his enthusiasm?" Jane asked with a smile. "Drums perhaps?"

"The thought has crossed my mind," Louise replied. "But for now, piano is what his parents pay me to teach him, so piano it is."

"Remind me to pick up some more earplugs next time I'm at the pharmacy," Jane said, clearing the empty cups.

Chapter Two

*I*t was a beautiful Wednesday afternoon, and this year's early colors were glorious. As Alice drove back from Potterston to Acorn Hill, the sun shone its bright promise, lighting up the colorful trees in a visual symphony. The sight of the rich hues flowing over the hills made her smile. She tuned her radio to a classical-music station and let the music add its beauty to the spectacular view that flowed past her.

Fall always brought out a sense of nostalgia in Alice. It signaled both an end and a beginning—an end to warm weather and sitting outside, and the beginning of school, church organizations and committees, and all the busyness that came with the new season.

She had already had the first meeting of her ANGELs group, young girls with whom she worked at church. They were enthusiastic for the coming year, and Alice had a few projects in mind for them already.

Maybe they could get involved with Barbara's project somehow. Since she was only working part-time at the hospital, she could devote some hours to this project. Though she was excited about it, she wasn't so sure Louise was. Louise often took a little longer to warm up to new ideas than Jane did.

She made a stop at the General Store to purchase items from the list that Jane had given her. Alice didn't recognize some of them—bean thread noodles, galanga, peanut sauce—but the proprietor did. He helped her fill the list without batting an eye at some of the more unusual products.

"Looks like Thai food is on the menu," he said, handing her a package of red curry that would soon enrich the inn's kitchen with its exotic fragrance.

"I leave all the cooking in Jane's capable hands," Alice said, putting the curry, along with a pungent gingerroot, on the growing pile of items in the cart. The owner called a young boy over to help her load the bags in the car, and soon Alice was on her way again.

As Alice turned in to Chapel Road, she made a mental note to call Barbara to see what she would require for the fund-raiser. The inn still had a couple of openings for the weekend of Halloween, and she wanted to advertise the murder mystery as an extra attraction to fill the inn with guests.

As she pulled up to the inn, she saw an unfamiliar car parked in front. *Must be a new guest who didn't know about our parking area,* Alice thought.

From her car's trunk she pulled out a small cart that Jane had bought to help with shopping and hold all the groceries.

As she opened the back door to the kitchen, she heard the sounds of muffled laughter, sounds that suggested her sisters were having a lot of fun without her.

When she entered, her momentary funk immediately switched to pleasure. Barbara Bedreau sat at the table, her streaked blond hair layered and fluffed in a youthful style. She wore a soft, tan suede jacket over a deep brown turtle-neck the exact shade of her pants. An elaborate pendant hung from a string of chunky beads. She looked stylish and fun all at the same time.

"Hello, Barbara," Alice said, moving her shopping cart to one side. "Welcome to our home."

As soon as she saw her sister, Jane jumped up from the table and took hold of the wheeled basket. "Is there more in the car?"

"Yes. Just a few more bags."

"I'll get them. Louise, can you put these away? Barbara, can you pour our dear sister some tea?" Jane flashed Alice a smile. "Barbara just arrived. Now go sit down, but don't make any more plans until I'm back." She wagged her finger in warning. "I don't want to miss out on anything."

In a matter of moments, Jane returned with the rest of the groceries, which Louise put away in the pantry and the spacious refrigerator. Alice was settled in beside Barbara, drinking tea.

"It is so lovely to see you again," Barbara said with a warm smile. "I'm sorry for barging in on you like this. I was passing through Acorn Hill and on impulse decided to stop by. I had forgotten that you were working this afternoon."

"I would have been here sooner, but I had a few errands to run." Alice took another sip of her tea and sighed in satisfaction. "I'm glad you came, Barbara. I'm hoping you can explain to my sisters what exactly your charity is all about and what it aims to do."

Barbara's sea-green eyes flicked eagerly from sister to sister. "What I do in my spare time is raise funds for a group of doctors who travel overseas to do simple surgeries in poor countries. The doctors offer their services free of charge, and we get a number of donations from medical companies for supplies."

"It sounds like you have many of your needs covered," Louise said.

"I know it looks that way, but somehow there are always unexpected expenses. And often, once the doctors get to the countries, the need is greater than the donations. That's where the foundation I volunteer for comes in." Barbara leaned forward, her eyes shining. "I have had the privilege of going on a trip with the doctors. What I saw was absolutely amazing. It was as the Bible says, 'The blind receive sight, the lame walk ... the deaf hear' (Luke 7:22). So many of these people lack basic medical supplies and attention. It takes so little to make such a difference. I saw things that brought tears to my eyes, and the experience made me more determined to help these people in any way I could."

The emotion in her voice and the intensity of her delivery impressed upon Jane the depth of Barbara's commitment. She understood now why Alice had been so excited about what Barbara was doing. Jane, too, found herself caught up in Barbara's enthusiasm.

"I only have so much time off from my regular work in public relations," Barbara continued, "but I devote whatever I can to try to help this organization. As I said, we always need more money. I have been trying to find different ways to raise funds for this organization, and one of the things I want to do is a mystery weekend."

"Which is where we come in," said Alice.

"That will depend on whether your sisters are in agreement," Barbara said carefully. "I can only devote part of my time to this project, so much of the work will fall on your shoulders. I was hesitant to do this, but Alice encouraged me to come and talk to you. So here I am. I don't want to push any of you beyond your comfort level."

"I certainly want to help out," Jane said with fervor.

Barbara opened a bright red file folder lying in front of her on the table. "This is a basic outline of how the mystery weekend will work. Do you want me to explain it?"

"That would be wonderful if you could give us an overview," Alice said.

"In its basic form, the mystery weekend is simple." Barbara handed Louise, Jane and Alice each a typed piece of paper. "You have a victim and about five to eight suspects. Each suspect is given a story to tell and a background story that will help each one answer interview questions. On the first night, the characters are introduced and provide the audience with significant details about themselves. On the second, the murder is revealed, and the suspects have to provide explanations and answer questions in order to be cleared of blame. They don't need to rehearse anything, and they may or may not be in costume, depending on how much work you want to do. Those in the audience will be divided into teams that try to expose the murderer." Barbara waited a moment, as if to give them a chance to ask questions. "You will need one person in charge of the proceedings. He or she will introduce the characters, direct the movement and time of the interviews, and give out clues from time to time."

"And how would the food be worked into this?" Jane asked, fiddling with a strand of hair as she looked over the paper.

"That depends on what you want to serve and how you want to serve it. Ordinarily, light refreshments are served the first night, and a buffet the second." Barbara handed Jane another piece of paper. "Alice told me that you are the chef here, so I brought along a few sample menus."

Alice watched Jane as she read and was pleased to see a smile tease the corners of her mouth. It looked like Jane would be on board.

Louise, however, was frowning. "I see from the outline that you can have up to eighty people. Surely that is far too many." She turned to Alice. "Alice, you can't be agreeing to all this hurry and scurry?"

"I don't think we'd have that many, and it wouldn't be 'hurry and scurry,'" Alice said in what she hoped was a placating tone. "We can have as many or as few people as we want."

"What if it doesn't turn out?" Louise murmured. "I wouldn't want the inn's reputation to suffer because of this."

"I think it could be a lot of fun for our guests, Louise," Jane said, "and that would balance out the work."

"Do you have confidence that this could be successful?" Louise asked, adjusting her glasses so she could look at Barbara. "I believe Alice told us you've never done this kind of thing before."

Barbara lifted her shoulders in a careful shrug, her eyes troubled. "That's correct. As I told Alice, you would be my guinea pigs."

Silence answered this comment. Alice saw Louise glance at the paper, then back at Barbara. The faint frown creasing her forehead wasn't a good sign.

"This same format has been used in many places with much success," Barbara said softly. "I have been to a couple similar events, and I know of a few places that make a living doing this."

"None of us here has had any experience with or exposure to this kind of thing before," Louise said.

"Speak for yourself, Louise." Jane laid a hand on her chest. "I personally have had long conversations with a friend who went to one."

"That is hardly experience," Louise said, adjusting her glasses.

Jane blinked in an innocent fashion. "She was very, very descriptive."

To Alice's relief, Louise smiled at Jane's silly comment. Jane and Louise had their differences, but, to the credit of both women, they could also laugh about them.

"I'm still hesitant," Louise continued. "We would have to inform the guests already booked for that weekend. What if they don't want to participate?"

"They wouldn't have to, of course, but it would make things easier," Barbara conceded.

"Maybe our first order of business is to send an e-mail to these guests to let them know what will be going on while they are with us." Louise sat back. From the expression on her face, Alice could see that Louise was wondering if this would cause some problems.

"We should think positively," said Jane. "I'll send out the notices this afternoon." She glanced down at the paper. "And from the looks of this list, the very next thing we're going to have to do is find a murder victim."

"I wonder who would be willing," Alice murmured as she ran her finger down the list of characters. She was choosing to think positively. All she and Jane needed to do was give Louise enough time for the idea to grow on her. The weekend would be for a good cause, and Louise's heart was big enough to eventually recognize the benefits. "We need someone who can ham it up a bit."

A knock on the back door made Alice look up.

"Yoo-hoo," the familiar voice of Ethel Buckley called out.

Alice caught Jane's eye.

As Ethel bustled into the kitchen, Alice returned Jane's smile. Jane winked at her, and Alice knew that precisely the same thought was going through her head.

"Aunt Ethel," Jane said, turning to her aunt as Ethel shrugged off her light sweater and finger-combed her short, bright red hair. "How would you like to be murdered?"

Chapter Three

*W*hy? Did I slam the door too hard? Or maybe you have your heart set on inheriting those diamonds I have hidden beneath my floorboards."

"No, no, nothing like that, Auntie," Jane said, laughing as she rose to give Ethel a hug and introduce her to Barbara. "We were planning a mystery weekend for the inn, and we need someone to be a murder victim."

Ethel looked stern as she pondered Jane's explanation. Then she reached out one hand to the kitchen counter as if she needed to steady herself, while she raised the other to her forehead in fine theatrical style. "And since you consider me to be at death's door anyway, you thought I'd be just right for the part." She closed her eyes and shook her head slowly.

"And the Oscar for best actress goes to . . . *Ethel Buckley*," Jane announced with mock formality.

Barbara clapped her hands, smiling at Ethel.

"After that miniperformance, Ethel, the part is yours for the asking," Alice added.

"Good, I'm all for it . . . the acting, that is, not the dying."

Ethel sat at the table.

"I'll get you some coffee right away to celebrate." Jane poured her aunt a generous mug of java, then put some muffins on a plate and set them in front of Ethel.

"Are these pumpkin muffins?" In seconds Ethel had cut one open, buttered it and taken a healthy bite.

"Oh, just one more thing, Auntie." Jane stifled a smile. "Do you *really* have diamonds under the floorboards?"

"You wish. Now pass the sugar."

The front doorbell announced new guests.

"The Malones, I suppose," Louise said, laying down her napkin. "They weren't due for another hour."

"I'll take care of them," Jane said, stopping her sister with a light hand on her shoulder. "You look over those papers." She really wanted Louise to approve of the mystery weekend. Jane knew from past experience that once Louise was excited about an idea, or at least interested, she would bring her considerable organizational abilities to bear on it, and the project would be all the more successful for it.

Jane felt hopeful as she walked through the dining room to the foyer, where the guests would be waiting.

A couple and their three children stood in the entrance hall, and Jane greeted them with a smile. The Malones had come to do some early "leaf peeping" with their children, who had a brief vacation from their school. This was the first time that Jane could remember all the rooms being booked by one family.

"Welcome to Grace Chapel Inn," she said.

The children smiled politely.

She signed in the family and took them upstairs to show them their rooms. The daughter got the Garden Room; one boy, the Sunrise Room; the other boy, the Symphony Room.

"These rooms are absolutely charming," Mrs. Malone said as she inspected each. "You and your sisters have a lovely, lovely place here. So very rustic and cozy. What do you think, Archer?"

Mr. Malone, a tall, imposing man, didn't share his thoughts but did give his wife a brief nod. As his wife toured the rooms, he pulled out a cell phone and frowned at it.

"I'm sorry, but the cell phone reception isn't very good here," Jane said to Mr. Malone.

He frowned at his wife. "Natalie, you didn't tell me that."

"We don't have cell phones ourselves," Jane said, "but a few of our other guests have commented on it."

"How do you do business?"

"We have a land line that serves our purposes," Jane replied. "If you need to make a call, you are welcome to use it. It's at the front desk."

"I'd like to do that directly if I may."

"Please go ahead," Jane said, and Mr. Malone lost no time in hurrying down the stairs as if the business at hand could not wait one more second.

"I'm glad we could all stay here," Mrs. Malone was saying as Jane led her to the Sunset Room. "We haven't been on a vacation with our whole family for some time now."

"I sincerely hope you enjoy your stay here," Jane said.

"Oh I'm sure we will. It's not easy for my husband to find time away from work." Mrs. Malone looked around the Sunset Room. "This is really very cozy. Archer had hoped we could stay in Potterston, but I wanted the peace and quiet."

"I should explain to you that my sister Louise has piano students, but the room they work in is soundproof."

"Oh, that's just fine. Peace and quiet for us means having no heavy traffic. I hope my husband has some time to relax."

"I hope so too. So I will leave you all to get settled in." Jane explained to her when breakfast was served, then left.

Mrs. Malone had made it clear that the family would be spending much of its time away from the inn, which meant that Alice, Louise and Jane could devote any extra time they had to the mystery weekend.

When Jane came back down the stairs, she could hear the muffled strains of tortured notes coming from Louise's beloved grand piano. The piano had been a gift from Eliot Smith, Louise's late husband, who was a musician. Jane wondered what he would think of the sounds emanating from it today.

When she went into the kitchen, Alice greeted her with a smile and a thumbs-up. Obviously, Louise had given her approval before Charles Matthews came for his lesson.

"It's a go, Jane," Aunt Ethel said, looking up from the papers in front of her. "And I get to be a writer who dies a mysterious death."

"I'm so glad," Jane said.

"That Aunt Ethel gets murdered?" Alice asked.

Jane threw Alice a wry look. "No, my dear sister. I'm glad that we are going to do this thing after all."

"I am thankful, too, that Louise is in favor," Barbara said.

"So we have our victim and we have the venue. What's the next step?" Jane asked, all business now, as she sat at the table.

"I made out a very rough budget that explains what the initial expenses will be," Barbara said. The charity I work for has some money we can use for start-up, and the rest I will put in myself." Barbara handed Alice and Jane another piece of paper.

"What is our biggest cost?" Jane asked, glancing over the figures.

"Initially it will be advertising. As people start purchasing tickets, we will receive more operating money. And when it is all over, we hope there will be some money in the bank." Barbara folded her arms on the table and leaned forward. "I want to emphasize that this is a first-time project for me, and I am thankful for your help. But I would be lying to myself and to you if I claimed to guarantee that this is going to make money. Before we begin, I want you to know that I will make up any shortfalls in the budget."

Jane could see by the frown puckering Alice's brow that she wasn't pleased with the risk to her new friend at all. But at the same time, the sisters could not afford to do more than allow the event to take place at the inn and to help in any nonfinancial way they could.

Jane chose to be positive. "This looks like so much fun. I'm sure it will be a great hit both with our guests and with the people in town. I'm going to predict that we will end up with money in the bank." She flashed Barbara, Ethel and Alice her brightest smile as if to underline her statement. "So what is our next step?"

"The first thing you need to do—as you've already said you would—is inform the guests who will be staying that weekend of what we are planning. If you have a Web site, you also might want to post it on there. After that we need to decide how many people we can handle here." Barbara brushed away a strand of blond hair from her face in a graceful gesture. "Then you need to find people willing to volunteer to be suspects."

"You said five to eight suspects?" Alice asked, going down the list in front of her.

"That number varies depending on which scenario we are going to use," Barbara replied. She tapped her pen on the paper in front of her. "I would suggest that we go with five suspects for now. I don't want to overburden either you or the inn. This way, if we have five teams of four to six people apiece, you will have a minimum of twenty and a maximum of thirty people trying to solve the mystery."

Jane whistled softly. "That seems like a lot for the inn."

"Is that too many?" Barbara asked, suddenly anxious. "If it will be too difficult—"

"No. I think it would be an interesting challenge," Jane replied. "If we want to involve the community, I think I could talk to June at the Coffee Shop and Clarissa at the Good Apple Bakery. I am sure they could help me with the food."

"The main thing to remember is that the food has to be easy to eat, so we're not looking at fancy dishes. Finger foods and appetizers would probably work the best."

"And will I need to memorize lines?" Ethel asked, wiping the crumbs from another muffin from her mouth.

"Only a few," Barbara said.

"If you want, Ethel, you could be the victim for the first night, and maybe we could find another job for you to do the next night," Alice said.

"That would be fun." Ethel sat back, satisfied.

With an apologetic look, Barbara pulled out another sheaf of papers. "Sorry for inundating you with all this material, but I made up some rough notes about how the two evenings will work. I don't have a fully developed story as yet. That will be something I hope to work out over the next couple of weeks. As I said, you can keep this as simple or make it as complicated as you want. Your suspects can show up in regular outfits or they can dress in clothing that will help illustrate their character."

"If you have an Easter bunny in the mystery, Lloyd could play that part." Ethel looked up from the paper that described the murder victim. "He's the mayor of Acorn Hill and my beau," Ethel said to Barbara, as if that explained it all.

"Lloyd Tynan was gracious enough to dress up as the Easter bunny at our Easter-egg hunt one spring," Alice added. "He has a penchant for acting."

"Unfortunately, there are no murderous bunnies in this production," Barbara said with a smile, "but there are other roles he might want to tackle."

"Oh, I can't wait to tell him," said Ethel.

"After the guests are split into teams, each team will work together interrogating the suspects, one team at a time. The suspects, at that point, will answer the questions from a script that they will be given, and they will be sequestered in separate rooms so that the other teams won't hear what they are saying. Then the members of the team, without telling the other teams what they know, will try to figure out, based on the questions they've asked the suspects, who murdered the victim."

"So no memorizing?" Ethel asked.

"Well, not much." Barbara glanced at the clock on the kitchen wall. "I am sorry to say this, but I have to leave. I have to be at another meeting in an hour, and I need to go home first."

"This will be such an interesting challenge," Jane said.

"As you are setting things up, I will stay in contact with you." Barbara gathered up her things and slipped them into a soft leather briefcase. "But anytime you need anything, please don't hesitate to call." She reached into her briefcase and pulled out a couple of business cards. "These cards have my cell phone number, my pager number and my office number. Just keep trying until we connect. You can try sending an e-mail or a text. For now, you might think about how you can roust out some volunteers to be murder suspects."

They said their good-byes, and Barbara left, leaving behind the vague scent of her perfume.

"She certainly seems like a very lovely young woman." Ethel folded her hands on the table. "I think this murder mystery weekend could work out."

"It will mean extra work for us," Alice said, reading over the papers once more, "but I do like the idea that we will be helping her and her charity."

"And helping people is a good thing," Ethel said, pushing herself away from the table. "I had better get going. I have things to do."

Jane and Alice exchanged a quick glance, stifling their smiles. They knew exactly what Ethel meant by "things"— talking to anyone who would listen about the plans for the mystery weekend. Barbara spoke of the need for extensive advertising and how the costs could cut into potential profits. It was obvious that Barbara did not realize what an asset Ethel was going to be in that respect.

"I think things are going to turn out just peachy." Jane got up from the table.

"I hate to be a pessimist," Alice said, frowning lightly, "but I sure hope that we don't get any cancellations because of this."

"Then don't be pessimistic. Be an optimist. Repeat after me: 'Everything is going to turn out fine.'"

"I sincerely hope so," Alice said, gathering up the plates and cups. "I really want to see this production work as much for Barbara's sake as for the sake of the charity. Her dedication is admirable."

"I couldn't agree more."

Chapter Four

S o much for thinking positively," Jane muttered, printing out the e-mail she just received. On Wednesday, after Barbara left, Jane had sent out notification of the mystery weekend to their guests. It was only Friday, and she had already received a cancellation for the weekend of the mystery event. The party said they had booked the inn for some peace and quiet over the Halloween weekend and didn't want to be involved in some strange game.

"You look disturbed, Jane."

Jane looked up from the computer to Louise, who stood on the other side of the desk eyeing Jane over her glasses, her hand full of letters. She must have just gotten around to opening the day's mail.

If Jane told Louise about the cancellation, her sister would have enough ammunition to say the dreaded words, "I told you so." Jane wasn't in the mood for recriminations, so she opted for evasiveness.

"Just a temporary glitch," Jane said, hoping Louise would interpret that to mean something was wrong with the computer.

"Now you know why I prefer paper and pen," Louise sniffed with a faint air of condescension. Louise did all the accounting work for the inn but still used an old-fashioned ledger and a calculator. Jane was the one with the most computer expertise. She maintained their Web site and corresponded with the customers who made their reservations through it. Some people still telephoned, and some still wrote, but the bulk of their reservations were now made via e-mail.

While Ethel had eagerly embraced the new technology and loved to check out chat rooms from time to time, Louise preferred to stay away from the computer completely.

"It's nothing that can't be fixed," Jane said with an airy optimism that she didn't really feel. *What if I can't fill those rooms?*

"As long as we don't have any cancellations because of this event, I will be happy," Louise said absently as she glanced through the mail.

"And your happiness is my goal in life," Jane said charmingly, plucking the e-mail from the printer and filing it away. She would handle it later; right now she had more pumpkins to attend to, and right after that, a list of potential suspects that she had to talk to. Fortunately, they had easy guests this week.

"I requested clean sheets yesterday. But last night we slept on the same sheets we had the first night we arrived." Mr. Malone drummed his fingers on the reception desk.

Louise frowned as she mentally reviewed the events of the previous day. Yesterday was Thursday, and the Malones had come on Wednesday, the same day Barbara Bedreau had visited. Surely she would not have forgotten to give them fresh linens? Then she remembered. In each room they had placed a card that guests could put on their pillows if they wanted their sheets changed. Giving guests the option was a way to save some money, water and time. Jane had gleaned the idea from an e-mail group of innkeepers that she belonged to. Many five-star hotels also offered the same policy.

Louise distinctly remembered seeing the card in Mr. and Mrs. Malone's room standing on the bedside table—not on a pillow—on Thursday morning. She had not thought it unusual. They had only checked in on Wednesday.

"I am sorry for the inconvenience, Mr. Malone," Louise said, "but as we explained when you checked in, laying the laundry card on your pillow is a signal to us that you want clean sheets. The card was not on the pillow yesterday."

Mr. Malone looked down from his imposing height, his dark eyebrows pulled together in a frown. "This is totally unacceptable. I know I placed the card on the pillow. This does not speak well for the reputation of your inn. Perhaps you need more capable help."

Louise tried hard not to bristle. She sent up a quick prayer for patience, took a long, slow breath and forced a smile to her face. As innkeepers, she and her sisters had to deal with a variety of people. Most of their guests were pleasant and grateful, but on occasion they had to work with difficult people.

"Again, I apologize, Mr. Malone." Louise kept her smile in place. "I will see to it immediately that the linens are changed."

She really did not have time for this. Alice was working an extra shift at the hospital; she was balancing the checkbook and in ten minutes she had a piano student coming. Jane was around and about town talking to potential suspects for the mystery weekend.

The mystery weekend wouldn't take place for another three weeks, and already it seemed that they were far too busy. She would have to talk to her sisters about this. It wasn't too late. They could back out.

"This really is a hick town." Mr. Malone harrumphed, obviously put out. "I told my wife that we should have made reservations in Potterston, but she had some foolish notion of staying in a quiet place."

"It is quiet and relaxing here," Louise said, trying to placate him.

He did not seem placated. "I took the liberty of using the inn's number to forward calls to me. Have you received any messages for me?"

Louise quickly flipped through the phone-message pad. "Unfortunately, there are no messages here for you or your wife."

"Like I said, hick town." He drew in his breath through his nostrils as if containing his anger. "May I use your phone?"

"Certainly," Louise said, excusing herself as she went to get fresh bedding and also to see if she could muster some patience. When she returned, she could hear Mr. Malone's voice raised in anger.

"What do you mean, 'not in yet'? It was supposed to be in two weeks ago." He paused, his lips pressed together. "I don't want excuses. I want results. Now you make sure this happens and happens immediately." Without saying good-bye, he hung up the phone and turned, glaring at Louise as if this were all her fault.

For a moment Louise felt a flash of sympathy for Mr. Malone's family. Here they were on a supposed vacation, and all he could think of was business.

"I don't think I could be a suspect," Sylvia said, carefully slipping a pin through the soft material of the dress she was working on. "But I could volunteer to make some costumes. That sounds like fun." She was bent over her sewing table, her strawberry blond hair brushing her cheeks. She wore a quilted vest over a bright blue T-shirt, and a tape measure draped over her shoulders. A long flowing skirt completed her ensemble. Jane was often teased about her unusual clothing, but sometimes Sylvia could give her a run for her money in that department.

"We have a limited budget, but we do have some money for costumes, and I think that would add a nice touch." Jane perched on a chair across from Sylvia in the back of the store, watching her dear friend as she worked. In the front of the shop, Sylvia's Buttons, bolts of fabric were set out in orderly fashion, sorted according to color and type, inviting even the most reluctant seamstress to finger material and dream. But here, in Sylvia's workroom, fabric of all colors spilled out from shelves in glorious disarray.

"What are you making now?" Jane asked, arranging the ceramic-headed pins in Sylvia's pincushion in an artistic pattern.

"I'm sewing a dress for Rose Bellwood. She and Samuel have an important agricultural function to attend, and she couldn't find a dress at Nellie's that suited her. So she asked me, and I said yes." Sylvia straightened and glanced critically over the layout of the pattern pieces. Then she took a straightedge and began measuring.

"What are you doing now?" Jane asked.

"See this long line?" Sylvia pointed to a line that ran all the way down each pattern piece almost from top to bottom.

"That's the grain line. I have to make sure that I have it running exactly along the grain of the fabric, or the fabric will hang wrong when the dress is completed."

"Such a smart friend I have," Jane teased, setting down the pincushion. She hopped off the chair and retied her ponytail. "Well, I have to run. I still need to gather up four more suspects."

"Who do you have already?"

"Aunt Ethel is the victim, and Joseph Holzmann offered to be one of the suspects. I have a few more prospects up my sleeve."

"Let me know about the costumes," Sylvia mumbled around a pin she had put in her mouth. "Like I said, I have the time."

"I'll be in touch." Jane waved good-bye to her friend and left the store. She took in a deep breath of fall air tinged with the nostalgia-inducing scent of burning leaves. *Each season has its own beauty, its own memories*, she thought as she walked down the sidewalk.

She greeted several people as she went. Acorn Hill was small enough that it was almost impossible to walk down the street without meeting someone she knew. Jane considered this a blessing, but at times, stopping to chat and catch up made for stressful delays.

Wonderful, mouthwatering smells drifted out from the Good Apple Bakery as she walked past. Jane didn't know how Sylvia could work so close to temptation every day. She herself had to fight the urge to dip too often into the cookie jar or sample too many of her own baked goods when they were cooling on the counter.

It was a blessing that she could still run for exercise every day. She knew the activity helped her stay trim and healthy.

She crossed Hill Street and walked to Wilhelm Wood's store, Time for Tea. A bell tinkled happily as she opened the door, and she was welcomed by the dark and mysterious scents of the different teas that Wilhelm stocked. Shining tins of various sizes and hues lined the wooden shelves, and ornate teapots and tea services were set out in display cases.

Wilhelm stood at the counter, tall and slim, his graying blond hair brushed back from his face. He was deep in discussion with a woman, the two of them bent over a large book. As Jane went farther into the shop, Josie, a lively blonde eight-year-old, came bouncing around one of the display units.

"Hi, Ms. Howard," Josie chirped, her curls bouncing on her shoulders. "My mommy is going to help Mr. Wood."

Puzzled, Jane walked to the counter and saw that it was Josie's mother, Justine, standing beside Wilhelm. "Hi, Justine, Wilhelm."

"Hello, Jane," Justine responded.

"Good afternoon, Jane," Wilhelm said, tugging gently on one lapel of his suit coat to straighten it. "What can I do for you today?"

"I'm canvassing the community," Jane said. "Alice, Louise and I are putting on a mystery weekend at the end of the month. It's going to involve a number of volunteers, and I was hoping you might be one of them."

Wilhelm gave her a broad smile. "I'm honored you thought of me," he said. "But I must inform you that in three days I'm leaving for Europe."

"Again?" Jane asked. It didn't seem so long ago that he had returned from another trip. It was amazing that he managed to keep his business going. His mother took over the shop when he left, but obviously Wilhelm had figured she needed extra assistance this time.

"I had a chance to go on a tour with a friend, and I hated to turn it down. I will be gone for about three weeks."

"We're certainly going to miss you." Jane smiled at Justine. "But I'm glad Justine will be working here in the meantime."

"I'm thankful not to be here all by myself," Justine said. "Wilhelm's mother knows how to run the store. I'm sure I'll be asking her all kinds of questions."

This should prove to be interesting, Jane thought. The last time Wilhelm took a vacation, his mother had "helped" him out by mixing a unique blend of oolong tea and tobacco.

"I wanted to make sure my mother had some good help," Wilhelm said, winking at Jane as if he had heard her thoughts.

"I guess if you will be working here you can't help at the inn," Jane said. Justine helped out periodically when the inn was full, and Jane had secretly hoped she could ask Justine to come a little more often while they were preparing for the mystery weekend. It looked as though she and her sisters would be on their own.

Justine nodded. "I'm sorry about that. But I was excited about the idea of running a shop for three weeks. So was Josie."

"I understand," Jane said, smiling. She pulled out her list and scratched Wilhelm's name from it. "I hope I can find someone to replace you, Wilhelm."

"I'm sure that you will."

"I'll go and pack up those mail orders," Justine told Wilhelm. She said good-bye to Jane and disappeared into the back room.

Wilhelm scratched his chin, momentarily lost in thought. He glanced at the door as if making sure Justine was gone, then turned back to Jane. "I have a favor to ask of you. Carlene Moss found out about my trip and was hoping that I would send reports back to her for the *Acorn Nutshell*. However, I'm not always very careful about my spelling and grammar, and I know my handwriting is atrocious. I don't want to appear foolish, so I wonder if I could send you my reports and you could turn them into real stories."

"I'm not so sure I'm the person you want," Jane said. "I'm more of a chef than an editor. I don't know if I could do your trip justice."

"You could do it more justice than I," Wilhelm said with an encouraging smile. "You would just have to work from my material."

Jane tapped her fingers on the glass countertop. She could probably squeeze it in. And perhaps she could get help. How hard could it be to write up something from what he gave her? In addition to helping him out, it could be interesting to experience traveling through his letters.

"I suppose I could do it, as long as your reports aren't too lengthy."

"Oh no. I'm not verbose, just unorganized."

"Okay. Send your letters to the inn, and I'll try to get Carlene her articles on time." Jane looked down at Josie, who was now standing beside her.

"My mommy said if I was good, I would be allowed to give people their money," Josie said, rocking back and forth from the toes to the heels of her sneakers. "But I'm not allowed to touch any of the pretty things. And there's a lot of pretty things in here, aren't there?" Josie tucked her hands in her pockets as if resisting the temptation to finger one of the china tea sets.

"There certainly are." Jane crouched down to Josie's level and pointed at an ivory tea set decorated with pale blue and mauve flowers. "That is one of my favorites."

Josie nodded, her hands still in her pockets. "When I have enough money, I want to buy that for my mommy."

Jane ruffled Josie's curls and stood up again. "That would make a lovely gift." She turned to Wilhelm. "If I don't see you before you leave, I hope you have a wonderful trip. Make sure you take lots of pictures so we can share your trip when you come back. As far as your letters go, will I be able to contact you in case I don't understand something?"

Wilhelm slowly shook his head. "My friend wishes to travel extensively while I am along, so we will be frequently on the move and hard to get in touch with. But you will do fine."

Jane bit her lip, wishing she had the same confidence that Wilhelm had in her. She said good-bye to Josie and Wilhelm, but as she left the shop, she wondered exactly how Wilhelm's mother managed to mix tobacco in the tea on that one occasion. She hoped it didn't have anything to do with Wilhelm's handwriting.

Alice parked her car by the inn and released a tired sigh. She rotated her neck, working the kinks out. One of the young nurses had phoned in sick, so Alice had to take over that nurse's patient, an elderly, extremely overweight woman who needed a bath. The experience reaffirmed Alice's gratitude that she was down to part-time hours now. She couldn't imagine putting in a full day of this kind of labor.

She got out of the car and walked to the house, a smile curving her lips and a sense of peace reaching out to her. The inn beckoned with the promise of comfort and a cup of tea.

"But we can't change plans now," Alice heard Jane say as she moved toward the kitchen. "I've already had a few people asking me for details about it, and half the town knows about it."

Alice paused, frowning at the sound of Jane's voice. Her sister wasn't precisely angry, but Alice could tell that there was no peace in the inn. She sent up a prayer for patience and fortitude, guessing that Jane and Louise were discussing the mystery weekend.

For a moment she almost felt bad that she had introduced the idea, but it seemed such a good way to help Barbara.

Dear Lord, she prayed, *make me a channel of Your peace. Help me to keep peace at our home.*

And with that she entered the kitchen.

"I didn't like the idea in the winter, and I don't like the idea now," Louise said quietly. She was scrubbing vegetables for dinner, her vigorous movements belying the soft tone of her voice. "It is making us all far too busy. And the last thing Alice needs when she comes home from hours of work is to be faced with more work. I think we should call it off."

"I would have changed the sheets if the Malones had put the card out where it was supposed to be. It won't be a problem because—" Jane looked up from the pastry dough that she was rolling out with quick, decisive strokes. Then she closed her lips, as if shutting off the next thing she was going to say. "Hello, Alice. How was work?"

"Just fine," Alice said as she looked from one sister to the other. "Just fine."

Smile nice and big, she thought. *Don't let them see how tired you are. Don't give Louise any excuse to call off the mystery weekend.* Like Jane, Alice didn't want anything to get in the way.

"We have a problem," Louise said, setting the vegetables on the cutting board and pulling out a knife.

"From the frown on your face, I hope handling that knife won't be a problem," Alice joked.

Louise's frown eased. Slightly.

Alice relaxed. Slightly.

"Louise had a run-in with Mr. Malone this morning, and we weren't around to help her out." Jane carefully lifted the dough and lined a pie plate with it. "I was canvassing for volunteers, and you were working."

"I will be home for the next week," Alice assured Louise.

"I don't know about that. One of the nurses you work with called before you arrived," Louise said, chopping the carrots with quick motions. Louise was not a stellar cook, but she was efficient when it came to the "prep work," as Jane called it.

"Don't tell me she's canceling one of the shifts she's taking," Alice moaned, sinking into the nearest kitchen chair. "I just traded some to give myself time off for the coming week."

"She isn't," Louise said.

Alice sighed in relief.

"She's canceling them both," Louise said, sliding the chopped vegetables into a bowl.

Alice sighed. "I'll simply have to get back on the phone and try someone else. I have some free time coming up the next week."

"If you do that, you will be busier the week of the mystery weekend," Louise said quietly.

She was right.

"So what should we do?" Jane asked.

"The only thing we can do at this stage," Louise said. She wiped her hands and turned from Alice to Jane with a look of inevitability. "I'm sorry, but I don't see a way around this. We have no choice but to call off the mystery weekend."

Chapter Five

"No, we can't do that," Jane cried out. She turned to Alice. "I know *you're* looking forward to doing it."

Alice glanced from one sister to the other, feeling torn. "I am looking forward to it. But Louise is also right. If this is going to make us so busy that we neglect our guests, we have to call it off."

Jane bit her lip, then turned back to her preparations. She didn't say anything, but Alice could easily read her disappointment because it mirrored her own.

She got up and patted her sister on the shoulder. "It was fun to think of, but we have to be realistic."

"Of course we do. I'm also feeling bad for the people who offered to volunteer. They were all so excited about the idea, especially Vera and Fred." Jane shrugged and gave her sister a smile of regret. "Now, who will tell Barbara?"

"I'll telephone her right away." Alice met Louise's eyes. Even though Louise had technically won the argument, Alice could see that she also shared their disappointment.

"I'm sorry," Louise said. "But the inn and our guests are our priority. We can't neglect them for the sake of someone else, no matter how worthy the cause."

As though expecting the call, Barbara answered the phone right away.

Alice explained the situation and told her that though they were still excited about the idea, it wasn't feasible for them to do it at this time.

"Would it help if I came?" Barbara asked.

"Probably, but you said yourself that you are busy. I don't want to take you away from your own work."

"Let me think about this," Barbara said. "Don't call anything off yet. I'll be in touch with you in the next couple of days to see if there's a way that we can work around this. Don't worry. It will all be fine, I'm sure."

Barbara said good-bye, then hung up.

Alice wished she had Barbara's confidence. She was tired and wanted a few moments' peace from obligations and concerns.

She rested her elbows on the desk and her chin in her hands as she stared into space, thinking and, for now, allowing herself some alone time.

She and her sisters had grown up in this house. It was a home of love and caring. After their mother had passed away giving birth to Jane, the sisters and their father continued to make this house a home.

Now, it was more than a home. It was a place for other people to stay and experience a time of peace and also to experience the sisters' hospitality. Overall, Grace Chapel Inn represented a good life for the sisters.

The inn's usual serenity had been upset ever since she offered to do this mystery weekend. For a moment Alice had second thoughts about volunteering the inn and her sisters' services to Barbara. It had obviously created tension between Louise and Jane.

Not that it mattered now. She felt a twinge of regret. Barbara's enthusiasm for the project had been infectious, and it also appealed to the nurturing part of Alice.

Maybe they could work on some other project some other day.

Please Lord, she prayed, *if this can't happen, then help us to be open to other opportunities to serve You and people who haven't been as richly blessed as we have. Thank You for our blessings. Help us to use them to help others.*

She smiled lightly, stood and walked back to the kitchen to help her sisters. She told them that Barbara had asked her not to call off anything yet. Jane was relieved and Louise looked resigned. And supper was a quiet affair.

Jane placed another pumpkin in the wagon she had pulled out of the garden shed. She glared at the bright orange globes that dotted the garden, glowing in the early morning sun, the picture of health and abundance. It seemed as if she hadn't made a dent in the pumpkin population.

"You aren't multiplying overnight, are you?" she grumbled as she lifted one more pumpkin into the wagon. She had set aside this Saturday for making pumpkin pies and tarts. She had even taken to giving away pies in an effort to share the garden's abundance; their pastor, Rev. Kenneth Thompson, said he would stop by this morning to pick up a couple of promised pies. But there were many more to take the place of those. She shook her finger at the pumpkins as she arched her back to ease the kinks. "Stop growing so much, would you?"

"I thought when you talked to plants, it was supposed to be soothing."

Jane gasped and whirled around, the voice behind her catching her off guard.

Barbara stood there, smiling, her sea-green eyes sparkling at her own joke. She wore a soft blue tailored suit, and today her briefcase was navy blue leather.

"Goodness, Barbara, you scared the life out of me." Jane placed her hand on her chest as if to hold her heart in place.

"I'm sorry, Jane." Barbara laid a hand on Jane's arm, trying without success to stifle her smile. "You sounded so funny grumbling at your pumpkins."

"I've been reprimanding them for being so prolific. Now I have to figure out what to do with the silly things."

"Maybe we should get Alice's ANGELs to carve some, and we could give them away to the participants in the mystery weekend."

Jane brushed dirt from one arm to avoid looking at Barbara. She didn't want to see her disappointment.

"Alice told me about your problems, and I'm here to tell you that I have a solution." Barbara bent over and with one arm caught a pumpkin that threatened to spill out of the wagon. "I decided to dedicate all my time to this event," she said, holding the captured pumpkin against her pale blue jacket.

Jane was so surprised she forgot to warn Barbara that the pumpkin would leave a streak of dust on her lovely suit. "But what about your job? I thought you didn't have much time to help us."

Barbara shrugged aside the comment. "I got rid of some obligations, and I subbed out some clients to another consultant, a friend of mine who needed the extra work."

Jane started walking toward the inn, pulling her load of orange treasures, but it didn't feel as heavy as it had before. If Barbara helped them, no one's job would suffer. As she was considering this, another thought slipped into Jane's mind. "Aren't you afraid of losing business?"

Barbara shook her head. "No. I'm more afraid of losing my mind. My work was getting far too stressful. I really want to make this event work. Helping these doctors is where my heart is. I've already found a number of organizations willing to host something similar for the charity." Barbara juggled the pumpkin and her briefcase and held the door to the kitchen open. She stood aside to let Jane pass with an armload of autumn's harvest. "If this mystery weekend is successful, I can convince other places to do the same, and I will have found a good way to raise funds for my doctors." She followed Jane into the kitchen, set her pumpkin on the counter and brushed the dust from her suit.

"Will you be all right financially?" Jane glanced at Barbara's elegantly tailored suit, her silk shirt and the gold necklace with its single large diamond, which matched the diamond earrings winking from her ears.

Barbara fiddled with the chain around her neck, understanding the implication in Jane's questions. "My job has made it possible to satisfy a lot of my own desires." She gave Jane a gentle smile and set her briefcase on the floor by the kitchen table. "I've made a lot of money, that's true, but it hasn't bought me happiness. Or love."

Jane heard a hint of regret in Barbara's voice. On impulse, she laid her hand lightly on Barbara's shoulder. "I understand what you're saying," she said. "Love is elusive enough in ordinary circumstances."

"Not that I'm pining, mind you. I've had enough offers . . ."

"I can believe that," Jane said. Barbara was a beautiful woman, with added beauty that came from within.

"I need a break from work. It's only a short leave of absence, and it could just do the trick. And it will help you out as well. So here I am, ready and willing to make sure that this dinner is a success."

Jane felt as if a load of concern had slipped off her shoulders. "I'm sure it will be."

A tap at the back door made her glance at the clock. She could hear the faint sounds of music coming from the parlor, so their visitor wasn't a student of Louise's, and Ethel usually announced her presence.

Jane excused herself and opened the back door.

Rev. Thompson stood on the back step, half-turned away from her, the remainder of the pumpkins in his arms. In spite of the breeze that teased leaves out of the trees, his dark hair was perfectly groomed. His shirt was rolled up neatly over his elbows, and as usual the crease in his pants was as sharp as a knife. A faint smile played on his lips, softening his usually serious demeanor.

"Come in, Kenneth," Jane said, pulling open the door. "Thank you for helping—just put those on the counter. You know that here we don't stand on porches or on ceremony."

He gave her a quick smile as he stepped inside. "I'm sorry. Blame it on my Boston manners, which my time here hasn't seemed to erase," he said, following Jane into the kitchen.

Barbara was sitting at the table. She turned to the minister with a polite smile on her face. He glanced at her, his features equally composed.

"Barbara, this is Rev. Kenneth Thompson, our pastor. Kenneth, I'd like you to meet Barbara Bedreau," Jane said.

"Hello, Barbara. Welcome to Acorn Hill." The pastor shook her extended hand.

"Thank you. I'm pleased to be here," Barbara said. "It's a lovely town."

"I think so too. I . . . like it . . . a lot."

"I can see why you would. It's . . . it's lovely."

"I like it."

Then silence.

Jane frowned slightly, surprised at the inanity of their comments. They were both intelligent, articulate people.

But as she looked at them, puzzled, she noticed that they weren't looking away from each other, and neither had moved. And as their gazes held, the pastor's smile grew warmer, and Barbara's cheeks grew pinker.

The reality of the situation dawned on Jane. She felt suddenly superfluous in the face of their obvious attraction to each other. But it would look odd if she left.

She hesitantly cleared her throat. Instantly, the pastor glanced aside, and Barbara looked down at her hands as she fiddled with one of her rings.

"Barbara will be here periodically over the next couple of weeks," Jane said. "She's going to help us murder Aunt Ethel."

Both the pastor and Barbara turned to Jane with curious looks on their faces. Then they both laughed, and the indefinable tension in the room eased.

"I'm assuming this has to do with the murder mystery weekend you were hoping to put on," the pastor said to Jane.

But as he spoke to her, his glance slipped back to Barbara, who was watching him.

"You will be glad to know that 'were hoping to put on' has changed to 'is going to put on.' Barbara has graciously agreed to put her considerable organizational talents to work to help us pull it off."

The pastor nodded slowly. "Really?" The single word held a wealth of meaning.

"I will become a regular nuisance," Barbara said with a light wave of her hand.

"I am sure that Jane, Alice and Louise will be glad for your help," he said, his deep voice holding a note Jane had never heard before from her friend.

Barbara must have heard it too, because her cheeks went from pink to red.

"I imagine you've come for your pies," Jane said, walking to the refrigerator and removing two cardboard boxes.

"Pardon me?" Rev. Thompson said, sounding distracted.

"The pumpkin pies. You were going to keep one and take one on a pastoral visit."

"Yes. Yes, of course." He turned back to Barbara, giving her a careful smile. "I imagine we'll be seeing you from time to time."

"I hope so," she said, returning his smile.

The pastor took the pies from Jane with a murmured "thank you," then, before he left, glanced back at Barbara again.

A certain excitement seemed to leave with him. Jane felt a gentle sigh build in her along with a feeling of anticipation. Rev. Thompson was a good friend of Jane's, and she was very interested to see how the situation would develop.

"How long has Rev. Thompson been your pastor?" Barbara asked.

Jane could see that she was trying to make the question sound casual, and she would have been fooled had she not seen the looks the pair had exchanged.

"For a few years now. He comes from Boston originally, but he enjoys life down here in Acorn Hill."

"I see," Barbara said, her voice soft. She smiled lightly. Then she tugged her jacket straight as if pulling her attention back to the business at hand. "I . . . uh, I brought some more information along. It's . . . uh, here." She picked up her briefcase, thumbing the latches. It took her three tries to get them both open. "I also brought along an outline . . . for the characters . . . the mystery . . . that we are going to do . . ." She stopped abruptly, then looked at Jane. "Am I babbling?"

Jane laughed. "A little."

"I'm sorry. It's just that I . . . he . . ." Barbara paused.

"Kenneth," Jane said helpfully.

"Rev. Thompson seems like a very nice man."

"Oh, very nice," Jane said, a teasing note in her voice. "And I'm guessing he thinks you're a very nice woman."

"You think so?"

"I do."

Barbara's smile grew, then she laughed. "Listen to me. I sound like a junior high school girl with her first crush."

"That's okay. As long as you don't expect me to pass notes to him, I think we'll get along famously." Jane decided to rescue her new friend and joined her at the table. "Now about this murder mystery. I already have the so-called suspects. I need to know what roles they are going to play and what our next step is."

Barbara was suddenly all business and she pulled out the necessary papers, setting them on the table. Half an hour later she and Jane had mapped out a plan of attack for the next few days.

"Now that I'm able to take over much of the coordinating, you and your sisters won't be overburdened with work," Barbara said as she ran her pen down the list, doublechecking the items on it. "I'll take care of ordering, and the publicity and invitations, and all you lovely ladies have to do is what I tell you."

"Oh goody," Jane said, clapping her hands. "I like the easy jobs."

"If you think being in charge of food is easy, then you need help. Our next step is to advertise. Did you put the notice on your Web site?"

"And e-mailed our guests for that week. I got one cancellation."

Barbara put down her pen. "I'm sorry, Jane. I didn't think this would cause that kind of problem."

"Don't worry, Barbara. We'll get other guests," Jane assured her. She thought of something. "Maybe I can offer a free pumpkin for every day they stay?"

"Or offer to *not* give them a free pumpkin for every day they stay," Barbara joked.

"That might work better," Jane agreed.

"So what are you going to do?"

Jane sighed. "Hope and pray that someone fills the canceled spot soon."

The Malones left Sunday evening, which meant that the rooms needed to be prepared for the next guests.

Monday morning found Alice in a flurry of cleaning. The Malone children had managed to leave their rooms in a jumble, with pillows and blankets strewn over the floors and the furniture rearranged.

As Alice worked, Wendell, the inn's cat, was making a nuisance of himself, threading himself through her legs as she vacuumed and rubbing against her face when she was bent over trying to retrieve a throw pillow from under a bed in the Symphony Room.

She took a moment to pet him, but that didn't seem to satisfy him at all. Finally, as if realizing he wasn't going to get enough affection from Alice, he sauntered off, head high, looking for attention elsewhere.

Not that he was going to get it.

Louise was balancing the checkbook, which would keep her busy, and Jane was in the kitchen with Barbara writing up the murder mystery as well as making chocolates for Halloween. Besides cooking and baking for her sisters and inn guests, Jane was in partnership with Exquisite Chocolatiers in Philadelphia. This week, however, she was working on special items that she sold in Time for Tea.

When Barbara found out that Alice enjoyed reading mysteries, she had invited Alice to help. But Alice soon discovered that reading a mystery was much easier than planning one. She offered what advice she could and gave Barbara a few ideas, but soon she felt superfluous and went back to cleaning, sharing suggestions only from time to time as she passed through the kitchen.

With Wendell out of the way, it took Alice only an hour to finish the cleaning. Before she went downstairs, she checked the rooms once more, making sure that all was in order. One guest would arrive later this afternoon, and two in the evening.

She took a moment to tweak the pale blue and yellow quilt of the Sunrise Room, then left.

Louise was bent over the calculator as Alice passed by, but the eldest sister looked up and gave a quick smile before diving back into the muddle of debits and credits. The doorbell rang before Alice reached the kitchen, so she turned around to answer it.

Wilhelm Wood stood on the doorstep, his topcoat draped over his arm, an envelope in his hands.

"Good morning, Wilhelm. I thought you were leaving today." Alice said, ushering him into the inn.

"I am, so I don't have much time. I was wondering if you could give this to Jane. It's my itinerary."

Alice took it, wondering why Jane would need the information. "I will. She's in the kitchen making chocolates for your shop if you want to speak with her."

He waved the suggestion away. "She will have to speak to Justine if she has questions, as I'm already running a little late. I had to explain a few things to Justine this morning, and then some customers came." He ran his hand over his thinning blond hair. "If you could do that for me, I would be most grateful."

"Of course," Alice said. "And have a wonderful trip."

"I will. I hope that Jane will be able to understand what I send her. Good-bye." And with that, he left, striding down the walk, whistling an upbeat song, obviously eager to be off on his latest adventure.

Alice glanced down at the envelope, then walked to the kitchen.

Jane was humming along softly with the radio playing in the background. The entire countertop was covered with chocolates of various shapes and sizes. Barbara sat at the table typing into her laptop.

"How is the work going?" Alice asked Barbara.

"It's coming along. We're going to have to tweak the mystery a little so that it will run a little better over two days. I think I'll have to see about getting in some extra entertainment for the first evening. Maybe a singer . . . or a fiddler. I'll work on it." She typed a few more notes into her laptop, then looked at Jane.

"Jane, what do you think of having Tex Holdem have a close connection to the young girl?" Barbara asked, tapping her fingers against her cheek. Her eyes returned to the laptop screen. "It could throw people off of Peter Proxy's scent if we introduce that later on in the evening."

"Depends on what we do with Wilma Wannabe and Gilbert Gopher."

"I have no idea what you ladies are talking about," Alice said with a laugh, "but I was wondering if there is anything else I can do to help besides trying to come up with a mystery?"

"Not right now, but in a couple of days, Jane and I will probably like to run the setup by you and Louise, and you can tell us if we've made things too obvious," Barbara said, tapping away at the keys again. Alice wondered how she could type and talk and think all at once.

"You can help *me*," Jane said, holding up what looked like a Day-Glo orange golf ball. "What do you think? These are going to Wilhelm's store."

"What are they supposed to be?"

"Obviously not the right shape." Jane pressed her hand down on the top of it, making it more oblong. "Now what do you think?"

"I'm guessing a pumpkin."

"You get the prize."

Alice laid the envelope on the table, careful not to disturb the papers Barbara had strewn over it. "Wilhelm dropped off his itinerary. He seemed to think you needed it."

Jane gave Alice a blank look, then realization dawned. "I had forgotten I was going to edit his travel articles for Carlene Moss."

"You'll still have time for that?" Alice said.

"I hope so. I hate not following through on my promises. Oh well, one thing at a time. For now I have to finish these pumpkins." Jane picked up a piping bag and gently ran narrow lines of brown down the sides of her candy pumpkin, then stood back to appraise it. "I think we're getting there, though it's a mystery how I'm going to change that color."

"How long will you be here?" Alice asked Barbara.

"She's staying for dinner," Jane said.

"That's wonderful," Alice said, pleased that she would have a little more time with Barbara.

A rap at the door caught their attention. Alice and Jane called out, "Come in," at the same time. The door opened and Rev. Thompson walked into the kitchen.

"Good morning, Kenneth," Alice said, surprised to see him. "What brings you to our inn so early?"

He stood in the doorway, glancing from Alice to Barbara to Jane to Barbara. He held a pie plate in his hand. "I thought I would return this," he said, holding it out. "Thank you very much for the pies. They were delicious. I took one to Martha Bevins and I ate one by myself."

"Oh, thank you, but you really didn't need to return that," Alice said, taking the disposable pie plate from him and heading to the garbage can. "These are made to throw away."

Jane whisked it from Alice's hands before she could dispose of it.

"Sometimes I like to reuse them." She set the now-dented pie plate on the counter.

"Aren't they a bit difficult to reuse?" Alice asked, remembering how Jane had told her to throw away a disposable plate just last week.

"Not if a person is careful." Jane turned her back to the minister, giving Alice a warning look. "And I think it was very considerate of Kenneth to recycle it."

Alice frowned, wondering what Jane was trying to tell her. It wasn't difficult to sense a change in the atmosphere, but she couldn't put her finger on it. Jane was acting strangely, and though Rev. Thompson stopped in from time to time, he rarely came over unexpectedly.

Jane turned back to him, a smile curving her lips. "I am trying out a new recipe tonight, Kenneth. Would you like to join us for dinner? Barbara will be staying as well."

"I'd love to," he replied. "Thank you very much."

Barbara had been pecking away at her laptop during this entire exchange, saying nothing, which Alice found most unlike her new friend. Barbara was vivacious and outgoing. It also puzzled her that Jane hadn't made proper introductions.

She was about to do so when Barbara made a half-turn and glanced toward the pastor.

It was just a quick look, and in other circumstances Alice would have missed it. But the awkwardness of the moment made her more aware. That and the faint blush creeping up Barbara's neck as he smiled at her.

And as Alice "got it," she felt a motherly warmth take over her heart. She felt as if she should excuse herself and leave these two alone. Jane still stood at the counter, looking away from the couple, her stiff posture suggesting she felt the same.

But they couldn't very well both leave, and it would only draw attention to Barbara and the pastor.

"Did you know that Barbara volunteers for Doctors Without Borders?" Alice asked, trying to find a safe conversational topic for all present.

The minister blinked, then reluctantly drew his gaze from Barbara to Alice. "Really? And what does that entail?"

"Right now aren't you mostly involved in the fundraising aspect?" Alice asked Barbara.

Barbara nodded, seeming relieved to be talking about something familiar. "I discovered the organization a few months ago, and since then I've become more and more involved with it," Barbara said, turning in her seat. "It's a wonderful thing they do, using the gifts God has given them to help others who simply don't have the same resources that we have." Barbara grew more animated as she explained the organization, and Alice could see that the minister was catching her enthusiasm.

"How does this tie in with the mystery weekend?" Rev. Thompson asked.

"It's a pilot project to see if I can use it to raise funds in other places. Alice, Louise and Jane very generously offered the use of the inn for my first production," Barbara said, brushing a strand of hair from her face.

Rev. Thompson smiled at Alice and Jane. "The Howard sisters are known for their generosity, and I'm glad you can partake of it." He turned back to Barbara. "I have to leave for Potterston, but I will look forward to hearing more about your project this evening." His smile was warm, friendly. "Until then," he said, his voice low as if speaking only to her.

Barbara nodded, watching the pastor as he left. As the door clicked closed behind him, Alice felt like sighing.

Where were the violins when one needed them?

Chapter Six

The rest of the day went smoothly, and dinner was a most enjoyable affair with lively conversation and wonderful food.

"How do you like living in a small town after big-city life?" Barbara asked the pastor as she cradled her coffee cup in her hands, her elbows resting on the table.

"It has its challenges," he said, carefully rolling up his sleeves and leaning back in his chair. "But overall I like the closeness of the community and how people come together to help each other when a need arises."

"Do you miss your privacy?" Barbara asked, glancing at him over the rim of her cup.

"One advantage of the small-town rumor mill is that if people are talking about me, sooner or later I get word of it." The pastor winked at Jane, and Jane knew he was referring to Ethel and her penchant for spreading "news," regardless of whom it was about or who the recipient was. Ethel was an equal-opportunity gossip.

"I don't know if I would like that," Barbara said, blowing lightly on her coffee. "But I surely do enjoy the hospitality."

She glanced around the table with a thankful look. "And you three have certainly opened your home to me."

"Acorn Hill can definitely learn something from how Jane, Louise and Alice treat strangers and welcome them into the community," the pastor said.

"When we first started the inn, we hoped to make it a place where people feel at home," Alice said.

"I believe the plaque we mounted on the front door sums up our mission." Louise glanced around the table. "It reads, 'A place where one can be refreshed and encouraged / A place of hope and healing / A place where God is at home.' This is our wish for the people who come and stay. I can humbly state that in the past we have been able to offer our guests some of that in one way or another."

"We've had our share of interesting guests, that's for sure," Jane said, thinking back over the variety of people who had stayed at the inn.

"And where is your family?" Louise asked Barbara.

"My parents and most of my family live in Florida, where I'm from originally. I have two brothers who used to tease me unmercifully. They still do. I also have two sisters, one older and one younger. The younger one lives in Washington, D.C., and works for the government doing Web design for various departments."

"That's a very large family," Louise said. "Are they all married?"

"All except me," Barbara said with a quick smile. "My parents would dearly love for me to be married, as would my sisters. My brothers claim I'm going to grow up to be an old, miserable spinster who gives all her money to obscure charities."

"I can't believe that," Jane protested. Barbara was so beautiful and fun. Jane knew that someday she would find someone.

As that thought crossed her mind, she glanced at Rev. Thompson, who was looking at Barbara with more than casual interest. Was romance blossoming right in front of them all?

"Maybe not a miserable spinster," Barbara said with a light laugh. "But who knows what my future holds?" She took a sip of coffee, as if embarrassed by her brief revelation, but as she set down her cup, Jane could not help noticing how Barbara flashed the pastor a quick, sideways glance.

Who knows, indeed? Jane thought, wondering how she could encourage this potential romance while ensuring that neither Barbara nor Rev. Thompson realized what she was doing.

Chapter Seven

*J*ane picked up her large butcher knife and gripped it tightly in her hands. Did she dare do it in one swift attack? The job required confidence. She couldn't hold back.

Clenching her teeth, she plunged the knife downward. Right into the heart of the pumpkin.

"If anything should inspire me, that little drama should," Barbara said, pushing herself away from her laptop. She tunneled her fingers through her hair, rearranging its neat waves.

Aside from Jane's evisceration of the pumpkin, it was a quiet Thursday morning at the inn. Their guests had gone on a tour to see the fall colors. Jane was working her way through her pumpkins, and Barbara was parked at the kitchen table.

"This is not coming together," Barbara said with a heavy sigh. "I can't seem to figure out a way to plant the clues without making it so obvious that people solve it right away. But if I make it too hard, people will get frustrated."

She looked at Jane and shook her head. "Do you want to trade jobs for the morning?"

"Pass," Jane said, scooping out the now halved pumpkin. "Give me a recipe to follow or a subject to paint and I'm your girl, but writing? Sorry. Not my strength."

"It doesn't appear to be mine either. I wish Alice could have helped us out. I'm sure she has some good ideas." Barbara got up from the table and started pacing. "I can't seem to get motivated today. And I still have to get those tickets that Alice printed up handed out to local businesses. And put up some posters." She blew out a sigh that lifted her bangs from her forehead.

Jane looked up from her pumpkin seeds, surprised at the frustrated note in Barbara's voice. Usually Barbara was upbeat and full of energy, but this morning she seemed distracted and fidgety.

"How much more do you need to get done?"

"I can't seem to weave all the stories together properly," Barbara said, leaning her elbows on the counter. She rested her chin in her hands, biting her lip. "It's like each time I make a change in one character's story, I mess up the other one."

"Did you try working backward?" Jane asked.

"And forward and sideways. I haven't tried upside down yet." Barbara pushed herself off the counter and started pacing again.

"As soon as I get done here, I'll see if I can help you," Jane offered. "Except with the upside-down part. It's too bad we can't use a prewritten script," Jane said. "It would make your job easier."

"I know. We probably could if we weren't charging admission. Most of the scripts I've looked at are copyrighted, and publishers are very fussy about how they are used."

"I'm surprised."

"It would be equivalent to renting a DVD and then charging people to come and watch it."

Louise came into the kitchen carrying her cleaning bucket. She had been washing windows and looked a little flushed. "Jane, have you called Jose yet?" She set the bucket in the storage room off the back of the kitchen. Jose Morales, who worked at Fred's Hardware, often did odd jobs at the inn.

Jane set the clean pumpkins in the microwave to cook and gave Louise a puzzled look. "Was I supposed to call him?"

"About coming to clean the outside windows and helping us put up the storm windows."

Jane sorted through her thoughts, trying to remember. She couldn't. She gave Louise a shrug. "Sorry, I don't remember."

Louise's glance slid to Barbara then back to Jane, and from the frown deepening between Louise's delicate eyebrows, Jane could tell what was coming next. Time for some deflection.

She held one hand out toward Louise, waving it back and forth, and put her other hand over her eyes. "I am catching negative waves," she intoned in a sepulchral voice. "I am picking up thoughts that are...frustrated. A sister, thinking that maybe her other sister is not paying enough attention...is not doing her job...is spending too much time on the murder mystery weekend." Jane peeked through her fingers to gauge Louise's mood.

"I am thinking that you are getting a little too much into the Halloween spirit," Louise said. Her frown had eased a bit, but not enough to show Jane that she was forgiven.

"At least I'm not getting into the spirits," Jane joked, giving Louise a smile.

Louise's lips twitched a bit, but then Jane saw them straighten. "I guess I should call Jose myself."

"No. Don't do that. I'll call him," Jane said, serious now. She knew when to back off. In spite of Barbara's help, Louise was still not convinced that the fund-raiser was a good idea. Louise enjoyed routine and order, and somehow she had it in her head that this mystery weekend would involve too much disruption.

It was a good thing she hadn't found out about the canceled reservation, which had yet to be filled. Jane was still hoping for a last-minute reprieve, but as each day passed, she grew more anxious.

"By the way," Louise said before she left the kitchen, "I got a call from a young couple who want to stay at the inn for a week or so. They said they would be on their honeymoon. Their call was a stroke of good fortune." Louise gave Jane a wry look. "Perhaps we'll be just as fortunate in filling the reservation that was canceled because of the mystery weekend."

"How? But… I… I …" Had she spoken her previous thoughts aloud?

"You were hoping we would get a new reservation before I found out?"

Jane had the good sense to look ashamed. "Something like that. But how did you know?"

"I am not going to tell you all my secrets," Louise said. "I know how much you love a mystery." And with a satisfied look, she strode out of the kitchen, leaving behind a baffled Jane.

Barbara was trying, without success, to muffle her giggles.

Jane spun toward her, then had to laugh. "Isn't my sister amazing?" Jane shook her head. "I thought I hid that cancellation notice."

"I could have told you that you can't hide things from a sister," Barbara said, still laughing. "Especially not one as capable as Louise." Her face grew serious. "But I still get the feeling she's not too keen on this mystery weekend."

"She's not keen on disruption, that's all. I think she's worried what our guests will think. Her worry was confirmed when she found out about that cancellation. Though how she did that, I'll never know." Jane shook her head, then joined Barbara by the kitchen table. Pieces of paper full of notes and scribbles were strewn across its top. "So, what do I need to help you with?"

"Background story," Barbara said, folding her arms over her chest as she frowned at the computer screen. "Each guest's history has to be woven into the victim's but in such a way that each could easily be a suspect. And they must each have motive and opportunity. I'm having a little trouble with a couple of the people's motives. They seem contrived."

"What have you got?"

Barbara explained the history of the characters she had already fleshed out. The two women threw around ideas while Jane turned her cooked pumpkin into pumpkin squares. When the timer sounded, she pulled them out of the oven and set them on the counter to cool. Just as she was about to mix up some frosting, a knock sounded at the back door.

Jane saw Barbara straighten the collar of her cotton shirt, then self-consciously run her fingers through her hair. Then Jane knew who was at the door.

"Come in, Kenneth," she called out.

The door opened, and Rev. Thompson stepped inside. Jane had to look twice to make sure it was he. He wore blue jeans and a soft leather jacket in a golden brown that accented his dark hair and brought out golden tints in his hazel eyes.

He looked dashing, she thought.

And from the faint flush that tinged Barbara's cheeks, Jane presumed that Barbara thought so too.

"Good afternoon, ladies," the pastor said. "I was going downtown and remembered that Alice had taken your car, Jane. I was wondering if you need anything?"

Jane stifled her faint smile. For a Boston-educated man, that excuse was about as transparent as the plastic wrap she used to cover her leftovers. If Jane really needed to go shopping, most of the town was within walking distance.

But she recognized the ruse for what it was, an excuse to see Barbara.

"I don't really need anything, but I had hoped to go for a drive with Barbara to check out the fall colors," Jane said, helping him along. "Would you like to come too? I'm sure you could use a bit of a break."

Barbara shot Jane a glance, which Jane ignored.

"That sounds like a great idea," he said. "The sun is shining right now, and if you'll permit me to drive, we can take my car."

"Great," Jane said, putting aside the mixing bowl. "What do you think, Barbara?"

"I suppose I could use a break as well," Barbara said with a nonchalance that Jane was fairly sure was assumed.

"Excellent. Let's go."

A few minutes later they were settled in the minister's Chrysler. Jane had coaxed Barbara to sit in the front seat.

Jane smiled as they drove, enjoying the sunshine and how it made the gold and red of the trees burst with color.

A sudden flash of guilt went through her. She had promised Louise to call Jose, and here she was gallivanting around the countryside.

She pulled out her purse and scribbled a quick note to herself. The last thing she needed to do was irritate Louise further. She would have time to make the call when she got back. The minister assured her they wouldn't be gone long.

"Where do you want to go?" he asked as they drove out of Acorn Hill.

"I had hoped to walk on the trails at the nature preserve about five miles out of town."

"I know the place," the pastor said.

From time to time Jane saw Barbara glance at the minister, but she was uncharacteristically quiet. So was he, which surprised Jane. He was usually at ease with people. In his work as a pastor, people often commented on how warm and open he was.

It looked like Jane would have to help things along.

"Do you like baseball, Barbara?" Jane asked. "Our minister is an avid Red Sox fan, but we try not to hold that against him."

"Jane is jealous because my beloved Sox have become winners," the pastor said, always eager to discuss sports.

"Actually, I'm not much of a sports person," Barbara said. Scratch that.

"Kenneth hails from Boston originally. Have you ever been there, Barbara?" Jane continued.

"No. But I would love to visit sometime. My father always wanted to take part in the Boston Marathon, but things fell apart when he realized that he would actually have to run, not walk it."

"Boston is a lovely city," the minister offered. "There are some wonderful older buildings that reflect a variety of architectural styles."

"I remember seeing a picture of the Old State House, built in 1713, I believe it was," Barbara said.

"Yes. The Declaration of Independence was first read from the balcony of the Old State House," he replied. "I grew up in Beacon Hill, so I have to confess I've been somewhat spoiled when it comes to old architecture and history."

Soon they were discussing various architectural styles and buildings and history, and Jane sat back content to hear them talk about neoclassical and Romanesque and Greek Revival. Not the most romantic of conversations, but at least they were speaking to each other.

Jane was happy enough to focus on the view, enjoying God's own architecture, the first and the best.

In no time they reached the nature preserve, and the conversation shifted easily to other topics as they walked along the tree-lined paths.

Barbara found out more about Rev. Thompson's upbringing, including the fact that his grandfather was a cod fisherman and that his parents were antiques dealers.

He found out that Barbara had put herself through business school and had successfuly advanced within two other companies before forming her own public relations firm.

Jane followed at a distance, feigning interest in gathering leaves, and soon she lagged far behind. The pastor and Barbara seemed not to notice.

Rev. Thompson had a quiet reserve about him that some strangers might misconstrue as austere. *No one could say that about him now*, Jane thought, as he gestured while he spoke, smiling down at Barbara, who was smiling back at him.

Things were progressing as Jane had hoped. And, as fortune would have it, when they came to a creek, the pastor took Barbara by the hand and ushered her across the few rocks that were used as stepping-stones.

Happiness fluttered through Jane as he and Barbara disappeared around a bend in the path. She could still hear the faint sounds of their voices and Barbara's light laugh. Things were going better than she had hoped.

But then Jane heard the pastor call her by name, and she hurried to catch up to them without the benefit of a helping hand to cross the creek.

The three walked along for a while longer, talking about Acorn Hill and its residents. Barbara was fascinated by the characters and by the various stories Jane and the pastor told her about remarkable events of the recent past.

"You've met Aunt Ethel haven't you?" Rev. Thompson asked as they walked.

"Our murder victim. Yes, I have. She seems like a sweet, energetic lady."

"She is that," he agreed with a laugh, looking down at Barbara again with a fondness that made Jane sigh inwardly.

A faint breeze sent some leaves drifting down onto the path ahead of them and around them. One snagged Barbara's hair, and before she could reach up to take it out, the pastor plucked it out instead, handing it to her. "Here you are," he said. "One of autumn's flowers."

"Thank you," she said softly as she twirled the leaf in her fingers. She glanced up at him, then away. "I should gather a few more and press them."

"I've got more than enough for both of us," Jane said, holding up her bouquet of leaves.

They walked on in companionable silence. Though Jane felt like a third wheel, she knew it would look strange if she tried to fall back again, so she talked to Barbara about the people who were helping with the murder mystery.

Once back in the sedan, however, Barbara sat in the backseat with Jane. As they drove home, they chatted about inconsequential things. But Jane noticed that the pastor had angled his rearview mirror so that he could see Barbara, and Barbara looked up at the mirror often during the ride home.

"Louise, I'm sorry I didn't mention the cancellation," Jane said as she added some flour to her bread dough the next morning. She was grateful that she had remembered to call Jose after she and Barbara returned the day before, or she would be apologizing about that too. She was also glad it was Friday. The week was almost over. Next week she could start fresh and be back to her usual organized self. "I should have said something sooner, but I was hoping the problem would be resolved before you found out." Jane started kneading the dough, hoping Louise would forgive her.

"That's fine, Jane," Louise said, glancing at her sister over her reading glasses. "It will work out fine in the end. I know you often assure me of that, and in this case I trust that you are right."

"Why do you do that?" Jane asked.

Louise frowned at her. "What do you mean?"

"Give me points when I'm up to my elbows in bread dough and I can't go mark it down somewhere."

"Points?" Louise was genuinely baffled.

"Yes, points. I give myself a point every time you admit that I'm right, and you get a point every time I have to admit that you are right."

"You keep track?"

"There's a book in the reception area . . . a *thick* book. Two shelves down, brown cover. I write it in there."

Louise was taken aback but relaxed when Jane laughed. "I'm kidding, dear sister. It's just that you are so wise. I really treasure the times when you tell me I'm right."

Louise shook her head, but she gave Jane an affectionate pat on the shoulder. "I'm glad you treasure them, and I'm glad you don't keep track. I would be concerned if you did."

"Kenneth gave an especially wonderful sermon this morning," Louise said as she laid the plates out for Sunday lunch. "I always appreciate how he presents a challenge to use what God has given us to help those in need."

The inn's most recent visitors had left the day before, and the sisters were enjoying a brief respite that would end with the arrival of their next guests in two days.

"He certainly practices what he preaches," Alice said, handing Louise the napkins for the table. "He's an example to all of us to take care of the poor, the widowed and the fatherless."

"God has blessed us with all that we need and more," Louise said. "We can choose what we want to eat. We have more clothes than we need. We have our own transportation. We would be considered extremely wealthy in many parts of the world."

"Well said, Louise," Jane agreed, bringing the soup to the table. "We are truly rich beyond measure."

"And at this time of the year, I really appreciate the bounty God has given us," Alice said. "Eating produce from our own garden, filling the pantry with food for the winter. And not only that, but also seeing the beauty of the changing seasons, with all the gorgeous colors. Such a glorious atmosphere! It makes me think of our honeymooning couple and what a lovely time of the year they chose to get married."

"I think it would be fun to plan a fall wedding," Jane agreed, her artistic mind imagining the color arrangements.

"Yoo-hoo," a dearly familiar voice called out, and Ethel entered the kitchen. "My goodness," she said, her eyes flicking from the set table to Alice, who was already putting out another setting. "I am not interrupting anything, am I? I know you girls have been busy and all."

"Come in and sit down, Aunt Ethel. Your place is prepared for you," Jane said, pulling back a chair for her aunt with a flourish worthy of a maître d'.

"Why, that would be lovely. Thank you, I think I will."

As they sat, Louise looked at Alice. "Is Barbara joining us for lunch? I saw her in church."

Alice glanced at Ethel, then shook her head as if warning her sisters. "I invited her to join us, but it seemed she had other plans."

"She has been spending a lot of time here," Ethel said. "I was surprised to see her in our church this morning and thought she might come here to work on that dinner thing again. I heard there are a lot of people interested. I know Viola has sold most of her tickets already, and Justine at Wilhelm's shop sold most of hers. She hasn't heard from Wilhelm yet but expects to get a letter soon. He is quite the traveler. I was talking to Barbara after church, and she said she liked to travel too. Doesn't she usually attend in Potterston?"

It never ceased to amaze Louise how Ethel could wander all over a conversation like a curious puppy, sniffing here and there and going down side trails, yet always manage to come back to her point.

"She does," Alice was saying, "But I told her about our services, and she seemed interested. So I invited her to come and see for herself." Alice turned to Louise. "I believe it is your turn to say grace."

Louise sensed that Alice wanted to end the conversation about Barbara, so she nodded and bowed her head.

"Thank You, Lord, for food and blessings, for friends and family, for the opportunity to serve You. Help us to be open to the needs of those around us, the people You place in our paths. Help us to use the gifts You have given us wisely for the glory of Your name and the furtherance of Your kingdom. We thank You for our food, that we have enough. Thank You for the hands that prepared it. In Your name. Amen."

Ethel watched as Jane served some soup. "What kind of soup is it?"

"I'll give you a hint. It's orange."

"You are determined to use up all those pumpkins, aren't you?" Louise asked with a laugh.

"The last hurrah of my garden. I'm glad I don't have to spend as much time weeding as I did before."

"Wedding?" Ethel asked, sitting up straighter, her eyes bright with anticipation. "What wedding? I thought I heard you talking about a wedding when I came in."

"I was talking about *weeding* the garden, but before you came we were saying that fall would be a perfect time for a wedding."

"Kenneth said something interesting when we went for a walk with Barbara the other day," Jane said with a melancholy smile. "He called the leaves 'autumn's flowers.' That's lovely, isn't it?"

"I noticed you gathered some of those 'flowers,' Jane," Alice said. "What are you going to do with them?"

"I thought I would press them. I found a wonderful picture frame made of two pieces of glass. I was thinking of putting the leaves between the glass. They would seem to float."

"You are so artistic, Jane," Ethel said. "I don't know how you come up with all your wonderful ideas."

"I buy them wholesale over the Internet," Jane said with a wink at her aunt.

Ethel frowned. "You can do that?"

"And if I want a used one, I go to one of those Internet auction sites."

Ethel narrowed her eyes, as if thinking. Her face cleared. "You are teasing me, Jane. That's not very nice."

"It isn't." Jane leaned over and gave her aunt a quick kiss on the cheek. "And I am very sorry, but I couldn't resist." She got up to fetch the next course, a spinach quiche. "So you said Justine hasn't heard from Wilhelm yet?"

"Not yet. I do hope he's okay."

"I'm sure he's fine. I haven't heard from him either. He will be sending me reports to give to Carlene Moss for the newspaper." Jane sighed. "I wish I had never taken that on."

"Surely it can't be that much work," Louise said. "Wilhelm is a very intelligent man. I am surprised he doesn't send his own reports directly to Carlene."

Jane set the golden quiche on the table, and as she cut it into wedges, steam wafted up with an inviting aroma. "I was too. He didn't seem to share my confidence in his writing, though, and asked me to make something of it. But I don't think I'll have the time. I might have to simply send them on to Carlene without any editing. I'm sure they'll be fine."

Louise knew how much Jane was helping Barbara with the mystery weekend, and though she initially hadn't approved of it, she was slowly starting to recognize the interest that it had kindled. She was out and about the town yesterday, and everywhere she went, people mentioned it. Many were eagerly looking forward to it.

On top of it all, they had received a reservation this morning from a couple who wanted to participate in the mystery weekend and were willing to take up the canceled reservation. The sisters still had one more space to fill, but Louise was sure it would come together.

Indeed, it had all worked out.

"If you want any help, Jane, I would be willing to look over Wilhelm's pieces," Louise offered. "If it's just a matter of checking spelling."

Jane put down the spoon and impulsively got up and hugged her sister. "You are a darling. Thank you. Though

Wilhelm led me to believe his letters might need a little more help than that."

Louise patted Jane on the arm and smoothed her own hair back in place. "That's fine, Jane."

"I could kiss you," Jane said.

"That's fine too," Louise said, holding up a warning hand. "We will leave it at hugs and thanks for now."

"That does take a load off my mind. I could probably do it, but it's nice to have one less thing to think about."

"I'm glad I could help out," Louise said. "How much trouble could a little editing be?"

Chapter Eight

Tuesday morning, Louise sat in the back of Viola's shop, Nine Lives Bookstore, working her way through Wilhelm's first letter. Louise had done some shopping in town and decided to stop at her friend's bookstore to visit and to return a book she had borrowed. When Viola left for a moment to serve a customer, Louise retrieved Wilhelm's letter from her purse.

As she read it, her heart dropped. This was not the simple editing job that Jane had said it would be. Wilhelm's message was scrawled all over the page, littered with abbreviations, odd contractions, strikeouts and the messiest handwriting Louise had seen since taking a prescription to the pharmacist. She turned to Viola for help, but she, too, was confounded by Wilhelm's writing.

"What in the world does 'LOL' mean?" Viola squinted through her glasses and tipped the letter away from her as if to read it better.

"I have no idea," Louise murmured as she scanned the second page of the letter, wondering once more what she had taken on.

"I remember reading something about this kind of abbreviation in an ad for a nonfiction book. Something about chat rooms and the like," Viola said, putting down the letter. She adjusted her glasses and got up from the table, huffing as she worked her way past a stack of boxes to a shelf of magazines. "This is a catalog for technical books, and, if I'm not mistaken, I think . . ." She flipped through the pile and pulled one out. "This is what I'm looking for."

"Did you say chat room?" Louise set down the letter as Viola thumbed through the catalog.

"Yes. The book described was an introduction to using some kind of message thing." She ran her finger down a page, then nodded, her glasses glinting. "Here it is. 'Have you always wondered what IMHO means? How about LOL? Or ROFL? This book will untangle the mysteries of the language of chat rooms and text messaging, decipher the code of abbreviations,' and it goes on," Viola said. "And it says at the end that LOL is shorthand for laughing out loud, and the other one is rolling on the floor laughing. Sounds silly to me."

"Do you have the book?"

"No. I could order it, but that would take awhile."

"You're right." Louise removed her glasses. "But I know that Aunt Ethel spends time in chat rooms. I wonder if she would know. I shall have to seek her out."

"Nonsense," Viola said, settling her ample frame into a wooden rocking chair next to Louise. "All we need to do is talk gossip. She'll show up soon enough."

Louise frowned at her friend, who simply smiled back and flipped one end of her colorful scarf over her shoulder. One of Viola's many cats delicately picked its way across the room and came to curl up on Viola's lap. This made Louise think of their own cat. She hadn't seen him for a couple of days. She would have been more concerned, but his food was disappearing as regularly as it used to, so he was around. Maybe he was sulking because they had been so busy with preparations for the mystery weekend that he had not received his usual share of attention.

"I heard that your friend Barbara has been spending a lot of time at the inn," Viola said, stroking the cat. "How are plans for the dinner coming? I've noticed a lot of interest in it."

"I am not that terribly involved," Louise said, setting Wilhelm's letter aside for the moment. "I have to confess I did not approve of it in the first place, though it certainly seems that many people are looking forward to it."

"I think it's a marvelous idea, and I also think that it's very generous of you and your sisters to allow Barbara to use the inn for the venue."

"I'm still not sure how this will all play out. All those people gathered in one place." Louise couldn't picture the logistics, but Barbara kept assuring her that "the inn will work perfectly."

Viola rocked her chair. "Is Rev. Thompson helping you ladies with the production?"

"No. Why do you ask?"

Viola leaned sideways as if checking to see if anyone was in the store, then gave Louise a secretive smile. "Because I saw him and Barbara the other day. They were talking intently."

"Where was this?" Louise wondered what they could have been discussing.

"At a coffee shop in Potterston. They were sitting across the table from each other, but leaning very close." As another cat made its way to Viola's lap, she moved the first one aside to make room. "Very close," she added.

Louise frowned. "You are not passing on gossip are you?"

The bell on the front door tinkled, and Viola set the cats aside, leaning sideways again to see past Louise to the main area of her shop. She gave Louise a thumbs-up. "I am gossiping. You did say you needed to speak with your aunt, didn't you?"

Louise turned around in time to see Ethel in front of a bookshelf, pulling out a book, then putting it back. She was chatting with someone. Florence Simpson.

"How in the world?"

"I'm psychic. I knew that if I started talking about other people, your aunt would come." Viola chuckled, brushed the cats' fur off her black skirt, adjusted the drape of her scarf over her pale ivory sweater, then pushed herself off her chair with a mild grunt. "But mostly, I saw her looking at your car parked in front of the store and I knew she would come in here to find you."

Viola headed out to see if she could assist Ethel. Louise opted to stay behind and try to work on Wilhelm's letter. She picked it up, pulled a pen out of a cat-shaped ceramic pot sitting on Viola's table and got to work.

She could hear Ethel and Florence chatting with Viola. It seemed Florence was looking for a book on etiquette and was asking Viola to order it for her.

Louise laid the letter on the table and smoothed the wrinkles out of the page, wishing she could as easily smooth out the writing.

"... *wnt to* [something] *town in N Hol*" Louise took a stab at it and guessed he went to a town in the northern Netherlands. According to the itinerary he had given Jane, this was his first stop. The only thing she could make out from the name of the town was that it started with an *M* and had a *K* in it. She would simply write "town" and leave it at that. The next few phrases were harder to read. All she could decipher from it was "rats" and "house" and "stocks" and "kettle." Maybe "kennel." She held the paper at a distance and managed to figure out that Wilhelm had gone to a kennel that had rats in it. It was one of the oldest in the Netherlands. He had his picture taken with a "stick"? He would need one if there were rats around. Louise shuddered. This didn't seem like a pleasant trip to her at all. It appeared there were many such "kennels." But this time he spelled it with a C.

She would have to do some research to find out about these rat kennels in the Netherlands. Maybe they put all the rats they found in a kennel, thinking it a humane way to deal with them. It sounded horrid, and she had a hard time imagining the fastidious Wilhelm being remotely interested in such a thing.

By the time Viola was finished with Ethel and Florence, Louise had managed to transcribe about half of the first page. Wilhelm had told Jane that he hoped she would make the information he gave her more interesting. She presumed her best course of action was to "translate" it for now and try to give it some narrative flow once she conquered the worst part.

"Well, Ethel and Florence could see that you were hard at work, so—with a little persuasion from me—they decided not to disturb you. And your aunt promised to be on hand if you need her chat-room expertise."

"I'm sure that she will, bless her. And thank you for being my first line of defense."

"You are making some headway," Viola said, glancing over Louise's shoulder at what she had so far.

"My headway is making my head ache," Louise said, rubbing her temples as if hoping to ease the pain.

"I'll see what I can do with this second page," Viola said, studying it with a serious effort. "Once I'm done transcribing it, we can polish it up a bit."

They worked in silence until Louise heard a swift intake of breath from Viola.

"This is unbelievable," Viola said, her hand over her mouth as if holding back her surprise. "From the looks of what I'm reading, Wilhelm has been going *horse* hunting close to the Black Forest." She looked at Louise, her eyes wide as she handed her the paper. "See what you can make of it."

Louise read slowly, struggling through the penmanship and the words, but came to the same conclusion. "I'm afraid you are right."

"We can't put that in the paper, can we? What would people think?"

"Well . . . hunting is a sport, as is fishing. If he had gone fishing you wouldn't think twice about writing that up." Louise was trying to be diplomatic, but again, this trip did not seem like the kind Wilhelm would take. Maybe he was going through some kind of life change.

"But fishing is a different kind of sport. It's less, well, *barbaric*. Besides, people have a different relationship with fish than with horses," Viola said. "I have stacks of those frivolous books that are so popular with young girls about horses. People raise them and have them as pets. You don't do the same with a bass or a catfish."

"What about goldfish?" Louise asked in a teasing note.

"That's not the same thing, Louise. Stop baiting me."

"I hope that pun was unintentional," Louise said.

Viola looked puzzled, then laughed. "Entirely unintentional. But to get back to Wilhelm's letter, why, we can't put that in."

Louise tapped her pen on the paper as she mulled this over. She couldn't imagine Wilhelm hunting, period. But she couldn't imagine him visiting rat kennels either. "This is what he wrote. I think we should put it in as he sent it to us."

Viola glanced down at the letter and shook her head as if still unable to believe what she had read. "I've never heard of such a thing in my life. I shall have to have a talk with him when he gets back. Horse hunting, indeed."

Louise had to laugh at her friend's expression. She read on, and then backtracked and read again.

"Does this make sense to you? From what I read here, Wilhelm went on a bike, and then he says something about watching, then dreaming and sleeping. Then something about getting blown up?"

Viola read the passage that Louise pointed out. "It could be that he went for a bike ride and almost fell asleep and his tire blew up," Viola said, biting her lip. "Which makes sense, because on this page he talks about bolts that were found. So he must have had a flat tire and needed some bolts to fix his wheel."

"I wish we could contact him to make sure," Louise said, tapping her finger against her chin.

"You could wait until he's back to verify the story."

"But Carlene called me yesterday about this. She is expecting me to get a story to her by this afternoon at the latest. She's left space for it." Louise wrote down what she thought Wilhelm had written. "We'll have to do the best we can for now. If we need to make a correction, it will just have to go in next week's *Nutshell*."

Early that afternoon Alice whisked a dust cloth over the dresser in the Sunrise Room and straightened one of the vases of leaves that Jane had arranged. There was one in each guest room. Their next guests were due at any moment, and thankfully Alice was ready for them. The ringing of the bell from downstairs announced them. She presumed they were the young couple on their honeymoon, Mr. and Mrs. Moreau.

As she went down the stairs, she saw a young couple standing by the registration desk. They were both smiling, which was always a good sign. Smiling guests were happy guests. And taking care of happy guests always made the sisters' job easier.

Young Mrs. Moreau had short black hair cut in fringy wisps that framed her face. She wore a snug T-shirt over tight-fitting blue jeans. Her pants were ripped at the knee and hung low on her hips. Though this type of clothing was not uncommon, it still bothered Alice to see young women dressed in such a manner. She looked more like a Miss than a Mrs., at least in Alice's estimation.

Mr. Moreau was more conservatively dressed. He wore a corduroy blazer over a soft wool sweater. He also wore blue jeans, but his were loose and pressed. His light blond hair was neatly trimmed.

She had heard the saying "opposites attract," and she supposed this was definitely the case with this young couple.

"Good afternoon, and welcome to Grace Chapel Inn," Alice said, reaching out her hand to shake theirs. "My name is Alice Howard. I understand you have reservations for the next few days."

Young Mrs. Moreau giggled, but Mr. Moreau shook her hand with a firm grip. "My name is Neville Moreau, and this is my wife, Summer." He gave his spouse a smile warm with affection.

"This is such a totally awesome place," Summer said, looking around the main entrance of the inn. "I've never seen gold used like this in wallpaper before." She walked to the wallpaper in question and touched it. "It even feels sorta slippery. Cool. Oh, and look, Nevvie, this hat rack looks like it came right out of some of those old movies that you like to watch." She admired it a moment, then walked back to the desk where Alice had opened the appointment book to confirm their reservation.

"We've simply got to sit out on that swing on the front porch. Wouldn't that be just so romantic? Just like in the old days." Summer sighed and slipped her hand through Neville's arm. "I'm so glad we could come. This is an awesome place to spend a honeymoon." She glanced at Alice.

Neville looked around the inn, then back at his young wife. "I have to confess, I had other plans, but Summer kept talking about this inn and how she always wanted to stay here."

"This was cheaper than going where all your other buddies went for their honeymoons," Summer said, giving him a nudge.

He scratched his name on the reservation book with the fountain pen that Jane liked guests to use.

"What kind of pen is that?" Summer asked, picking up the pen when Neville was done with it.

"It's an old-style fountain pen. My father used to use it."

Summer turned it over in her hands, then laid it gently down on the desk. "Did your dad used to live here?"

"Yes, he did. I grew up in this house."

"Cool! You have family?"

"Two sisters. We run the inn together."

"Neat!" Summer stuck her hands in the back pocket of her jeans and rocked back and forth, looking around, seemingly fascinated with the place. "You're lucky. This is an awesome house. My little brothers would like totally overrun the place. Good thing they're not here."

Neville gave Summer a smile and handed Alice a credit card. She addressed herself to the paperwork required for payment. While Alice worked, Summer detached herself from Neville and again moved slowly around the front entrance commenting on the inn's various antiques.

"Do you have many suitcases?" Alice asked Neville when she was finished.

"We have three. I'll bring those up later," Neville said.

Summer giggled. "Nevvie took more clothes than I did. Not too normal for a guy, is it?"

Neville gave her an indulgent smile. Though she and her sisters practiced discretion when it came to their guests, Alice could not help speculating about this oddly opposite couple.

She led them up the stairs, but Summer paused at the landing to look at some old pictures of Madeleine Howard.

"Who is this lady?" Summer asked, touching the picture frame with one slender finger.

"That is my mother," Alice said. "That picture was taken shortly before she passed away."

"Oh, she must have been quite young."

"She died at thirty-nine giving birth to my youngest sister," Alice said quietly, thinking of how this fact had often caused Jane pain.

Summer's expression became serious, and she gave Alice a level glance. "That stinks, doesn't it? That your sister never met her mom?"

Alice held the young woman's steady gaze and realized that in spite of her immature language, she was capable of genuine sympathy for someone she hadn't met. Perhaps there was more to Summer than met the eye.

"It has been difficult, but she has us and a wonderful community."

"I thought I read something about God on the plaque in the front of the house," Summer said. "I have to check it out again. That's cool. Where did the inn get the name?"

"The inn is named after Grace Chapel, which is next door. My father was the chief pastor there until he died a couple of years ago."

"Church. Wow!" She turned to her husband. "I wanna go on Sunday. Can we?"

Neville looked taken aback, but nodded. "I suppose we could, if we are here on Sunday," he said slowly. He glanced at Alice. "Is that possible? Could we attend?"

"Of course. Guests are always welcome." Alice glanced at Summer again, seeing her in a new light. She turned and led them the rest of the way up the stairs. "You will be staying in the Garden Room," she said, standing aside to let the couple in.

"Oh, now this is an amazing room," Summer said as she walked past Alice into the room. "I can see why you call it the Garden Room." She dropped onto the bed. "All these cool shades of green and that awesome trim on the wainscoting. This is amazing." She turned to Neville with a huge smile. "Thanks, hon, for agreeing to come here." She jumped off the bed and threw her arms around her husband.

Neville gave Alice an embarrassed glance but hugged his young wife back.

"Will you need any help with your bags?" Alice asked as she handed Neville the key to the room.

"The two of us will be able to manage," Neville said.

"We serve breakfast in the mornings in the dining room," Alice said, going through her usual speech for new guests. "We'll have other guests staying with us, so you may be eating with them as well. We have brochures of the local businesses and attractions at the check-in counter. Dinner can be purchased at the Coffee Shop or at Zachary's, a fine eating establishment in town. If you have any other questions, please let us know, and we'll be happy to help you."

"So, you guys don't have supper for us?" Summer asked as she inspected the large rosewood chest that was part of the bedroom suite.

"No. We're strictly a bed-and-breakfast. But occasionally we have a high tea."

"High tea sounds cool. Are you going to do it while we're here?"

"Unfortunately, no." They were far too busy with the mystery weekend to contemplate even more work.

"Oh well. That's okay."

Neville pulled out his wallet and Alice realized what he was about to do. She was puzzled as to why he thought he should tip her. She had done nothing more than show them to their rooms.

"As for gratuities," she said smoothly, as if this were also part of her speech for newcomers, "we have a policy of not accepting them. Everything we do for you is included in the package price, and we do it gladly and thankfully. We want your stay here to be as enjoyable as possible, and we don't want you to think that we expect extra for our services."

Neville looked puzzled, as if this was highly unusual in his experience.

Summer giggled. "Nevvie works with money all the time, so he's used to handing cash to anyone who comes his way. He works at a bank that his family is connected with, but I'm trying to talk him into getting in touch with his inner mechanic. He likes to fiddle with cars, but his parents didn't think that was a very good job for him." She looked up at him with an admiring glance and stroked his arm in a loving gesture. "When I was working as a waitress, he was always my favorite customer. Guess that's why he married me. Saved himself a pile of money on tips."

Neville grinned.

Alice started her retreat. "I will leave you two alone to unpack and get settled in. Again, if there is anything you need, please come and talk to us. One of us is generally around the house, usually in the kitchen."

"There is another thing," Summer said.

Neville frowned down at her and shook his head. "It's okay. I'm sure it will be fine."

"I told them, and I don't want to miss them," Summer said, louder.

"Please, Summer. It's not going to happen."

Summer turned to Alice, her eyes intent. "We might get a call from another Mr. and Mrs. Moreau. If they call, we need to know right away."

The intensity of her glance surprised Alice.

"Of course. That is not a problem."

"Thanks a bunch," Summer said with a relieved smile.

"Don't count on it," Neville said.

"I can dream, can't I?"

And as Alice made her way down the stairs, she wondered anew at the young couple's relationship. It was another mystery to add to the mix.

Chapter Nine

*J*ane, I'm just heading out and wondering if you need anything," Alice said as she entered the kitchen Wednesday morning. "I have to go to Potterston to pick up a few things for Barbara."

Jane looked up from the script she had been going over and felt a lick of panic. "Is it Wednesday already?"

"All day," Alice said, buttoning up her light jacket.

Jane glanced over her shoulder at the calendar hanging on the wall behind her. The days were speeding along. They had only a week and a half until the mystery weekend, and she still had to finalize a menu. In addition, the script wasn't ready.

"Don't tell Louise, but I'm starting to feel hysteria coming on."

"Your secret is safe with me," Alice said. "Have you seen our young honeymooners today?"

Jane made a quick note in the margin of the script, then looked up at her sister. "No, haven't seen them since last night. They weren't in their room this morning. I imagine they're out and about."

"I'm sure they will let us know if they need anything."
Alice said good-bye and left.

Jane had some baking to catch up on, a few more pumpkins to deal with, and she still had to put finishing touches
on plans for the mystery weekend. For a moment she wondered if she had taken on more than she could handle, but
she was determined to make this succeed. Barbara was so
excited about the event, and she had already received
inquiries from other groups who were interested in using
the same means to help raise funds for Barbara's charity.

Jane enjoyed being a part of a worthy cause. She liked
knowing that the work she was doing with Barbara had
broader repercussions, that it would help people who
needed it. Though she saw her work at the inn as a ministry,
at times she liked to know she was helping others beyond
their guests and the people of Acorn Hill.

Some time later a light rap at the door made her look
up at the clock with a nip of frustration. She had hoped to
squeeze out a few more minutes of work on the script
before her other obligations demanded her time. She had
bread baking in the oven, and after that she had promised
Louise she would clean some windows.

"Come in," she called, putting down her pen and gathering up her papers, hiding them safely in the folder. She
didn't want anyone to have any hint of what the mystery
was about.

Rev. Thompson stepped inside the kitchen and glanced around.

Jane stifled a smile. It was hard not to see the disappointment on his face when he noted Barbara was not present. "I was…uh…wondering if Louise was here?"

"Louise has gone shopping," Jane said, getting up from the table. Though Barbara was not present, Jane expected her soon. She would stall the pastor until Barbara's arrival. "Would you like a cup of decaf?"

"No, thank you. I don't want to bother you." His eyes went to the folder lying on the table. "I am between duties right now, so I thought I would stop in, but I know you are busy."

That was true. But Jane was never too busy to play Cupid. "Nonsense," she said, waving her hand as if brushing away his protests. "I always have time for my friends."

She prepared the coffeepot as if it was a foregone conclusion that he would stay. He hovered in the doorway a moment, and as the scent of the freshly ground coffee wafted toward him, he gave in and sat at the table.

"How are things going with the story for the mystery weekend?" he asked, folding his hands on the table. "Barbara said you are having some difficulty weaving the different strands of the story together."

Jane hid her pleasure. Obviously he and Barbara had been spending time together if he knew that much.

While the coffee brewed, she put together a plate of pumpkin squares and sugar cookies. "The writers of mysteries make it seem so easy," Jane said with a note of petulance in her voice, "but it's hard to give out just enough information for people to make an informed guess, but not so much that the solution is easy. In addition, when the mystery is solved, people should be able to have an 'aha' moment."

"Have you thought of asking Alice to help? I know she likes to read mysteries."

"She tried but said she had better luck solving mysteries than trying to concoct one. Besides, Alice is busy enough these days."

Jane heard a light cough, then looked behind her. Summer stood in the doorway between the kitchen and dining room, biting her lip, her hands in the back pockets of her snug blue jeans.

"Hello, Summer. You're back," Jane said.

"Yeah. And I, uh, was wondering if anyone called for us while we were gone?" she asked. She exchanged smiles with Rev. Thompson.

Jane shook her head. "But if anyone does, I'll let you know."

Summer nodded, biting her lip again. "Sure thing. I know Nevvie doesn't want as much as me to connect with anyone, but I was kinda hoping…" She gave a noncommittal shrug, then said, "Please don't tell Neville I asked, okay?"

Jane didn't know what to make of that, but she nodded anyway.

"Thanks a bunch for that." Summer looked relieved, then turned and went off, her steps fading away as she jogged up the stairs.

Jane turned to her friend, thoroughly confused. "That was enlightening." She glanced back over her shoulder as if hoping to see the solution to this interesting problem. "One is waiting for phone calls, the other doesn't want any. I wonder what is going on."

"I think you have been delving too deeply into your mystery play," he said with a laugh. "It could easily be that one wants more privacy than the other, that's all." He took another sip of his decaf and glanced out the window. Then he pushed the sugar bowl around and took another sip. Carefully, he rolled up the sleeves of his pale green shirt.

Jane couldn't stand it any longer. "Kenneth, you didn't come to sit and drink coffee and talk about our mystery guests, did you?"

The pastor looked up, his eyes wide with surprise. Then his expression turned sheepish. "Your intuition serves you well, Jane." He rested his elbows on the table and leaned forward. "I wish I knew exactly how to bring this up." He fidgeted with the sugar bowl again. "Something has been on my mind of late."

Jane knew he needed a little more of her intuition. "I am going to go out on a limb and guess this has something to do with Barbara."

Without looking up, he smiled, still pushing the sugar bowl back and forth. "Correct limb."

"You're attracted to her."

He looked up, and Jane was surprised to see a light flush color his cheeks. "Yes. I am. And to tell you the truth, I'm not certain what I should do about it."

"Is it a problem?" Jane was surprised at his reluctance. When he and Barbara were together she could feel the connection between them, it was that tangible. She wondered why this bothered him.

The pastor smiled a gentle smile, but Jane could see a touch of melancholy in it. "When Catherine died, I thought I would never find anyone like her again. In fact, I never thought I could love again." He paused, his finger running up and down the side of his mug. "Barbara is a wonderful person. Vivacious and outgoing…" He glanced over at Jane.

No one in Acorn Hill had ever met Catherine, Rev. Thompson's first wife. She died about ten years ago, before he came to Grace Chapel and Acorn Hill. He spoke of her only occasionally, so Jane and her sisters knew little more about her than that she was a talented painter and that she had died, childless, of a heart condition.

It was this hint of experienced sorrow in his life that made him such a compassionate listener and gave him a heart for those who suffered.

"Are you feeling guilty because of your feelings for Barbara?" Jane gently prodded.

He chuckled. "Seems silly, doesn't it? I loved Catherine so deeply and for so long. I struggled with my faith when she was taken away, but I know that God upheld me through that time. I was so sad . . . the pain was so great I thought I would never recover. But I did. And now, I find I am attracted to another woman for the first time in many years, and I feel that somehow demeans the love I have for Catherine."

Jane could see his struggle. She reached across the table and put her hand on his. "Catherine loved you, didn't she?"

His smile told her more than any words could.

"If you love someone, don't you want the best for them?" Jane continued.

Her friend looked up at her, as if he knew where she was going. "You're going to say that Catherine would want me to be happy."

"I was going to try something less cliché, but, yes, that about covers it," Jane said.

"I have to confess, it is an interesting situation," the pastor said. "This feeling of attraction."

"Now don't go and overanalyze this thing with that Boston-educated mind of yours," Jane warned. "Sometimes you need to go with the flow and simply let things happen."

"Now that's the San Franciscan in you talking."

"Actually, it's the Jane in me. Living in San Francisco only enhanced it," she said with a wink as she withdrew her hand. "Barbara is a wonderful person, and I sense she thinks you're quite a hunk."

He shot her a frown, but Jane laughed. "It's true," she said. "And the nice part about Barbara is that she understands the obligations of your work as a pastor, because she is so committed to the charity she is supporting. She also has a heart for people in need. I think you should allow this to happen."

There was a light knock at the back door, and she knew that it was Barbara. "Come on in."

She couldn't resist a quick look at Rev. Thompson to catch his reaction, and she was pleased to see him rise, smiling.

The door swung open and Barbara backed into the room, balancing the briefcase slung over her shoulder and a stack of papers in her arms.

"Should have used the front door," she huffed, shifting her load. She turned in time to see Rev. Thompson standing in front of her, his hands out for the papers. She blushed.

"Why, thank you, kind sir," she said with a smile, as she handed them to him. "You're my own knight in shining armor."

"Actually, today it's cotton and wool," he said, smiling back.

"Looks good too," Barbara said.

They paused, looking at each other. Then, as if just realizing Jane was in the kitchen, they looked away.

"Do you want some coffee, Barbara?" Jane asked, her question breaking the silence.

"That would be great." Barbara slipped her briefcase off her shoulder and dropped it on the chair by the table. "Please put those on the table, Kenneth," she said, her tone noncommittal. But Jane caught the look she gave him. And it warmed her heart.

She made up a lame excuse to check on something at the front desk. Somehow she had to find a way to encourage these two to pursue this relationship, but how?

Both Barbara and Rev. Thompson had jobs that kept them busy. He held a prominent position in town. And privacy in Acorn Hill was as rare as snow in July.

The leaf tour had worked, to a point. She also knew that the pair had spent time alone this past Sunday.

Jane was determined to see these two people, who were so obviously suited for each other, together.

Think, Jane. Think.

She waited awhile longer, but she had to get her bread out of the oven before it burned. She returned to the kitchen.

And entered in time to see the pastor and Barbara quickly draw away from each other.

Romance hung in the air, as surely as the smell of bread baking. Rev. Thompson cleared his throat and quickly got up. "I . . . must be going . . ." he gave Jane a half-hearted smile, then looked back at Barbara. His expression softened, and he rested his hand on her shoulder.

"I'll be seeing you later," he said softly.

She looked up at him, as coquettish as any young girl with a crush, and nodded as he left.

Jane affected a casual air that she hoped Barbara noticed and pulled the bread out of the oven.

Okay, Emily Post, Jane thought as she carefully shook the bread out of her seasoned pans, *what is the proper topic of conversation for a situation like this?*

"You don't need to feel awkward, Jane," Barbara said as Jane set the last of the loaves out to cool. "We should have been . . . well . . . more discreet."

Jane shook off her oven mitts and set them on the counter, then turned to her friend. "No. That's fine. I'm glad you two are comfortable around each other . . . or rather that you aren't afraid to express your affection . . ." She stumbled verbally, then finally threw her hands in the air.

"Okay. I'm glad that you and Kenneth are in love with each other. How about that?"

Barbara pretended to be inspecting her manicure, which was, as always, immaculate. "How about that?" she said softly, then gave Jane a coy look. "I don't know about the 'in love' part, but 'in like' sure sums it up."

"I can do 'in like' as easily as the other." Jane sat across from Barbara at the table, allowing herself a huge smile that almost made her face hurt. "I'm happy for you."

Barbara folded her hands on the table, tapping her thumbs together. "I also would like it if . . ." She stopped, as if she was unsure what to say next. "Kenneth is quite a high-profile member of this community . . . and things are so unsure."

"And you don't want any gossip spreading."

"And you have read my mind."

"I'm very literate when it comes to that," Jane said with a light laugh.

"Thanks for that, Jane. You are a good friend." Barbara reached across the table and squeezed her hand. "I don't know what will come of this. But I guess I'm willing to give it a try."

"Has anyone phoned yet?" Summer drummed her fingers on the reception desk, the bright red of her nails flashing in the late afternoon sun.

Louise looked up from the checkbook and lowered her glasses so she could see the young girl better. "I'm not sure. I haven't been here all afternoon," she said. Jane had mentioned Summer's earlier request in the kitchen.

Summer pursed her lips, nodding absently. "Neville and I are going to go for a walk," she said. "It's so beautiful outside. Jane told me about a pond a ways from here that I want to see." She gave Louise a smile, then ran back up the stairs. A few moments later she and her new husband walked out the door, hand in hand, looking like the picture of a loving couple.

Louise went back to work. An hour later she had all the bills paid and entered, and she had one more chance to review Wilhelm's letter.

She and Viola had hoped to get it to Carlene for inclusion in today's edition of the *Nutshell*, but it took her and Viola most of yesterday to transcribe it, and they couldn't get it to Carlene on time. It would simply have to wait for next week.

The front door opened, and in walked their latest guests, Donna Lyster and her daughters, Patti and Maria, their arms full of rustling bags. It looked like the young women had a successful shopping trip. Donna had only one bag, but she was smiling just the same.

The Lysters had arrived earlier this afternoon. From what Louise understood, they were in town for a week to help plan the wedding of Patti, the older daughter, to a young man from Potterston.

"Welcome back," Louise said, putting down her pen. "How was your shopping trip?"

"It was great," Maria said, holding up her bags as if for inspection. She shook back her dark hair as she smiled with pleasure. "Patti got some wicked great shoes, and I got a sweet sweatshirt, and we got a whole bunch of other stuff."

Louise merely smiled, though she failed to comprehend how shoes could be both evil and good simultaneously. "I'm glad you had a good time."

Donna inhaled appreciatively. "It smells wonderful in here. Is your sister Jane baking again?"

Louise nodded. "We are hoping to host a mystery weekend here in a week and a half, and I imagine she's trying to get as much food prepared and put in the freezer as she possibly can."

"I heard there was a couple here on their honeymoon," Patti said. "I wonder if she might have any wedding-planning suggestions for me."

"They are out for a walk at the moment, but you will probably be seeing them around," Louise said. "The inn is not that large, and breakfast is a communal affair here."

"Now, darling," Donna said with an indulgent smile, "you don't need any help from a complete stranger. Your future mother-in-law and I are more than capable of making all the arrangements."

Patti shrugged. "I know, but maybe she has some helpful tips."

Louise took in Patti's sweater set and pressed khaki pants and thought of Summer and her faded and torn blue jeans. Somehow, she doubted they would have much in common.

Chapter Ten

Thursday morning, only Summer and Neville were among the guests who were down early for breakfast, as were all three sisters. Their newest guest, an older man who had checked in late Wednesday, was still sleeping, and Donna, Patti and Maria were still in their rooms.

When Summer realized that the sisters were planning to eat in the kitchen, as was their usual procedure, she implored them to join her and her husband. "It would be like way cozier."

Moved by the obvious sincerity in Summer's voice, the sisters smiled, thanked her and moved into the dining room with their cups and saucers.

"What do you call this?" Summer asked, looking at the golden brown pastry that Jane had set on the table.

"It's a pecan ring, a sweet biscuit rolled in cinnamon and layered with pecans and a caramel sauce." Ribbons of steam and the comforting scent of cinnamon floated up when Jane cut it open. She served a piece to Summer.

"It looks amazing." She took a bite while it was still warm and sighed in satisfaction. "I think I could get fat staying here."

Alice glanced at the young woman's slim figure and doubted that such a thing could happen.

"Are you about finished?" Neville eventually asked his young wife with an indulgent smile.

"I wouldn't mind another cup of coffee," she said, wiping her fingers on her napkin. "We're not in any rush, are we? It's so homey here."

"No. We can wait. I'm sure the shops of Acorn Hill won't be missing us." Neville laid his hand on Summer's shoulder. Alice smiled at the gentle interaction between the two. It still surprised her, considering how different they were.

Summer was about to get up and clear the table, when Louise held up her hand. "I'll get it for you," she said. "You are our guest."

Summer laughed as she glanced from Alice to Jane. "I'm not used to this fussing. It's strange for a waitress to be the one drinking the coffee instead of the one pouring the coffee. Of course at home, I was always running around pouring and serving too."

"Do you have family, Summer?" Alice asked.

"Yeah. Big one." Summer shot Neville a grin. "Nevvie is still getting used to the noise at our place when we're all together. He's an only child so it's a bit tough for him— especially at suppertime. Depending on how many extras are at the table, it's fast and furious, so you have to grab what you can. At his place, you sit and wait while someone brings you first this plate, then another plate." She gave Neville an apologetic look. "I don't mean to slam your family. I mean, it's always really nice with the different glasses and the rows of silverware on each side of the plate." She shrugged. "It's just that I'm not used to all that fuss."

"Where do your parents live, Summer?" Alice asked. The more she and her sisters got to know them, the more dramatic their differences seemed. She was starting, however, to see the appeal that this girl held. She seemed like she could be a lot of fun.

"Oh, we live in Potterston. I've heard such good things about your inn for ages."

"And what about your family, Neville?" Alice asked. "Do they live in Potterston as well?"

He shook his head and carefully wiped a trace of the muffin from his lips. "No. They live in Pittsburgh."

"It's a pretty amazing house they have," Summer said. "Tall, brick, lots of windows. They even have this kind of turret part in the house. Way cool. And half of the house is covered with this ivy. Looks like something you see in those English movies. We could put all my brothers and sisters in that house and still have room for the aunts and uncles and their kids." Summer related all of this with a big smile on her face and not a touch of rancor in her voice. She seemed genuinely impressed by it all.

"Summer," Neville warned, as if she was moving onto a topic he didn't want to discuss.

"It's true. It's crazy how big their place is." She shook her head as if she couldn't understand it one bit. "But hey, Neville's right. I shouldn't carry on so. How much money they have is their business, not mine, right? I shouldn't be critical. God knows the heart of people, I don't." She looked around the table, smiling, as if looking for confirmation of her comment, and Alice smiled back. In that quick statement she caught a glimpse of wisdom beyond the girl's young years. And she also caught a glimpse of the appeal she probably held for Neville.

"You are absolutely correct," Louise said, laying her napkin beside her plate. "We can't presume to judge others. We must leave that up to our Lord."

"Preach it, sister!" Summer said, emphasizing her glib comment with an upraised fist.

Jane glanced at Louise's surprised face, and before her younger sister could make some smart comment, Alice spoke up. "Is Barbara coming today, Jane?" she asked. "I need to talk to her about the ticket sales."

"She can't come until this afternoon," Jane replied. "She has, let's say, other commitments."

Alice wondered why Jane was being so vague but let it slide.

"Is Barbara the lady helping you with the mystery weekend?" Summer asked.

"Oh, you know about the supper?" Jane asked.

"It's the talk of the town," Summer said, glancing at Neville. "I'm trying to talk Neville into coming back for it instead of going to New York for the rest of our honeymoon like he planned. Do you have any rooms?"

"We do have a vacancy if you're interested," Jane said.

"What do you say?" Summer said to Neville, her eyes dancing with excitement. "It sounds like a riot."

"*Riot* might be exaggerating somewhat," Louise commented as she got up. "But I think it will be fun."

As Summer had done moments before, Jane pumped her fist in the air behind Louise's back. Louise was finally coming around.

"I don't know, Summer," Neville said. "I think we should stay in New York. You might be disappointed if we come back and you don't make the contact you've been hoping for."

Summer held his gaze. "If we come back, we'll have a good time. And I'd sooner come back here than go scampering around the country until it's time for you to go back to work."

"Things may not happen the way you want them to," the young husband said cryptically.

Summer shrugged off his comments. "Maybe, maybe not. But in the meantime, I think this mystery weekend sounds like fun." She turned back to Louise. "Count us in if you have the room."

"We can work out the arrangements when you have your plans settled," Jane said.

"So this Barbara lady," Summer said, stirring some more sugar into her coffee, "I heard she and the preacher have a thing going."

Jane's eyes grew wide, and she sent a horrified look to Alice. "Why would you say that?" she asked. This was supposed to be hush-hush. She hadn't said much to her sisters for fear they might let it slip accidentally.

"We had supper last night at the Coffee Shop and heard it there," Summer said. Then she cocked her head as if listening. "Hey. It sounds like someone else is up. Maybe it's those girls."

"Who was discussing Barbara and Rev. Thompson?" Jane asked, wanting to know more about the talk at the Coffee Shop.

Patti and Maria entered the dining room, pulling Summer's attention away from Jane's question.

Glancing from Summer to Neville, Patti greeted all present. "Good morning, everybody."

Maria echoed her sister.

"Girls, these are the Moreaus, Summer and Neville. Summer, Neville, this is Patti and Maria Lyster," Louise said as Alice placed extra chairs at the table.

"Nice to meet you both," Patti said, giving Summer a smile. Then she and her sister glanced at the sideboard.

"Help yourselves to breakfast," Jane said, getting up. "Would you like coffee or tea with breakfast?"

"Shouldn't we wait for Mom?" Maria said, glancing back over her shoulder.

"She'll be coming down pretty soon," Patti said, filling up her plate. "This looks wonderful." She looked over her shoulder at Jane, Alice and Louise. "Is breakfast like this every morning?"

"We have something different every morning."

Patti sat and started eating. "This is so good. I hope the caterer for our wedding will do as well."

"You're getting married?" Summer asked, leaning forward, interested.

Patti nodded, then glanced at Maria. "If we can come to an agreement on things, that is the plan."

"Where are you getting married?"

"Potterston."

"No kidding? I'm from Potterston," Summer said. "Who are you getting hitched to?"

"David Duplesis."

"Tall? Black hair? Drives a Mustang?"

"You know him?"

Summer hesitated a moment, then said, "I know of him. We didn't exactly move in the same social circles. His parents have a few dollars to pitch around."

Patti buttered a muffin and shook her head. "Tell me about it. It's been causing some trouble in planning this wedding. Mom is scared that we're going to end up looking cheap. They invited us to stay with them, but Mom figured it was better if we didn't impose."

"Good morning," Donna sang from the doorway, stepping into the room. She glanced from Patti to Maria and smiled at Neville and Summer.

Alice introduced everyone and offered Donna some coffee, which she gratefully accepted.

"It's another wonderful morning," Donna said. "I had such a good sleep. What a peaceful place you have."

"I'm so glad you are enjoying your stay," Alice said.

"I was hoping to drive into Potterston today, Patti, to go over plans with Mrs. Duplesis. She was thinking of the country club for the reception. What do you think of that?"

"I don't know, Mother. It seems rather…" she shrugged as if unable to find the word.

"Expensive?" Summer put in.

Donna glanced at the young woman. "Are you familiar with Potterston?"

"My hometown," Summer said with a grin. "Mom and Dad still live there. We're going to visit them today. Dad has an old truck he wants Nevvie to look at. Something with the engine."

"I think it's a cracked head gasket," Neville said. "But I'll have a look at it in order to tell."

Jane could see Donna's puzzled frown as she sized up Neville in his neatly pressed pants and crisp shirt. Jane had to admit that the juxtaposition of Neville's looking like a banker and talking like a mechanic was a little hard to figure out.

"What part of Potterston do your parents live in, Summer?" Donna asked. "David lives on the east end of town, in the Blakely subdivision."

"I know. Snob Hill." Summer said, her wide smile pulling any ill will out of the comment. "My mom and dad live out of town."

"They own a farm?"

"Yep. Truck farm. Produce, some flowers. Kept us seven kids busy morning, noon and night."

"I see," Donna said, with a polite smile. She turned to Alice and her sisters. "We were wondering if there are any stores here in Acorn Hill that we might be interested in looking through."

Alice glanced at Jane, then Louise.

"You could try Nellie's for clothes," she said. "The Holzmanns have an antiques shop where you might find something interesting. Sylvia's Buttons sells fabric, and she does some custom sewing."

"That might have been fun," Patti said, glancing at her mother. "Getting a wedding dress sewn. I could have designed my own wedding dress."

"Hey, I could help," Summer said. "I like doing that kind of thing."

Alice saw Donna lift one eyebrow at the lacy camisole and corduroy jacket Summer wore this morning.

"Honey, we simply couldn't have done that," Donna said to Patti. "You had to buy your dress closer to home. I couldn't imagine coming back here all the time for the fittings."

"Actually, Mother, I wouldn't have minded."

Donna gave her a faint smile accompanied by a sigh. "Maybe not, but knowing how much trouble you have had making up your mind on anything associated with this wedding, I imagine it would have been close to impossible to design your own wedding dress." Donna took a sip of coffee. "It will be your wedding, darling. It's your special day. Your father and I want it to be the best it can be."

"I know, Mom," Patti said, pushing her plate away. "And I appreciate all you've been doing."

Donna seemed relieved. "I'm looking forward to meeting with David's family. They have been so kind and cooperative."

"Oh, Mr. and Mrs. Duplesis are great people," Summer put in. "Mr. Duplesis is always giving money away. They have it, but they're not stingy with it."

"I'm glad you shared that with us," Donna said, giving Summer another tight smile.

"There was this fund-raising dinner last spring. It was for the hospital." Summer said, glancing at Alice, who seemed not to notice Donna's irritation. "You work at the hospital, Miss Howard. Do you remember?"

"I do, actually. We needed some new medical equipment, an MRI machine."

"Mr. Duplesis, he gave a boatload of money to the cause."

"And how were you involved?" Patti asked.

"I worked the supper. As a waitress."

"That was generous of you," Louise said.

Summer shrugged. "Hey. It's what I do."

"You're a waitress?" Maria asked.

Summer nodded. "Yup. It's how I met Neville here." She reached out for Neville's hand. Alice felt sorry for him. He was absolutely surrounded by women who were talking about weddings.

"I'm looking forward to planning this wedding with Mrs. Duplesis," Donna said.

"I'm sure it will be a whoopin' party. Those Duplesis people really know how to put on a bash."

"A wedding is hardly a bash," Donna said.

Summer grinned at Donna, completely unfazed by the woman's attitude. "It's a party, isn't it? Fun, family and celebration." Her expression sobered a moment, her glance skittering to Neville. "At least that's how it should be."

Neville put his hand on Summer's arm and squeezed it. "We had a great wedding," he said, as if reassuring her. He looked from Patti to Donna. "We're on our honeymoon right now."

"So I understand," Patti said. "Congratulations. Did you get married in Potterston?"

"Yes, we did. In Summer's parents yard."

"Oh, I see." Donna's frown told Alice that she *didn't* see.

"It was just a little wedding." Summer kissed Neville's cheek. "Lots of fun."

The loving look he gave his young wife made Alice smile to herself.

"Do you have pictures?" Alice asked.

"Upstairs. Do you want to see them?"

"I'd love to," Alice said.

"Actually, I would too," Patti said. "I'm always looking out for something different."

"We had a different wedding all right." Neville buttered another muffin as Summer ran up the stairs to their room.

"What do you mean?" Donna asked.

"It was a memorable, meaningful wedding. Summer pretty much planned it all. I was away for a lot of the planning, so I let her have at it."

"Did you do anything special?"

Neville looked down at his muffin, his mouth curved up in a cockeyed grin. "Among other things, we had a horse-drawn carriage take us away from the reception."

Patti sighed. "That sounds so romantic."

Summer returned waving a small photo album. She set it down beside Patti and slipped into the empty chair beside her.

"My mom and dad have a digital camera, so they ran some pictures off right away for us."

Patti took the small album and opened it up. "Oh. You came in on a horse?"

"Yeah. Powder. I've had him since I was fourteen."

"Let me see." Maria jumped up from her chair and leaned over Patti's shoulder. "Cool. I think you should do that, Patti, instead of that great big car Mom was looking at getting."

"It's called a limousine, Maria," Donna said.

"Whatever. I like the horse."

"I don't think we need to worry about that." Donna took a careful sip of her coffee as if controlling herself. "I'm sure the Duplesis family is not interested in an equine wedding complete with all the . . . trimmings."

"Hey. You could borrow the carriage and horses if you want," Summer said as if she had not heard Donna.

"Don't even think about it!" Donna snapped.

Her harsh comment drew everyone's attention, and silence fell for a moment. But Summer did not seem perturbed.

"I'd like to have a look at your pictures as well," Alice said, breaking the tension.

"I would too," Jane said, and soon there was a small group around the album.

"Your horse is beautiful," Alice said.

"You didn't want your father to walk you down the aisle?" Jane asked.

"Dad is really shy, so I told him I would make it easy on him. My sister has a horse, and she was my bridesmaid. She rode in on hers." Summer pointed to another picture.

"And what is that you are wearing?" Alice asked.

"I couldn't very well have a long fancy dress, could I? So I got my mom to sew up a pair of really wide-legged white pants and a jacket to match."

"Weren't you afraid they'd get dirty?" Patti sounded intrigued, a fact that netted her another disapproving look from Donna. Fortunately, Patti was bent over the wedding album and didn't catch it. But Alice saw it.

"They did. A bit. But riding in was what I wanted, and Neville approved." Summer glanced over at Patti. "What do you want to do?"

Patti glanced at her mother, who was watching her and Summer with more than passing interest. "I'd love to have a small, intimate wedding . . ."

"I don't think the Duplesis family wants a small wedding," Donna swiped a smear of butter over her scone. "They said themselves that they won't spare any expense."

"That doesn't mean we need to make it expensive. We could still keep it simple. I mean, the dress . . ." Patti let her voice trail off as she glanced back at the picture of Summer's casual wedding outfit.

"Mrs. Duplesis would not want to see you in pants at your wedding," Donna said. "She was with us when we picked out the dress."

"When *you* picked out the dress," Patti said, a cool note in her voice. "I had another one in mind."

"Why didn't you go with that one?" Summer asked. "I'm sure Mrs. Duplesis wouldn't have cared. She's pretty cool."

"She has standards," Donna said.

Summer gave Donna a quick glance as if detecting the censure, then shrugged. "Hey, you gotta go with what you want, I think. It doesn't need to be a big splash to be a lot of fun. Besides, my mom always said that if people put twice as much energy into staying married as they do into getting married, more people would still be married."

"I agree," Patti murmured, leafing through the rest of the photo album. Alice could see page after page of pictures of laughing, happy people. Summer's wedding may have been unusual, but it was obviously a loving family affair. "So I'm guessing these are your parents. Where are Neville's?"

Alice saw Summer glance at Neville, then back at the album. "They didn't like the idea of Neville marrying me. They didn't come." Then she gave a light laugh. "But that's okay. We're married now. They'll come around eventually. He's their only kid after all."

"You see, Patti, that's something you don't have to worry about." Donna gave Summer a piercing gaze. "The Duplesis family thinks very highly of Patti."

"And they probably think highly of her taste," Summer said sincerely, but Alice could see that Donna was getting upset.

"Patti. Maria. Time to go."

"But Mom, we haven't finished looking at the pictures yet," Maria said.

Patti got up, thanking Alice, Jane and Louise for breakfast. "And thanks for letting me look at your pictures," Patti said to Summer. "It looks like you had a fun wedding."

"In spite of a few teeny glitches, yeah. We did." Summer's smile was as natural as ever, but Alice could see a faint glint in her eyes when she looked at Donna.

"That's nice," Donna said, looking away. "And now, girls, we should get going. We have a lot to do today."

The Lysters went back upstairs, and Summer glanced at Neville. "I did it again, didn't I?" she said. "Opened my big mouth too much."

Neville stood and reached for Summer's chair. "Don't worry about it, hon," he said, helping her up. "I'm sure it doesn't matter."

"At least I didn't say anything about David Duplesis," she said, looking in the direction that Patti, her mother and sister had gone. "That would just be nasty."

Neville dropped a light kiss on her forehead. "You don't have a nasty bone in your body, sweetie. Be yourself—that's the person I married."

Alice watched them go, her heart warming at the obvious love between them in spite of their differences.

But as they walked back up the stairs, she wondered what Summer meant about Patti's future husband.

"I'd better hurry and get the kitchen cleaned up," Jane said, clearing the dishes.

"There's no rush," Louise said, carrying a full tray back to the kitchen.

"I have a few errands I need to run."

"Such as?" Louise pressed.

"I need to talk to Sylvia about the costumes," Jane said, rinsing off her plate and setting it in the dishwasher.

"And I should see Craig Tracy at Wild Things about some arrangements for the mystery weekend," Alice added, trying to figure out how all this was going to happen.

"Why don't you both go on to town?" Louise asked, taking the dirty plates off the tray. "I'll finish cleaning up."

"Are you sure, Louise?" Alice did not want to give Louise another reason to complain about the supper. Not that she had any lately, but Alice preferred to stave off any objections before they became a problem.

"You don't mind?" Jane asked.

"Of course not," Louise said. "You go and run your errands. There's not much to do here except clean up."

Alice glanced at Jane, who paused a moment.

Louise fluttered her hands in a shooing motion. "Go now."

So they did.

I've got the best costume for the writer." Sylvia pulled out a bright red gown edged with gold. It positively glowed in the late-morning light. "Isn't it great?"

Jane let the silky fabric run over her fingers. "Where did you find this fabulous material?" It felt delightfully heavy and rich. Exactly the kind of thing a wealthy, best-selling author would be wearing. At least the author visiting Acorn Hill for the mystery weekend.

"I found it at a thrift store." Sylvia giggled as she lay the gown aside. "It used to be a robe. But I turned the fabric inside out, and this is what I ended up with."

"I hope this isn't too much for you." Jane was concerned that her friend might make herself so busy that she neglected her own customers. While Sylvia's business was doing well, she could not, Jane knew, afford to take too much time away from it.

"Oh no, not at all." Sylvia waved aside Jane's concerns with a flap of her hand. "I'm keeping things simple. Because you're not sure of the characters yet, I made sure to keep the costumes easy to adjust, which, in turn, makes them easy to make."

"It's perfect."

"Speaking of perfect, I heard of an absolutely perfect match." Sylvia gave Jane a knowing look. "Kenneth Thompson and Barbara Bedreau."

Jane snuffed a spark of annoyance; it wasn't Sylvia's fault that she had heard that. "Where did you hear this?"

"Hope Collins mentioned it to me this morning at the Coffee Shop. I think it's wonderful." Sylvia raised her eyebrows. "You don't seem impressed. I thought you and Barbara were working together. I thought you really liked her."

"I do. Very much. But that's not the problem." Jane absently ran her fingernail along the edge of the silky material.

"I was hoping, for Kenneth's sake, this could be kept quiet. I wonder how people found out."

"All I can tell you is that my information came via the Coffee Shop." Sylvia looked troubled. "I think I remember telling Craig Tracy. I'm sorry. I was so happy for Rev. Thompson I didn't think I needed to be cautious about it."

Jane smiled at her friend. "Don't worry about it, Sylvia. You didn't know." She held up the costume again. "You're doing a fabulous job with this. If you need any help, please let me know. I don't want you working too hard."

"This is all for a worthy cause." Sylvia returned the dress to its hanger. "I'm only too glad to be helping out."

"Thanks again," Jane said. "Let me know when the costumes are done, and I will pick them up."

But as she took leave of Sylvia's shop, she felt bad for her friends, Barbara and Rev. Thompson. How did the secret get out?

"I need to know the exact number the day before the actual event." Clarissa Cottrell lifted one thin shoulder to wipe some flour off her cheek, transferring a smear of white to her dark blue housedress. Her gray hair was tucked back under a hairnet that had slipped a bit. Clarissa was a tall, thin woman who, though past legal retirement age, was still running her own bakery. She loved it, and the people of Acorn Hill were thankful that she did. "I can have everything delivered to the inn right on time that way."

Though Alice was regularly surrounded by the delicious smells of Jane's baking, the scents that wafted through the bakery made her mouth water. "We should have the final number by next Thursday afternoon," Alice said, glancing down at the glass display case. Golden cookies crusted with fat chocolate chips, puffy pastries overflowing with whipped cream, glistening bars dipped in chocolate, delicately decorated petits fours nestled in pastel-colored paper cups—all sat in neat rows inviting customers to buy more than they had originally planned. And they usually did. Clarissa had been running the Good Apple Bakery for many years, and her skill and experience, combined with a deep love of what she did, made everything she baked extra special.

"I'm getting excited over this event." While Clarissa spoke, she deftly arranged a batch of freshly baked doughnuts sprinkled with sugar in the glass case. "There's hardly a ticket to be bought."

"I'm hoping it turns out. Barbara has done a tremendous amount of work and made a number of sacrifices to have this event succeed."

Clarissa leaned her elbows on the glass case and smiled. "And I'm sure our own Rev. Thompson would like to see Barbara succeed as well."

"What do you mean by that?" Alice asked carefully.

Clarissa laughed. "I understand that they are dating. In fact, I heard that it's just a matter of time before wedding invitations will be sent out."

"And where did you hear that?" Alice asked, thinking of what Summer had said only this morning. *How did news get out so fast? And false news at that?*

"I believe I overheard it in Viola's store yesterday when I went to pick up a magazine." Clarissa frowned. "You seem upset."

"Maybe a little." Alice eyed the croissants. "But I can tell you that as far as I know, there is no wedding in the works."

Clarissa showed a disappointed face. "I'm sorry to hear that. I was so excited for him."

"I'm sure if Rev. Thompson were getting married, he would announce it." Alice hoped she didn't sound prim. As much as she loved Acorn Hill, she wished people's lives weren't subject to so much speculation.

Clarissa pushed herself away from the case and removed the plastic gloves she had been wearing while working with the doughnuts. "Well, you have yourself a good day, Alice. And let me know the final count when you know it."

"I will. And thank you again so much for helping us out with this." She gave Clarissa a wave.

Right after she attended to some urgent details with Craig Tracy, she had to find Jane. They needed to find out how this false information was spreading.

Chapter Eleven

I 'll have the centerpieces delivered on Thursday evening," Craig Tracy said, glancing over the order sheet. He made a quick note with a pencil. "That's a week from today."

Alice glanced at the photograph of the autumn arrangements in gold and brown and orange lying on the counter of Wild Things, Craig Tracy's flower shop. "These will add a lovely touch to the supper."

"And I understand that Miss Bedreau will be paying for this?"

"Yes. She insisted."

Craig tucked the pencil behind his ear, and ran his hand over his light brown hair, as if smoothing down the stubborn cowlick in the front. "I wonder if she'll be ordering her own flowers here."

Alice knew she looked as puzzled as she felt when she saw Craig's smile fade away.

"It's just . . . I presumed that she and Rev. Thompson . . . that they were a couple . . ." Craig shrugged.

Though Alice had lived all her life in Acorn Hill, it still never ceased to surprise her how quickly news went around this town.

"There is no 'she and Rev. Thompson,'" Alice said.

"I'm sorry. I just heard . . ." Craig blushed and Alice immediately felt bad.

"No. *I'm* sorry. You didn't know. Barbara is simply a good friend of many people around Acorn Hill, myself and Jane and Louise included."

Craig nodded and folded up the order form, slipping it into the green gardener's apron he wore. "Of course. I should know better than to listen to gossip in this town." He absently pinched off a dead flower from some African violets displayed by the counter. "Mind you, one often has a hard time differentiating between gossip and news. Your father, Rev. Howard, often reminded me that words are like arrows—once released, you have lost control of them." He brushed his fingers over the deep green velvet of the leaves. "He was a wise man, your father."

"He was indeed." Alice waited a moment, acknowledging the compliment. She glanced down at her watch, then slipped her purse over her arm.

"I'm looking forward to seeing how this mystery weekend plays out," Craig said, pushing himself away from the counter. "And, of course, to solving the mystery."

"From the sound of what Jane and Barbara have been scheming, that might not be as simple as you think." Alice waved good-bye and stepped out of the shop in time to see Jane coming down the street from Sylvia's Buttons. Even from this distance, Alice could see Jane's frown.

Alice crossed the street and met Jane at the corner.

"You don't look very happy," Alice said. "Did you have some difficulty at Sylvia's?"

Jane did a double take, then shook her head. "No. Not at all. Sylvia is doing a fantastic job. I don't know how she manages to do so much with so little."

"Practice from when she was younger, I imagine," Alice said, referring to Sylvia's upbringing. The seamstress had been raised by a single mother who taught her to sew out of necessity as much as a desire to have her work with fabric.

"She's a good person, but I left her shop with a tad bit of concern."

"You did seem to have vestiges of a thundercloud following you down the street," Alice said with a chuckle.

Jane sighed. "Sylvia has heard the same thing that Summer mentioned to us this morning. About Kenneth and Barbara."

"This is getting out of hand. Clarissa had them as good as married. And Craig Tracy was hoping to do the flowers for their wedding."

"I wonder how this got started. They have been so discreet. And they wanted to keep it that way." Jane glanced around the calm streets of Acorn Hill, at the vehicles that drove by and the people who passed them as they stood on the corner, as if trying to spot the culprit.

"Clarissa said she heard it at Viola's store. Craig said he heard it around town."

"And Sylvia and Summer said they heard it at the Coffee Shop."

Alice thought a moment. A light wind slipped through her coat, making her shiver. A faint harbinger of winter.

"If Louise doesn't mind holding down the fort a little longer, we could make a stop at the Coffee Shop and ask around. I wouldn't mind a cup of tea before I go to work this afternoon."

"That sounds like a good idea," Jane said. They made their way down the street in the direction of the Coffee Shop at the other end. As they passed the Acorn Antique Shop, they both waved at Rachel Holzmann, who was working on a display in the window, then nodded a greeting to another resident of Acorn Hill, who mumbled a quick "hello" to the sisters as he passed.

The Coffee Shop was unusually busy, and Alice and Jane could not sit in their usual spot. A number of unfamiliar faces crowded the shop—people touring the countryside to look at the glorious fall colors, Alice guessed. The sisters slipped into a booth that was just vacated.

"Coffee for you, Jane, and tea for you, Alice," Hope Collins said, putting down a set of cups and saucers in front of them a few moments later. She poured Jane a cup of coffee right away from the carafe in her other hand. "I'll be right back with the tea. Did you want anything else?"

Jane glanced down at the one-page menu lying on the table. "Actually, I think I'll have a piece of pie. Anything but pumpkin."

"June has been experimenting with pineapple pie. I'll get you a piece of that." Hope's curls, blond today, bounced on her shoulders as she turned her head. "And you, Alice?"

Alice held up a hand to decline. "I haven't been going for my walks with Vera, so I'm going to pass for now."

"Be back in the fastest of flashes," Hope said. She left, easily maneuvering around the crowded tables, trading quips with some of the regulars as she went.

A low hum of conversation waxed and waned through the Coffee Shop. The smells of toast and coffee and bacon blended with the elusive scent of oatmeal, creating a warm, welcoming atmosphere.

Jane narrowed her eyes, looking around the shop. "So how does something like that get started?" she asked, her tone peevish. "They have barely acknowledged to themselves how they feel about each other." She paused, looking a bit sad. "I feel bad for Kenneth. The man gets no privacy, does he?"

Hope came back with a little teapot for Alice and set it carefully on the table along with the piece of pie. "There you are. Enjoy." She set some cutlery beside Jane's plate, pushing the sugar bowl out of the way. "And how are things coming with your mystery weekend?" she asked. "I'm excited about it." Hope, who had at one time stated her dreams of being a movie star, was going to be one of the suspects.

"You should see the lovely dress Sylvia is putting together for our victim," Jane said, unwrapping her cutlery from the paper napkin. "It's gorgeous."

"I can't wait," Hope said, tightening the strings of her apron. "But you haven't told me what the story is about. Do you know yet?"

"Barbara doesn't want anyone to know too soon what part they'll be playing," Jane said. "We want to keep things a surprise. If people discover anything about the characters beforehand, it might give them an advantage."

"I can see that. News spreads around this town quick enough as it is." She shook her head. "I mean, I keep hearing buzz about Rev. Thompson and this Barbara woman. I heard that they are seeing each other."

At least Hope doesn't have them married off, Alice thought.

"Who did you hear this from?" asked Jane.

"I believe I heard it at the Clip 'n' Curl when I was getting a rinse." Hope stroked her chin, as if trying to draw out the memory. "I think it was . . ." she bit her lip, frowned and then snapped her fingers. "Yes. It was Ethel Buckley who mentioned it. I was surprised. I hadn't heard anything about it here, and you know how quickly news travels when people are hanging around drinking coffee."

Jane caught Alice's eye and shook her head. Alice knew exactly what she was thinking.

Their dear aunt was at it again.

Unfortunately, they could no more stop the gossip than they could stop the rain. All they could do was attempt damage control and hope that the rumors wouldn't affect Rev. Thompson or Barbara.

"And how about that Wilhelm?" Hope continued. "I was talking to Viola when I went to Nine Lives, and she was telling me about his letters. Sounds like he's having quite the adventure. But checking out rats in Holland?" She shuddered. "Doesn't sound like much fun to me."

Jane had wondered herself about Wilhelm's trip. But when she talked to Louise about it, her older sister had only said that it was somewhat difficult to get the precise meaning of his letters. Jane only hoped they were getting it right, or Wilhelm was going to come back to some very curious townspeople.

"I'd better get back to my other customers," Hope said. "Enjoy your pie."

After she left, Jane turned her worried eyes to Alice. "How did Aunt Ethel find out about Kenneth and Barbara? It's simply beyond my imagining," she said, lowering her voice.

"Aunt Ethel definitely has her talents, and information-gathering is one of them."

"The CIA doesn't know what an unsung talent is hiding out here in Acorn Hill," Jane said.

"Heaven forbid that Aunt Ethel gets hold of a state secret. It would be all over our town in seconds."

"Yes, but think what she could be finding out for them. I tell you, she's wasted here."

Alice laughed, trying to imagine their dear aunt, with her bright, intent eyes, flitting around and ferreting out state secrets. "Kenneth and Barbara are going to have to weather this storm. The only thing we can console ourselves with is the fact that if it was meant to be, they will manage."

"I suppose so, though I know Barbara values her privacy, as does Kenneth."

They considered the repercussions of the gossip in silence.

"I don't know," a familiar voice was saying as Jane finished her pie. "This seat seems a bit close to the window. I don't want a draft on us."

Alice turned to see Clara Horn, standing at the table beside them, her hands gripping the handle of a baby buggy.

Her gray hair was pulled back in a bun today, emphasizing her pale features.

Alice looked from Clara to the buggy. She wouldn't dare, would she?

"Oh nonsense, Clara, it will be fine."

Alice's attention was drawn from Clara's buggy and her suspicions about its occupant to their aunt, Ethel Buckley.

Ethel glanced from Clara to them, and her face brightened. "I was hoping I would find you here. I haven't seen you as much as usual. I know you haven't had time to visit. You've been busy with that play or supper thing. I am so excited to be 'killed.' I've never been a murder victim before, though this morning Ned Arnold almost ran into me when I was crossing Acorn Avenue. I know I was jaywalking, but he should have seen me, I would think. But Lloyd was waiting, and I hate making him wait." Ethel put her hand to her bosom and raised her eyes heavenward, giving her enough time to draw breath for the next onslaught. "My goodness, my heart is still pounding. So I thought I would come here, and I saw Clara, and here we are."

"Here we are indeed," Alice said, glancing at Jane, who nudged her with her foot. "Ethel, we need to talk to you—"

"Oh, hi, ladies. Ethel, I think we better move," Clara laid a hand on Ethel's arm, distracting her. Clara darted a quick glance over her shoulder. "This doesn't look like a good spot at all. I'm worried about Daisy."

Alice glanced at the buggy, hating to ask but knowing, for the sake of the other patrons in the Coffee Shop, that she had to.

"Is Daisy in that buggy, Clara?"

Clara angled the buggy so Alice could clearly see the miniature potbellied pig nestled beneath a hand-crocheted blanket. Black button eyes stared back at her, and it looked as though the pig were smiling.

How could she diplomatically tell Clara that most people in the Coffee Shop would not be comfortable with the idea of a pig—even a miniature one—dining with them, especially June Carter, the owner? "Do you think you should bring her in here?" Alice asked.

"Oh, I know it might not be safe for my dear Daisy, but I can't let her out of my sight." Clara heaved a huge sigh. Her eyes darted around the Coffee Shop again. She pushed the buggy closer to Alice and Jane's table, then leaned closer. "I am so worried about my dear Daisy," she whispered. "I think someone is trying to kidnap her."

"You mean pig-nap," Jane put in, looking serious. But Alice could see from the subdued sparkle in her eye that her sister was having fun.

Clara frowned, as if trying to figure out if Jane was serious or not.

"You know, Clara, you are right. The Coffee Shop is probably not safe for poor Daisy," Alice said, reaching into the buggy and covering up the pig. "We should probably take her outside, and you can tell us more. This pig-nap... kidnapping sounds serious."

Clara bit her lip, then nodded. "That's a good idea." And she spun the buggy around and marched out of the Coffee Shop, past the indulgent smiles of locals and the shocked looks of strangers. The latter must have thought that Clara had a rather ugly grandchild with her. The former knew precisely what Clara had in the buggy.

After Jane left some money for their refreshments, they all got outside without incident and without being detected by June or Hope. They made it around the corner past the windows and stopped on the other side of the Coffee Shop, along Chapel Road.

In the lee of the Coffee Shop, they were protected from the fall breeze scattering leaves along Hill Street.

"Come with me to the inn," Alice said to Clara. "On the way you can tell me what is happening."

"She's worried about Daisy," Ethel put in, hovering between them.

"I can speak for myself, Ethel," Clara said in a surprising show of spirit. She rocked the baby buggy as if soothing poor Daisy, whose snuffling showed that she was the least concerned of everyone present. "Strange things have been going on at my house," Clara said as they walked along the street. "Two days ago I found a hole in the garden. I didn't think anything of it and filled it in. Yesterday I found another one. And this time I looked a little closer, and there were some dog treats in it. I don't have a dog, so I figured someone was trying to lure Daisy. Then, after that, I got an anonymous phone call, and a second one this morning."

"You should get that call-display thingy I told you about," Ethel said. "That way you can tell in a flash who is calling."

"But I don't have it and don't want to pay for it."

"You can easily afford it. Maybe play a little less bingo."

"I don't play that much bingo," Clara huffed.

"Did the caller say anything?" Jane asked, pulling Clara back to the point.

Clara blinked, then turned her attention back to Jane. "The first time I heard some laughing, which made me real scared. The second time it sounded like they were disguising their voices. They asked me if my pig still had its squeal." Clara shuddered. "Sounded like a death threat to me."

"And tell them the rest," Ethel encouraged, waving her hands ahead of her as if to hurry the words out of her friend.

"I will. I will." Clara shot her an annoyed scowl. "This morning I found a strange-looking blanket on the front step with a note attached. The blanket was made out of old cloths that had been stitched together with heavy yarn in uneven stitches. Looked scary to me."

Alice didn't know what to say. Clara was truly concerned. "That certainly is a mystery," she said.

"I guess one can expect these kinds of things around Halloween," Jane offered. "After all, 'tis the season."

"Thank you for the invitation to the inn, but I better be getting back," Clara said. "Daisy needs her rest—even if I don't feel comfortable at home."

"She will be fine," Alice said, patting her on the shoulder. "I'm sure there's a logical explanation for all of this."

"I hope so," Clara said, turning the buggy to check on her beloved pet. "I can't imagine why someone would want to do something to my Daisy."

She said good-bye and started back, heading toward her home.

"That is interesting," Jane said as they walked up the sidewalk to the inn. "And who said that nothing exciting goes on in this sleepy little town?"

"Lots of things go on," Ethel said, walking past Alice through the front entrance. "Social activities, fairs, and now you girls are putting on this mystery weekend. And soon, we'll have a wedding."

"That is something we need to discuss with you, Aunt Ethel," Alice said as they walked toward the kitchen.

Louise was at the kitchen table, reading a magazine. She looked up when they came in. "So, how are things in town?"

"Clara is concerned about someone pig-napping her dear Daisy, and we found out that there have been some rumors going around." Jane sat across from her sister.

"Really? What rumors?" Ethel asked.

Alice gave her a level glance. "Rumors about Rev. Thompson and Barbara Bedreau getting married."

"That's hardly a rumor," Ethel said with some authority. "I heard it right from Barbara herself."

"When?" Alice and Jane asked in unison.

Ethel's puzzled look bounced from one to the other. "Why, I was here. Barbara was talking about a wedding."

Alice and Jane traded puzzled looks.

"You heard it too, Jane."

"We were talking about some of our guests. They are newly married."

"I bet it's that young couple we see all over town. They seem like an odd pair, him so elegant and her looking so, well, tough with those strange outfits she wears." Ethel shuddered.

"Anyway," Alice said, firmly leading Ethel back to the topic at hand, "Barbara was not talking about herself."

Ethel pursed her lips. "But I saw her and Rev. Thompson here, at the inn. Alone. They looked rather intimate to me."

"They were probably just visiting. And do you think it was wise to pass on false information?" Alice gently prodded. "After all, he is our minister."

"I know how to keep a secret," Ethel said, affronted. "I know that people don't need to know about Rev. Thompson and Barbara. It's just that, well, I was getting my hair done, and we got to talking about romance and how it's hard to find a good romance novel, and I said I prefer the real thing, and Betty Dunkle was teasing me, saying I couldn't spot romance if it came up and kissed me on the cheek. And I said that I know romance when I see it, and she said, 'since when?' kind of like I'm not too bright, and I said that the way Rev. Thompson looked at Barbara was very romantic."

Alice glanced at Jane who rolled her eyes.

"And the part about them getting married?"

Ethel slowly lifted her hands in an "I don't know" gesture. "I just put that together with you and Barbara talking about weddings. Or rather the wedding of your guest, and well, I was just…"

"Overcome by the perming fumes," Jane grumped.

Ethel blinked, looking hurt.

Jane was immediately contrite and reached over and laid her hand on her aunt's arm. "I know you didn't mean any harm, Aunt Ethel. But this is our minister you are talking about. You can't go around saying things you don't know anything about."

"But I thought I did know," Ethel said, glancing from Alice to Louise as if looking for someone to take her side. "And maybe I shouldn't have told Florence and Clara. I wish they would have kept it to themselves. Some people can't keep a secret," she said plaintively, blissfully unaware of the irony in her statement.

"Even if it were true, it wasn't really your news, was it?" Louise put in finally. "You might have waited until some official announcement was made."

Alice felt a touch of relief. If anyone could make Ethel see reason, it was Louise with her careful and sensible comments.

Ethel looked down at her fingers and picked away at her dusty-rose nail polish. "I suppose you're right, Louise. It's just that I was so happy for him." She raised her head a bit, like a puppy looking for absolution. "That's not wrong is it?"

"No. Of course not," Alice said. "But now the whole town is thinking they are going to get married."

"But they should," Ethel said. "They are perfect for each other. They make a lovely couple." She placed her hand on her heart as if to hold it in. "And it seems like they are so in love."

In spite of the seriousness of the situation, Alice had to smile. Dear Aunt Ethel meant well; she just hadn't done well.

"Anyway, it is not a good idea to keep talking about them, okay?" Jane leveled a pointed glance at their aunt, who seemed to finally get the message.

"I'm sorry. I won't say anything to anyone anymore." She put her other hand over the first on her chest as if sealing the statement. "It's no one's business what our minister does in his spare time, is it?"

At least Ethel wouldn't be adding any more fuel to the fire.

There was a moment of silence, as if marking this occasion. Ethel's gaze flitted around the table. "So?" she asked, her expression brightening. "Are they going to get married here or in Potterston?"

Chapter Twelve

I'm starting to worry about myself." Jane dropped onto the sofa in the living room and rubbed her eyes with her fingertips. "I've been working on this mystery so long I'm starting to suspect the people who show up in my dreams."

Alice looked up from the book she was reading. It was a quiet Friday evening at the inn. Their guests had gone out for dinner, and, for the moment, the inn was empty.

"As long as you don't start sleepwalking past the knife block, I'm sure we'll be fine," Alice said calmly.

Jane dropped her head on the back of the burgundy sofa and sighed long and deep. "I'm wondering if this thing will ever come together in one week's time."

"It will be fine. A lot of the elements are in place," Alice assured her, turning another page in her book. She wasn't concerned. In spite of Louise's misgivings, none of their other work had suffered, thanks to Barbara's organizational skills.

They had all the suspects in place. The menu was planned. Barbara had hired an amateur magician for the first evening. All they could do now was wait for the actual day.

"I wish I had as much confidence in me as you do," Jane said, closing her eyes a moment. "Oh no," she groaned, holding out her hands as if pushing some imaginary thing away. "Here they come again. All those people. All those puzzles. It's a nightmare."

Alice shook her head at her sister's theatrics and turned her attention back to her book. The mystery she was reading was coming together, and though she had a good idea of who the culprit was, she wasn't entirely sure, which made reading on interesting.

"I don't suppose you could lend your expertise to my little project," Jane asked in a hopeful tone.

"We tried that, remember? I wasn't much help," Alice said, not looking up from her book. "I'm more of a consumer than a producer of puzzles."

Jane heaved another sigh, heavier than the first, but Alice pretended to not hear it. She wanted to read, and she couldn't help Jane anyway.

Wendell strolled by, his purr adding a cozy counterpoint to Jane's anxiety. He blinked slowly at Jane and Alice and then, making up his mind, jumped up onto the arm of Alice's chair. Alice lifted her book so he could sit more comfortably and kept reading.

After a while the doorbell rang. This time Alice did look up, in time to see Patti and Maria enter the front hall, their mother trailing behind.

"It's important to keep up appearances," Donna was saying. "We can't have the Duplesis family think we're cheap."

Patti raised her eyes heavenward. Maria looked bored, Donna concerned.

"I know your father would want you to have the best wedding you can."

Patti turned to say something to her mother, then caught sight of Jane and Alice in the living room. Her expression brightened, and she walked over to them. "This looks cozy. May we join you?"

"Of course," Alice said, closing her book.

"I could make you a pot of coffee or hot chocolate if you'd like," Jane offered.

"Hot chocolate would be awesome," Maria said with obvious relish, joining her sister. She sat down on the floor, then crawled over to Alice's chair to tickle Wendell under his chin. "I like this cat. He's so nice and quiet."

Alice looked down at Wendell and scratched his ears. "He's our mascot and loves all the attention."

Maria coaxed him off of Alice's lap. Wendell allowed her to pet him for a moment, then arched his back and trotted off.

Jane stretched, got up from the sofa and glanced at Donna. "Would you like some coffee or hot chocolate, Mrs. Lyster?"

Donna looked around the room. "Where is that . . . talkative girl?"

"I believe Summer and Neville went out for the evening," Alice said. She didn't like the way Donna referred to Summer, but Donna was a guest as well, so diplomacy had to prevail.

"In that case, I'd love some coffee," Donna said, settling down in a chair opposite the sofa. She looked around the room and smiled for the first time that evening. "I love the wainscoting in this room. It creates such a warm atmosphere. Actually, all the rooms that I've seen here are so cozy and welcoming."

"Thank you," Alice said. "Jane had a strong influence on the decorating we did, though it was a collaborative effort."

"A what?" Maria asked, leaning back against her mother's chair.

"It means they worked together, silly," Patti said, giving her sister a poke. Her grin, however, showed her younger sister that she was teasing.

"I think it would be awesome to run a bed-and-breakfast," Maria said, then yawned. "You could have all that good food every day."

"And you would have to *make* all that good food, dear," Donna said, gently brushing her daughter's light brown hair away from her face.

"Do you like making the food?" Maria asked Alice.

"Jane does most of the cooking and baking here," Alice said. "We help out from time to time, though neither Louise nor I is as good at it."

"I love baking," Maria said. "Patti doesn't. 'Course, when she marries David, she won't have to do any baking, will you, Patti? His family is so rich."

"It is poor manners to discuss money, Maria," Donna said. She glanced at her daughter and smiled. "But then again, it is nice to have some financial security."

Alice noted Patti's frustrated look. It seemed as though the daughter and the mother were definitely at cross-purposes.

Jane returned with a tray of steaming mugs and a plate of pumpkin bars and assorted cookies. Maria fell on them as if she hadn't eaten for days.

"This is lovely," Donna said, taking a sip of coffee. "You treat us so well here."

"I'm totally going to run a bed-and-breakfast when I'm older," Maria said, finishing off another cookie.

They sat and visited, chatting about Acorn Hill and Potterston and the Duplesis family. Patti was quiet, Donna animated. Maria finished off every last bit of food on the tray, and when Jane had refilled the plate, the girl ate heartily once more.

Oh, for the metabolism of a young teenager, Alice thought, aware of how hard she had to work to keep herself from gaining too much weight.

"I think it's time for bed, girls," Donna said, getting up. "I would like to get an early start tomorrow. Thank you for the coffee. It was lovely." Donna got up and glanced at Maria, then Patti. Maria got up, but Patti stayed, rocking in her chair.

Donna kept her eyes on Patti, but Patti avoided her gaze. "Don't stay up too late, honey. Tomorrow we have to start making some decisions. I can't keep Maria out of school forever, and you know how much she wants to be involved in the plans."

Patti nodded.

Shrugging, Donna turned and left.

"You don't mind if I sit here awhile?" Patti asked.

"Not at all. We're not the most interesting company, but you are more than welcome to join us," Alice said with a gentle smile.

"Did Neville and Summer say when they would be back?" Patti asked.

"Not really. I believe they went to Zachary's for supper. A local restaurant," Jane said.

Patti glanced around the room again. "You don't have a television, do you?"

"We have a small one in the kitchen. We watch the occasional program," Alice said. "Jane likes to watch cooking shows."

The front door opened again, letting in the sounds of laughter, and Patti sat up, craning her neck to see who had come in.

It was Neville and Summer.

As Summer closed the door, she glanced into the living room and saw Patti. She paused, her hand on the door.

"Better close it, honey. You're going to let all the cool air in." Neville was already heading up the stairs. He hadn't seen Alice, Jane and Patti in the parlor.

"You go on up, Nevvie. I'll be there later."

"What are you going to do?" he called down.

"I want to visit awhile." She looked back up the stairs. "Besides, all you're going to do is go straight back to that book you've been reading."

"Guilty," he said. "See ya later." They heard the sound of a door closing and Summer entered the living room.

"Would you like something to drink?" Jane offered. "Patti and Alice are having some hot chocolate, and I've got coffee."

"Is this part of the package?"

"We offer evening refreshments to select guests," Jane said, giving Summer a wink.

"Cool. I'll have some hot chocolate."

"Considering that hot chocolate is by its nature hot, I don't think you mean *cool*," Jane said teasing the young girl.

Summer pointed at her and laughed. "Ladies and gentlemen, we have a comedienne in our midst."

"So how was your dinner at Zachary's?" Alice asked, closing her book and putting it aside. She was going to have to find out "whodunit" some other time.

"It was really good. I really enjoyed it." Summer sat in the chair that Donna had vacated and glanced sidelong at Patti, who was looking at her. "How are the wedding plans coming?"

Patti shrugged. "We went looking at wedding cakes today. Thought we might gather some ideas."

"Did you decide anything?" Alice asked.

"Not exactly. We have to decide if we want to go with a traditional tower cake. Mom saw something in a wedding magazine. It was a gazebo, and it had some kind of tree-looking thing with plates in it, and each plate held one part of the cake. So that means we'll have to go with a different kind of cake."

"A gazebo for the cake?" Summer lifted her eyebrows.

"Mrs. Duplesis was talking about a more traditional cake, so they had to discuss that. Mrs. Duplesis said she had heard about a baker in Pittsburgh who does something with hazelnut and cream and chocolate that is supposed to be fantastic. So now Mom wants to check that out, which means the cake is on hold for now." Patti smiled but Alice could see it was forced.

"You don't need a fancy baker. We just had a plain cake that had our names written on it. My mom baked it," Summer said.

"I can't see that happening."

"So what else did you do?" Alice asked.

"We checked out decorations at a wedding store." Patti shook her head. "I didn't know there were so many different things you could do with a wedding. Mom and Mrs. Duplesis were talking about favors for the table for about an hour or more. It was boring."

"An hour? That's craziness. We put out some candies in a dish and called it a party," Summer said with a laugh.

"They were talking about having a bud vase at each table with a rose in it, and silver plaques engraved with our names, or china napkin rings or three hundred other ideas." Patti's sigh of frustration showed Alice how little it seemed these things mattered to her.

"Did you decide on invitations?" Summer asked, helping herself to the single pumpkin bar that Maria had not eaten.

Patti waved her hand. "Mom has a huge book back at home that we have to wade through. Didn't have time before we came here. I dread the thought of making more decisions."

"You don't need to do them so fancy," Summer scoffed. "I made mine on the computer. It was real easy."

"I'm not good with the computer." Patti bit her lip. Alice dearly wanted to give her some advice, but she could see that for now, the last thing Patti needed was yet more advice.

"It's not hard. I could show you," Summer waved her hand. "I mean all you do is pick your pattern and write something up. I put a picture of two ropes twined on mine. Keeping with the whole horse theme. What theme do you have?"

"I don't have a theme." Patti slumped suddenly, clenching her hands together. "I don't know what my colors are supposed to be. I haven't decided on gifts for the attendants. I don't know if I want strapless, sleeveless, train, drape, fitted, loose, satin, *peau de soie*, cotton . . ." She stopped, lifting her hands in a gesture of surrender. "What kind of bride am I if I can't decide what kind of wedding I want?"

"Why don't you elope?" Summer asked.

Patti laughed at that. "Can you imagine what my mother would say if I did that?"

"Neville and I were talking about it," Summer said. "Just to make things simple, but I kept thinking of my family. They were so proud of us and so happy for us, and I knew they would want to be a part of the celebration. So we had the party at our place."

"At least you knew what you wanted." Patti covered her face with her hands. "I don't know what I want. And David doesn't care one way or the other. I wish he would care a little bit. It would make things a lot easier for me."

"Patti, I think Summer brought up an important point this morning at breakfast. People can put more energy into getting married than into staying married. Maybe you should start with what kind of life you want with David and go from there."

"But my mother has such definite ideas," Patti said.

"So did Neville's mother." Summer flashed a smile at Patti as if to show that she didn't hold it against her mother-in-law.

Patti turned to Summer. "I hate to be nosy, but why didn't Mr. and Mrs. Moreau want you to marry?"

Summer wiped her mouth with a napkin and carefully laid it down, her smile fading away. "Mom and Dad Moreau had, and I quote, 'better things in mind for Neville than just a waitress,' unquote. Which is what I was and am and proud of it. I'm really good at what I do. I don't have a degree, and I don't care. Doesn't make you a better person. They also didn't like it that I thought it was cool that Neville liked being involved in mechanics. At one time he wanted to do it for a living, but he changed his mind on his own. He's okay with his banking work now, but he likes to fiddle with cars in his spare time. They thought I was going to turn him into a grease monkey, and they were scared. They tried to push me away from Neville, but instead all they did was push us closer together." Summer wrinkled her nose. "I feel bummed for them that they chose not to come to their only son's wedding. But they'd been pushing him to break up with me for months, and Neville got sick of it. So he said, 'Let's get married.' He figures it's better to apologize than ask permission. His parents are really nice people, but they had different ideas for Neville."

Jane came in again with another mug of hot chocolate and another plate of baked treats.

"I am really going to get fat here." Summer picked up the mug and in spite of her protestations also took a cookie.

"So you're not scared to face Neville's parents?" Patti asked with an admiring look.

Summer dismissed the idea with a casual shrug. "They can't change anything now. I know they love their son, and that's cool. But Neville and I love the Lord first and each other next. His parents come third on the list."

Alice could not help smiling at Summer's confident declaration. At the same time she sensed a serious note in her conversation, and her positive opinion of the young woman grew more so.

Summer finished her cookie and licked her fingers, then picked up her mug of hot chocolate and looked at Patti again.

"So now *you're* getting married, and you're actually pretty lucky that his mom and dad really like you."

"They do. They're really nice people."

"I know. Always surprised me that David didn't turn out . . ." she stopped and winced. "Sorry," she mumbled.

"Sorry about what?" Patti said.

Summer glanced from Jane to Alice, then back to Patti. "Nothing. Just me spouting off again."

Alice knew Summer well enough by now to recognize that she was holding back something.

"You were going to say something about David," Patti pressed.

"No. I was just, well . . ."

Alice was surprised to see Summer blushing, and she wondered what the girl was going to say.

"About how he didn't turn out . . . what? Better?"

Summer turned to Alice and Jane. "So how are the plans for the mystery weekend coming along? Things falling into place? Do you need any help?"

"We're doing okay, thanks," Jane said. "I'm glad you're coming back for it."

"Yeah, well, it sounded like fun. I mean, I'm looking forward to going to New York for a visit, but this would be more my style." She took a final sip of her hot chocolate and set the mug on the tray with a *clunk*.

Patti leaned forward. "Summer, I want you to please tell me about David."

Summer flicked at an invisible crumb on her shirt.

"You know something about David that you're not telling me."

Summer glanced at Patti with uncharacteristic nervousness. "It's not my place to tell you."

Patti chewed her lip. "I wish you would help me out, Summer. I'm so confused."

Summer looked up at her, then away.

"Confused about what?" Jane asked, sensing Summer's reservations but also sensing that maybe she had information Patti should know.

"About this whole wedding thing. I can't get as excited as my mother or Mrs. Duplesis. In fact, I'm not sure I want to get married yet."

"Really? What is making you unsure, Patti?" Jane asked.

"Me, for one thing. Shouldn't I be thrilled that I don't have to pinch pennies? Shouldn't this make me the happiest bride in the world?" Patti folded and refolded the paper napkin that she had taken with her mug of hot chocolate. "But I'm not. I listen to you, Summer, talking about your wedding and how you had to save money and how you had so much fun planning it, and I'm jealous."

"What are you jealous of?" Summer asked, finally getting involved in the conversation again. "It was hardly the wedding of most girls' dreams. I got the definite idea from your mom that she thought it was hokey."

"But it was your dream. And you and Neville loved each other enough to go against his family and get married the way you wanted. If Mrs. Duplesis didn't like me, I don't know if I could, or would, go through with it. I don't think David would go against their wishes. In fact, I don't know if I even care anymore. About this wedding—or about David."

Summer looked at Patti, then took a quick breath as if making up her mind.

"You look like you have something to tell me, Summer. Please, if it's something I need to know, tell me now."

"You first have to promise you won't get mad at me."

"I won't," Patti said.

Summer looked at Alice, then Jane. "Please stand by me through this."

They both nodded at her, giving their assurance.

"This is really awkward, you know," Summer said, "but I guess before you start picking flowers and invitations and all that, I should tell you what I know about your David. And I want to tell you now because tomorrow we're leaving, and I don't know if we'll be back before you go." She leaned forward, her elbows resting on her knees. "You know I work as a waitress in the Potterston Café," Summer said. "That's how I met Neville. Anyway, I also met David there."

"What do you mean?"

Summer held up her hand. "I didn't meet him there as in *meet* him there. I mean, I just saw him there." She made a face. "And don't I sound like a total idiot. Anyway, he would come and sit by the window all the time and talk to me. I sorta knew him from school. He was always this important person 'cause he always had a real nice car and all. Anyway, he tried to ask me out, but I was already seeing Neville, so I told him no. He kept asking me."

"How long did he keep asking you?" Patti asked.

Summer blew out her breath. "Up until about a month ago."

"I see."

Summer held out her hand in a placating gesture, glancing from Alice to Jane. "It wasn't my fault, you know. I never encouraged him. I kept talking about Nevvie, about how much we loved each other. But David wouldn't listen, and he wouldn't stop."

"It's okay, Summer," Patti said. "I understand. I have had my doubts about him for a while now. I think that's why I was having such a hard time making up my mind about things."

Summer relaxed back in the chair. "That's good. Because he would show up at the restaurant with other girls too." She shook her head, looking at Patti. "Honestly, Patti, the guy is a louse. You're way, way too good for him."

"You hardly know me," Patti said with a bitter laugh.

"She's a great girl, isn't she?" Summer said to Alice. "She doesn't need this guy. Really." She turned back to Patti. "I'm sorry to lay it on you like this. I'm not really good with the fancy words. That's why I think Nevvie's mom and dad took our relationship so hard. They like using words like *actualization* and *agenda*, and I'm all about keeping it real. I never went to college, but I know how to treat people, and I know how to serve my Lord. And I know that David Duplesis is not the guy for you. You deserve a lot better."

Patti gave Summer a small smile. "Thanks for that. It's not what I wanted to hear, yet I'm not surprised." Then she let out a long, deep sigh and turned to Jane and Alice. "But now what am I supposed to do?"

"If you aren't sure about him, knowing what Summer has told you, I think you should do what your heart tells you," Jane said. "Think of this. If you called off the wedding, how would you feel?"

"Relieved." Patti said the single word without hesitation.

"That should tell you something right there," Alice said.

"But how am I going to tell my mother? How am I going to tell Mrs. Duplesis?"

"There's only one way to do it," Summer said. "Just tell them."

"Like you told Neville's parents."

"Right," Summer said. "We told them we weren't going to stop seeing each other, that we loved each other. It was hard, but it was for the best."

Patti bit her lip, then got up. "Okay. I will." She gave Summer a tremulous smile. "I want to thank you for telling me what you know. Thanks." She gave Summer a quick hug, and left.

Summer looked from Alice to Jane. "Did you see that? I dish the dirt on this girl's fiancé, and she gives me a hug. Funny old world, isn't it?"

"You did the right thing, though I sensed it was hard for you," Alice said.

"It was. I don't like being a gossip, you know." Summer sat a moment, a faint frown creasing her forehead. "But you know what I'd like to do with you two? I'd like to pray for Patti, that she has the strength to tell her mom and David's mom. And David."

Again Alice felt an outpouring of affection for this woman who seemed so youthful, yet was so grounded.

"I think that's a wonderful idea," Alice said. She glanced at Jane, who was smiling as well. And they bowed their heads and together prayed for the young woman upstairs whose life was about to take a dramatic turn.

Chapter Thirteen

*R*ev. Thompson was especially inspiring this morning, wasn't he?" Ethel asked, looking intently at Barbara as they walked with Ethel's three nieces along the sidewalk toward the inn. "I always enjoy hearing him preach. Every Sunday is such a blessing, and this Sunday morning was no different."

Louise had invited Barbara to come to the inn for lunch after church, an invitation wholeheartedly endorsed by Jane and Alice.

Ethel had made plans to spend the day with Lloyd Tynan, but at the last minute their plans changed, and now, to Louise's dismay, their aunt decided to join them, throwing out comments as subtle as a sledgehammer.

"Yes. He was," Barbara said. "I appreciate his challenge to us to help others. It's something I know I want to do more and more."

"I'm disappointed he couldn't come for lunch," Ethel said, her bright eyes watching Barbara.

"Rev. Thompson had other obligations," Louise said, sending her aunt a warning glance . . . for all the good it would do. Ethel was observant only when it seemed to suit her. "I am sure he would not want to renege on them simply to have lunch with us."

"I know, I know," Ethel said, waving Louise's comments away. "But it is still too bad. You are looking so very attractive today, Barbara. I really like that color on you. You look like fall walking. I'm sure Rev. Thompson noticed as well."

Barbara was wearing a deep-gold fitted sweater over a pair of camel-colored slacks. A gold, green and rust scarf tied at her neck gave her outfit a finishing touch. "How poetic of you, Ethel," Barbara said, diplomatically avoiding Ethel's transparent hint.

Indeed, she does look like fall, Louise thought, taking a moment to admire the vibrant colors of her clothes.

The sun shone brightly, melting away the crisp coolness that the fall mornings brought. Leaves crunched beneath their feet, swirling over the sidewalk in the faint breeze.

"Isn't this a glorious day?" Jane spread her arms wide with enthusiasm. "Fall is like summer holding its breath for the final plunge into winter."

"Please, Jane, I for one am not ready to contemplate winter yet," Louise said, shivering at the mere thought of snow and cold.

"No, but that is the beauty of fall, its appeal. We know that winter is coming, so we cling tenaciously to every scrap of warmth and appreciate more fully each beautiful day God blesses us with."

"You're in high spirits this morning," Alice said.

"I should be. Yesterday Barbara and I put the finishing touches on the mystery play. It is such a good feeling to be done."

"Wonderful," Louise said, brushing a fallen leaf off her coat. "That means you can now try to decipher the latest letter from Wilhelm." She would love nothing more than to hand that job back to Jane. Carlene had accepted the article Louise had finally given her for the newspaper with puzzlement. But she decided to run it as it was.

Wilhelm had promised pictures on his return, so Louise hoped that they would help to explain some of the more obscure items mentioned in his letter.

"Sorry, sister," Jane said with an apologetic look. "I've still got a bunch of things to catch up on. I am behind on my last order of chocolates, and you did want me to see about the storm windows."

"That last excuse sounds a bit flimsy," Louise said.

"Not really. Doing the windows is a burdensome chore." Jane nudged her arm. "But I will try to squeeze it in if you really want me to."

Louise knew she had the time to deal with the letter herself, and she also knew that some of Jane's other work had indeed fallen by the wayside while she worked on this mystery. "No. That's fine," she said, giving in. "Perhaps Viola and I have deciphered Wilhelm's code. It might be easier this time."

"When does his first article come out?" Alice held open the front door of the inn for Barbara, Ethel and her sisters. "It wasn't in the last *Acorn Nutshell*."

"It will be in this Wednesday's edition," Louise said, slipping off her sweater. As she hung it up, a slight movement in the living room caught her eye.

Patti was curled up in a chair, reading. Louise wondered if the girl was all right.

Before Summer and Neville left Saturday morning, Summer had asked if Patti was around, but she was still sleeping.

"Hey, Patti," Jane said, walking into the living room. "How are you doing?"

Patti looked up and, to Louise's relief, she was smiling. "I'm a whole lot better than my mother is."

"Where is your mother?" Alice asked, glancing past Patti to the dining room.

"She left shortly after breakfast and will be back later. She's taking Maria back home. She needs to go back to school tomorrow." Patti laid down her book. "She wanted me to come along, but I told her I needed to talk to David this morning."

"Who is David?" Ethel asked, peering around Jane to see what was going on.

"It doesn't matter," Louise said firmly.

"David is my . . . fiancé. Actually, my ex-fiancé."

"You're going to call off your wedding?" Ethel asked, all ears.

Louise stifled a groan. Had she known Patti would be there, she would have insisted that Ethel remain silent on the matter of the young woman's engagement. The last thing Patti needed was an inquisitive stranger.

"I did it already. He drove over, and we met at the Coffee Shop."

Louise stood closest to her, and she laid a hand on Patti's shoulder, squeezing it supportively. "I'm sorry to hear that, Patti. That must have been hard."

"It was. A bit. But I think he had a hint of what was coming. He told me that he had turned over a new leaf, but I tried to explain that, regardless, I wasn't ready for this step. Not with him." Patti looked up at her and to her surprise, Louise saw relief more than sorrow on the young woman's bright face.

"Oh. I'm so sorry," Ethel said, hurrying to Patti's other side. She slipped her arm around Patti's shoulders and gave her a hug. "You know what they always say: It's better to break an engagement than a marriage. And, I imagine, a whole lot easier."

Patti gave Ethel a puzzled look, obviously not knowing who this sympathetic older woman was, but smiled at her nonetheless.

"Patti, I would like you to meet our aunt, Ethel Buckley," Louise said. "She lives in the carriage house behind the inn. Aunt Ethel, this is Patti Lyster. She is a guest here, as you have probably surmised."

"I did. Surmise that is," Ethel said. She patted the girl on the shoulder. "You know, I wouldn't worry too much about this broken engagement. I know it will be hard, and you will probably be sad for a while, but you are such a lovely young lady. Why, you'll have someone new in your life like that." Ethel snapped her fingers as if to emphasize her point.

Patti chuckled. "Thank you so much for the compliment, Mrs. Buckley."

"Oh, call me Aunt Ethel. And I think you should join us for lunch instead of sitting here all by yourself."

"No, that's fine. I don't want to intrude," Patti said.

Louise, Jane and Alice added their invitation, and Patti overcame her initial hesitation and accepted.

Jane and Alice both took a moment to murmur their sympathies. Patti thanked them, and she continued to look relaxed, at peace. Louise realized that her previous indecision had been a symptom of her relationship with David.

Louise introduced Patti to Barbara, who had remained in the foyer. As they went into the kitchen, she heard Patti ask Barbara what she did. While Jane and Alice prepared lunch and Louise set the table, the two of them chatted amiably. Patti asked a number of questions, which Barbara answered willingly and with the enthusiasm that her work always brought out in her.

Ethel—always one to surprise—was content to listen and watch.

"What you do sounds so interesting," Patti was saying. "I've always wanted to do some kind of service project. Maria is going to go to Mexico with her youth group to help build a house there. But I would really like to be involved with something more long-term."

"Have you completed college?"

"I'll be done with my nursing degree in a couple of months. In fact, the wedding is, I mean *was*, supposed to be two weeks after that."

Louise was pleased to see that Patti's animated expression didn't falter when she made her slip of the tongue.

"There's always a need for nursing staff," Barbara said. "If you don't mind working in primitive conditions."

"I don't mind doing something that will make a difference," Patti said.

"I understand exactly what you mean. I am so blessed to be working with Doctors Without Borders. It has really changed, and is still changing, my life."

Louise caught the intensity in her voice and was again impressed by it. And for a moment she wondered about the state of Barbara's relationship with Rev. Thompson.

Lunch was put on the table, and as Jane said grace, Louise added a silent prayer for Patti. Although she sensed that the young woman was relieved, Louise also knew that such a drastic change of plans could result in some confusion for the young woman.

Please, Lord, she prayed silently, *help her to find a new direction to her life.*

In spite of what had transpired in Patti's life, lunch was an animated affair. People talked past and through each other, relating the events of the week, sharing stories and, in general, behaving like a family. Louise was pleased to see Patti smiling and laughing over some of the stories Ethel, a born storyteller, recounted of people in Acorn Hill and of her life as a farmer's wife.

"Has Clara spoken to you lately?" Ethel asked Alice. "She is so worried about what is happening, she said she didn't dare leave the house. In fact, she wasn't in church this morning."

"Should I go see her?" Alice asked.

"I know she would surely appreciate it," Ethel said, nodding for emphasis. "I've never seen her like this, and I don't like it one bit."

"What is wrong?" Barbara asked.

"Someone is trying to steal her Daisy," Jane said.

Barbara frowned. "Daisy being . . ."

"Her pig."

Louise saw Barbara press her lips together, holding back a laugh, and she had to smile herself.

"That *is* terrible," Barbara agreed, glancing at Louise, as if sensing her scrutiny.

Louise gave her a wink, and Barbara looked down.

"Daisy means a lot to dear Clara," Ethel said, her tone defensive, as if she detected their humor. "She is like a child to Clara. And Daisy isn't an ordinary, pig-sized pig. She's the cutest little potbellied pig. Just a miniature one."

"Of course, Aunt Ethel," Alice said, placing a placating hand on Ethel's arm. "As soon as we're done with lunch, I'll make sure to give her a call and see if there's anything I can do to help her."

"She would be very grateful. It's not fun being afraid of leaving your own house. I know I wouldn't appreciate it. I love being able to get out and about, though, to tell you the truth, I don't understand the depth of Clara's affection. But maybe it gives her purpose in life, and that's a good thing. We all need purpose, don't we?"

"I'll agree to that one hundred percent," Barbara said.

When lunch was over, Barbara got up to help with the dishes, but Louise would have none of it. "No. You sit and talk with Patti."

"I'll help," Ethel said, getting up from her chair.

So as the sisters and their aunt rinsed and loaded dishes into the dishwasher, Patti and Barbara remained deep in discussion. Barbara told her about her work and some of her experiences. Patti looked more enthusiastic about Barbara's stories than she ever had over her own wedding plans.

When the kitchen was tidy, Ethel returned to her house, and Alice gave Clara a phone call, telling her that she would be by on Tuesday.

After Louise had excused herself to practice on her piano and Jane had gone upstairs to take a nap, Alice poured Barbara and Patti more coffee, and the three went to the living room to visit awhile longer

Twenty minutes later, the front door of the inn opened slowly, and Alice glanced over to see Donna step inside. She closed the door and drooped against it. She looked tired and stressed, and Alice felt sorry for her.

It must be hard to think that your daughter is settled and then find out that you're wrong, and you have to cancel a hundred plans.

As Donna pushed herself away from the door, she looked over at the living room, straightened and walked in. She looked at Patti, her expression hopeful.

"You're still here," she said. "You didn't go to Potterston."

"No, Mom. David came to Acorn Hill."

Donna's hopeful expression disappeared. Her shoulders sagged inside her fashionable camel-colored coat, and she slid into the nearest empty chair. "And?"

Patti twisted a strand of hair around her finger. "I called it off."

Donna's eyes clamped shut, and she slowly shook her head. "Honey. Why?"

"Because it wasn't right, Mom. I have been feeling wrong about this for a while now. I didn't know how to tell you and Mrs. Duplesis. She was so good about everything, and so nice and so kind that I have to confess I hoped I would find these traits in David as well. But I never did, Mom. I never did."

Donna's sorrowful gaze turned to Alice. "You are a sensible woman. Tell her she's doing the wrong thing. Tell her that she won't find a better man than David. And she won't."

Alice paused as if summoning her strength and wisdom. Then she turned to Donna. "If Patti is unsure of her relationship with David, then she made the right choice. My sister lived through a divorce, and, trust me, that is not something you want your daughter to go through. As Summer said, it is easier to get married than to maintain a marriage. "

At the mention of Summer's name, Donna's face grew hard.

"This is her fault. She's the one who put this silly idea into your head."

"What silly idea, Mom?" Patti asked. "The silly idea that you should marry someone because you love him? Because he happens to be the greatest guy you know? I'm sorry, Mom. And I'm sorry for the Duplesis family. They are great people, but their son, unfortunately, is, as I was told, a louse."

"And why would you say that?"

"Summer told me that while he and I were engaged and she was dating Neville—and David knew about that—he asked her out."

Donna's eyes grew wide. "David Duplesis asked Summer out?" As if this were unimaginable.

"Mother, I don't really want to discuss this further," Patti pleaded.

Donna pressed her lips together but looked around the room, as if hoping to find someone on her side. When her eyes settled on Barbara, Alice realized that the two women had not met before, so she introduced them.

Barbara cast a look of compassion toward Donna. "I know that you have no reason to value my opinion, but I feel compelled to say that your daughter is a lovely person, and from talking to her I've discovered that she certainly has a level head on her shoulders." Barbara gave Patti a gentle smile, then looked back at Donna. "I don't think you need to worry about her future."

"Miss Bedreau was telling me about the work she does," Patti said, "with Doctors Without Borders. I think it could be something for me after I graduate from nursing school."

Donna's eyes grew wider still. "But honey, that would mean going to different countries where there's disease and horrible living situations."

"Exactly," said Patti.

"But . . . but . . . don't you want to have a home of your own? Don't you want to settle down? I mean, we had such a lovely crystal pattern picked out and you really liked it and now you'll never have it. At least not soon." Donna looked confused, and Alice had to bite back a smile. The poor woman really didn't know which way to turn.

"Truthfully, Mom, picking out crystal really doesn't excite me."

"Are you sure this is what you want, my dear?" Donna continued. "I mean, if you are going to cancel, now is the time, before we send out any invitations or spend more money. But David's family . . ."

"I'm sure, Mom," Patti said. "You are right about David's family. They are wonderful people, and it will be hard to tell them. But I've been having my doubts about David for some time now. I am sure I wouldn't be happy with him."

Donna folded and refolded the scarf on her lap. "I suppose if that's how you feel." She sighed again. "And I had picked out such lovely potholders for your new home."

Patti laughed, then got up and gave her mother a hug. "Mom, you are the best mother I could ask for. Why don't you keep the potholders for yourself?"

Donna patted her daughter's arm. "I just might have to." She dabbed at her eyes. "And now that I don't have to plan a wedding, the next few months won't be as hectic as I thought they would be."

Patti laughed. "I'm still young, Mother. There's a strong possibility you'll have a chance to plan a wedding for me yet."

"I'm hoping," Donna said, giving her daughter a tremulous smile. "But please, no horses, okay?"

"No promises, Mom. Except that when I do get married, it will be to someone I love as much as you love Dad."

"That *would* make me happy," Donna said.

Chapter Fourteen

"Are you sure that's what he wrote?" Louise asked Viola. "That he has seen *love?*"

It was Monday afternoon. Louise had picked up the mail, which included with it Wilhelm's most recent letter, which was more challenging than his previous one. She called Viola in a moment of confusion. Viola closed her shop for lunch and came over to the inn immediately. They sat together in the library.

"I know Wilhelm can come across as staid and fussy, but it seems that these days, love is in the air," Viola said. "If your pastor can find love, then who knows?"

"Kenneth and Barbara are friends," Louise murmured, glancing around, hoping that Ethel wasn't present. The sisters had a hard enough time keeping a rein on her as it was. Ethel had done as they had asked, but Louise knew she was convinced that wedding bells would be ringing in Grace Chapel before Christmas.

"That's precisely what representatives of movie stars say to similar rumors," Viola harrumphed.

Louise looked over her reading glasses at her friend, hiding her smile. "Now how would you know that, Viola?"

Viola didn't look up from the letter. "I know things," she said vaguely. "As for Wilhelm, I think his letter says that he found love in Paris. Which is not entirely unlikely. Though it is a cliché, Paris is the city of lovers." Viola shook her head. "When I was there after college, you couldn't turn around but you'd see some couple kissing."

"But how do we put that?" Louise asked.

"Diplomatically."

They had only a limited amount of time before Viola had to go back to her shop, and Louise wanted to get as much done as possible before then.

"Now then, I am willing to accept that Wilhelm may have found love in Paris, but this next paragraph doesn't flow at all," Viola said, holding up the last page of the letter for inspection. She frowned and adjusted her glasses, tilting her head up so she could see better. "He's saying something about widows, in a house?"

"Could he mean windows?"

"That is possible, but from what I can decipher it seems that one was flirting with him. Last I heard, windows don't flirt and I can't imagine that windows in a house would make him wax poetic. Or at least as poetic as I can decipher."

"Maybe that's how he met his true love?" Louise ventured.

"Maybe," Viola agreed, her pen scratching out what she presumed the missive said.

Louise continued reading her own page, then stopped and read it again.

"If you think you were working on something interesting, let me read you what I'm guessing *this* says. He writes that he was in jail for shooting someone." Louise felt her heartbeat quicken. "Now surely, *that* has to be wrong."

Viola held her hand out for the page, and Louise gave it to her.

"All I can read is 'in jail' and 'shot him.' Maybe he shot someone *while* he was in jail?"

"But Wilhelm? In jail?" Louise took the page back and read it once again. "I can't believe that. How could he write in such cavalier fashion about such a thing? And about finding love in Paris?"

"Maybe he fell in love with someone who had a boyfriend who was jealous? One of the cheerful widows he refers to," Viola suggested. She shook her head, as if negating the comment. "Oh, listen to me. I sound like I'm reviewing a melodrama."

"Wilhelm's trip sounds like a melodrama," Louise frowned and transcribed what she could. "I wish he wrote better. Thank goodness he's coming back in time to go over this before we give it to Carlene."

"I certainly would want an explanation from Wilhelm on this," Viola said.

Louise agreed and went over the letter again. And then once more.

She was transcribing the final page when the front door opened and Patti entered, all smiles. She had gone on a shopping trip through Acorn Hill. Just for fun.

Donna Lyster was lying down with a headache after being on the telephone all morning. Louise felt sorry for her. She had a daughter herself, and she knew that a loving mother's only wish is to see her children happy and secure.

As Patti hurried up the stairs with her shopping treasures, Louise realized that she hadn't seen Patti this happy since the young girl arrived. Obviously, breaking off the wedding was a huge load off her shoulders.

The ring of the phone broke into her thoughts.

It was Clara Horn, asking for Alice again. Alice was at work. Clara sounded distraught, and all Louise could do was reassure the old woman that she would leave a message for her sister. She reminded Clara that Alice had said she would visit on Tuesday.

"Is Clara still convinced that someone is trying to steal her precious Daisy?" Viola asked. "I can't believe she thinks anyone would want a pig."

"Some people feel the same way about cats, Viola," Louise said to her friend.

"Cats I can understand. Cats are friendly, kind and warm, and welcoming." Viola spoke with the true passion of a cat lover. She finished off the last of her page and gave her notes to Louise. "Here you go. It's the best I can do with what we have. I hope that you can make some kind of sense out of the rest."

"I will type it up but hold off on delivering it until the last minute." Louise looked over the notes again. "When Wilhelm comes back, I hope to go over it with him. It certainly needs some clarification."

Viola glanced at her watch and got to her feet. "Sorry I can't stay any longer—I have to get back to the shop. If you have any more trouble, come over tonight, and we can give it another try."

"Thanks so much for coming on such short notice."

"What are friends for?" Viola asked, adjusting the bright orange scarf draped over her tan dress.

"Deciphering letters, for one thing." Louise showed Viola to the door, then returned to the library to do whatever more she could.

The rest of the day seemed to slip through Louise's fingers. She and Jane cleaned the kitchen thoroughly and finally got the windows washed. She was glad Fred Humbert was able to spare Jose to help them put up the storm windows.

She had some music lessons in the afternoon, and before long it seemed that it was time for dinner.

When Alice came home from work, Louise gave her Clara's message, but the nurse was too tired to visit the old woman that night. Alice phoned Clara to reiterate her promise that she would be by the next day.

⌒

The street that Clara lived on was in a cozy part of Acorn Hill. Large, handsome maple trees arched over the street on both sides.

Clara was waiting for Alice at the end of her walkway. Clara wore a faded blue cardigan over a pale pink house-dress, and fuzzy blue slippers warmed her feet.

Her hair was in disarray, and she looked as if she hadn't slept since she first told Alice about the threats against Daisy.

For a moment, Alice regretted not having taken the poor woman more seriously; she looked that distraught.

"I'm sorry I couldn't come sooner," she said, as Clara ushered her up the walk. It was thick with leaves, and the yard was almost buried in a carpet of fading reds, oranges and yellows.

Large maple and ash trees grew higher than Clara's roof. In the summer it was difficult to see her tall Victorian, her grounds were so wooded.

"Doesn't matter, you're here now," Clara said, clutching Alice's arm as she glanced nervously over her shoulder. "The knocking, it's been getting worse."

Knocking? Alice frowned as Clara ducked into the house through a side door, almost pulling Alice in behind her. Once inside, Clara shut the blinds on the door.

She had drawn all the curtains in the house, giving it a dark, gloomy cast that was, to Alice, almost creepier than the mysterious goings-on.

"Do you want some tea or something?" Clara asked, hovering in the doorway, wringing her hands.

"I'm fine," Alice said, not wanting to add another burden to the poor woman. "Why don't you tell me what's been happening?"

"In a minute. I need to check on Daisy. Just sit down, sit down," Clara gestured toward the kitchen table and Alice complied, glancing curiously around Clara's kitchen as she did.

If the curtains hadn't been pulled, she suspected it would have been a bright, cheerful place. The kitchen cabinets were painted a bright yellow and the linoleum was a pale green with yellow flowers. The table Alice sat at was covered with an apple-green tablecloth.

But what really caught Alice's attention was a large, floor-to-ceiling glass cabinet in the dining room, just through the arched entryway.

The large curio cabinet held shelf after shelf of pigs. Plaster pigs, ceramic pigs and stuffed pigs. Clothed pigs prancing on hind feet, pigs with ribbons around their necks. Groups of pigs, single pigs. Pig teapots, pig salt and pepper shakers, pig plaques.

She had never seen so many porcine figures in one place in her life. Curious, she got up to have a closer look and could not help smiling.

It wasn't hard to see that Clara was as obsessed with pigs as Viola was with cats. Clara, however, had limited herself to one live animal, whereas Viola had a veritable menagerie of them.

"There, Daisy is fine for now." Clara huffed into the dining room. She stopped when she saw Alice looking at her display case. "Aren't they just the cutest?" she said.

"You have an extensive collection."

"Some I got as gifts. Most I bought. See those down there?" She pointed to a set of pigs wearing different-colored sweaters that almost looked real. Some held flowers, some vegetables and one a poinsettia, and Alice realized that each pig represented a month of the year. "I got those from Florence."

Alice was surprised. More than once Alice had had her conflicts with Florence on the church board. To see this token of a friendship prompted Alice to have a different view of the woman.

"They are very cute," she said, straightening. "Now, why don't you tell me what's been happening."

Clara dropped onto the nearest chair, fanning herself with her hand. "I already told you about the holes in the garden and that blanket thing."

"Do you still have it?"

"I threw it away." Clara's pale green eyes grew wide. "Oh no. Have I put the case in jeopardy? There might have been fingerprints."

"I doubt that we could get the local authorities to run a check on it," Alice said, trying not to smile. Alice knew that there had to be a logical explanation for the goings-on at Clara's house.

"The past two days, on top of all you already know about, someone has been knocking at the door, but when I go to answer, there's no one there."

"It's probably someone knocking and running away," Alice suggested.

"No. It isn't." Clara got up to take a quick peek from behind the curtains in the dining room. "I heard the knocker knock. Three times." She lowered her voice as if worried that the thing bothering her was hovering within earshot. "I was looking at the door the whole time. And no . . . one . . . was . . . there."

In spite of herself, Alice felt a chill. There had to be an explanation, but right now she could think of nothing to say to assure the distressed woman in front of her. "Did you report this to the police?"

"I don't know if I should. I'm afraid they might laugh at me."

They wouldn't laugh, Alice thought, *but they might not treat it seriously*. "What time was this?"

Clara glanced at the clock. "Seven o'clock. It was dark."

It was five-thirty now.

"Do you want me to stay and see if it happens tonight?" Maybe her presence would make Clara feel more secure. Besides, Alice's own curiosity was piqued.

"That would be nice," Clara said with obvious relief. "Can I make you something to eat while we wait? I'm not as good a cook as Jane, but I'm a fair hand with a biscuit."

"Thank you, Clara, that would be lovely." Alice phoned her sisters to let them know what was happening. Clara turned down her offer to help in the kitchen, asking her instead to check the windows and look in on Daisy from time to time.

As Alice made the rounds, separating the heavy blinds Clara had across the window, she felt like a criminal on the run. She saw some boys kicking a ball back and forth in a yard across the street; an older couple strolling down the sidewalk, enjoying the last bit of warm weather; and a woman pushing a baby buggy alarmingly like Daisy's. The woman glanced at Clara's house, then away.

When Alice saw that, her suspicions were aroused. But a quick check on Daisy showed her that the little pig was fine and that her buggy was still safely parked beside the house.

Daisy had her own little pen inside, complete with blankets and some chew toys. She slept, her feet sticking out and spasming as if she was running in her piggy dreams. She was perfectly content, blissfully unaware of the drama that swirled around her.

After Alice's second round, Clara called her to supper. While they ate, Clara told Alice about her children. About Daisy. About her relationships with Florence and Ethel. And some more about Daisy. Alice had, from time to time, felt sorry for Clara, who lived all alone, but it seemed that her life, not counting the momentary excitement now taking over, flowed along contentedly. Alice hoped she could help solve the mystery so that Clara's life could go back to her normal, happy routine.

Soon enough the dishes were done and the kitchen cleaned up. It was well past six o'clock, and the sun had set.

Alice found a game of Scrabble, and she managed to talk Clara into a match while they waited. At Clara's request, they played by the light of a small table lamp. The darkened house grew gloomier and the atmosphere more ominous as shadows pressed in on them. They were hunched over the table, a single cone of golden light the only illumination, creating odd figures that moved every time Clara bumped the lamp.

Alice knew there was nothing to be afraid of, but keeping company with an increasingly jumpy Clara made her feel nervous nonetheless.

"Did you hear that?" Clara would ask from time to time, cocking her head as if to catch any sound better.

But other than the occasional noise of a car driving by, or voices of people in the nearby yards, Alice heard nothing.

They were halfway through the game when a sudden, loud chiming startled Alice into dropping one of the tiles she was about to put down.

"What is that, what is it?"

But it was only the mantel clock striking seven.

They resumed the game, and Alice chided herself.

Just as she was starting to relax, she heard it—an ominous knocking on the front door.

"Do you hear it?" Clara whispered, clutching Alice's arm. "There it is again."

Alice got up and strode quickly to the window beside the front door. Carefully she eased the blinds aside as the knocker sounded again.

There was no one on the front step. Nor was there anyone running away down the empty, darkened street.

A chill tickled Alice's spine.

The knocker sounded again just as a cold, clammy hand touched her neck.

Her heart leaped in her chest.

"See," Clara whispered from behind her. "I told you. There's no one."

Alice drew a long steadying breath, willing her pounding heart to settle. She pulled the blind farther aside, but doing so revealed nothing more. "I need to go outside to look around," she whispered to Clara. "You stay here."

She went out through the kitchen door, and, trying to muster her courage, took a quick look around the yard. The trees seemed gloomy, the lights from the street barely penetrating the mass of branches and leaves that still clung to them. A soft breeze whispered in sinister tones, growing, then sighing away to nothing.

Alice looked all around, listening. She heard a different whispering sound, like distant human voices, but she couldn't see anything. She carefully worked her way around the side of the house, and, in spite of her show of bravery, shot quick glances behind her. The wind picked up a bit, knocking branches against the house with a hollow sound, and as she slipped around the side of the house, she heard the knocker rattle again . . . then again.

She looked intently at the knocker, then around the yard. A movement up in the tree made her jump and look up. It was an inquisitive squirrel.

As she watched it scamper back down the branches, she saw something above her glinting in the beam of the streetlight, something long and fine. She kept her eyes on it, and as they adjusted to the gloom, she realized what she was looking at—fishing line.

It led directly to Clara's front door. Following it, she discovered that it was threaded through an old plant hook on the veranda, then tied to the knocker. Someone had rigged this to knock from a distance, and whoever it was must have done this recently.

She laughed a shaky laugh and, turning, followed the line to its source. It ran through the branches of a tree over-hanging Clara's sidewalk and from there to some bushes. As she inspected the line, she heard a yelp, then the sound of scrambling, and two figures jumped up from the bushes.

"Stop right there," she called out. Even in the half light she could see they were not very old, maybe about nine and ten.

They stopped in their tracks. As they slowly turned around to face her, Alice recognized them. They were the two boys she had seen playing in their front yard earlier.

They stood now, looking down. One of them scuffed the ground with his running shoe; the other had his hands shoved in the pockets of his pants.

"Hello there," Alice said cheerfully, determined not to frighten them too much. "You boys have been busy. That's tricky what you have done here. You've done this before, haven't you?"

"Only once." The one looked quickly up as if to gauge her mood, but then looked down again. "Are we in big trouble?" he mumbled, his toe pushing the leaves around.

"Maybe a little trouble," she said, looking down on them kindly. "What are your names?"

"I'm Toby," the older of the two said, "And this is Skeeter, my brother." He pointed his chin toward the boy beside him.

"You won't call the police, will you?" Skeeter asked, looking up at her with a frightened expression. "I can't go to jail. I'll be in such big, big trouble if I go to jail."

Alice squatted down in front of them in order to look less intimidating. "No. I won't call the police, and you won't go to jail. I want to know what you boys were doing."

"We just wanted to see the pig," Toby said plaintively. "We thought that if she thought someone was at the door, she would come out. Then we could sneak in. So we tied up the fishing line. A friend showed me how. We took it down right away the last time we did it because it didn't work, so we wanted to try again."

The obvious flaw in their plan, of course, was the fact that Clara was too frightened to do more than poke her head out the door.

"We made the little piggy a blanket so it would be warm," Skeeter offered hopefully. "And we tried to make a pig trap, but she never lets the pig play outside. He's such a cute little pig."

"And that's why you dug the holes in the garden."

Skeeter slowly nodded his head, looking down again. "We are in trouble now." He elbowed his brother. "It's your fault."

"No it isn't. It's your fault."

Alice stopped them both. "Do you know how much you scared poor Mrs. Horn? She thought that there were ghosts in the neighborhood."

Toby's head shot up, his eyes wide. "She did? Cool!"

"No. Not cool. She was very, very scared."

Toby's pleased expression faded away. "I'm sorry. We didn't want to scare her."

Alice could see that they were genuinely contrite, but they had to understand the results of their actions.

"Are your mom and dad at home?" she asked, standing. At the least, she needed to talk to them about what had happened.

Toby shook his head. "My mom and dad are gone."

"We're staying with our gramma," Skeeter offered. "She lives there." He pointed to the house across the street from Clara's. "Gramma sleeps a lot," he said. "And she doesn't let us watch television."

"It's sorta boring," Toby offered.

Alice felt a flutter of sympathy for the two boys. "What is your grandma doing now?" she asked.

"Reading," they both said at once.

"I would like to talk to her, and I would like it if you boys came with me."

As Alice crossed the street and walked up the steps, she heard Toby mutter to Skeeter, "We are in bad, bad trouble."

But though Alice had felt bad for Clara, she was also sure that once the situation was explained to her, she would not be angry with the boys.

The boys' grandmother was a cheerful woman, and when Alice told her what had happened, she frowned at them, but Alice could see a glint of humor in her eyes.

"So you see, I would like them to meet Mrs. Horn and apologize and find out how they have frightened her," Alice explained.

The grandmother agreed. "Mrs. Horn is a lovely neighbor. I'm sorry they caused trouble, and I'm grateful for your interest. Their mom and dad had some important business to tend to in Florida, and they couldn't leave the boys anywhere else," she explained. "So they took them out of school and brought them here. I've tried to help them with their schoolwork so they don't fall behind, but they're quick learners and done by noon. I'm afraid they have been a bit bored."

Alice understood. Minutes later, the boys were following her across the street.

Clara was waiting at the door, clutching Daisy, when Alice returned. The older woman frowned when she saw the young boys. "Aren't you the boys staying across the street?"

Alice explained what had happened while the boys stared at Daisy. She told Clara that the boys were eager to get to know Daisy, and that was all it took.

Clara ushered them into the house, and while she introduced Daisy to the young boys, Alice turned on a few more lights. The house became cozy and inviting instead of threatening.

Clara and the two boys sat on the couch, and she carefully handed Daisy to Toby, the older boy. Daisy snuffled a few times, content with all the attention, and the boys were thrilled to finally get to hold the small pig.

Before Alice left, she suggested that maybe the boys could help Clara rake up the leaves on her lawn in the afternoons.

"If you do that," Clara said to the boys, "you can come and visit Daisy as much as you like."

"Really?" Skeeter held up the little pig and grinned at her. "We get to be best friends, Daisy."

"Could we push her in the buggy sometimes?" Toby asked.

"I think so. If you're careful."

Alice had to smile at the image of the two boys taking turns holding the pig, and she reluctantly agreed that Daisy was quite cute . . . in her own potbellied way.

Alice said good-bye, pleased to have Clara's mystery so easily and painlessly solved.

Chapter Fifteen

"We'll be checking out," Donna Lyster said, placing her key on the front desk Wednesday morning.

"I hope you enjoyed your stay," Louise said as she prepared an invoice for Donna. As soon as she spoke the words that were so automatic, Louise wished she could take them back. How could this poor woman have enjoyed a stay that resulted in her daughter's broken engagement?

As Louise studied Patti, however, she had to think that this was the most relaxed the woman had seemed since her arrival at Grace Chapel Inn.

Donna scribbled her signature on the bottom of the credit-card slip, and offered Louise a wan smile. "This is a lovely place to stay, and you and your sisters have been most hospitable." She tucked the invoice into her purse, and her smile turned melancholy. "I would be lying if I said that I'm excited about the outcome of this visit."

Patti lowered the brochure she was reading and gave her mother a quick, one-armed hug. "I know this was hard for you, Mom," she said, resting her head on her mother's shoulder. "But it was the right thing to do. It wouldn't be fair to David or his family to keep on pretending nothing was wrong."

Donna pressed a kiss to her daughter's forehead. "I know, sweetheart. But every mother likes to see her daughter taken care of, and I was pleased with David and his family. I knew you would have been well provided for."

"Money was not a problem, that's for sure." Patti smiled at her mother. "But you and Dad also taught me that money is not everything. And I guess I took that lesson to heart."

Louise was encouraged by the young woman's comments. "You can be proud of your daughter," she said to Donna. "It's rare to see such wisdom in someone so young, and I believe she has made a wise choice. C. S. Lewis once said, 'To love is to be vulnerable.' I think your daughter has done admirably in handling the challenges that have confronted her."

Patti gave Louise a look of gratitude. "I want to thank you and your sisters for all your help. Is Barbara around?"

"She is not at the inn at the moment. I believe that she and Jane went to the Coffee Shop to go over some final details for the mystery weekend."

Patti thanked her, said good-bye, and they left.

Louise said a prayer for the young woman. Though Patti seemed content with the decision she had made, Louise knew that there would be a brief period of emptiness in her life.

⌒

"If you could make sure that all the food is delivered to the inn by four thirty on Friday, that should be early enough," Jane said to Hope Collins. "And tell June thanks so much for her contribution. It will make a big difference."

Jane turned to Barbara. "You want another cup of coffee here before you have to leave?"

Barbara glanced at the delicate gold watch on her wrist. "I'm sorry. I don't have time. I have to be in Potterston this afternoon to meet with a client."

"I can't tell you how much I have appreciated your putting so much of your own work on hold while you helped us with this mystery weekend," Jane said as they walked toward the entrance.

"It wasn't a hard decision to make. This organization means so much to me that I would do anything to help it."

Jane wondered if she felt the same about Rev. Thompson. It seemed that Barbara talked more about Doctors Without Borders than she did about the pastor.

They passed Clara Horn, who was drinking hot chocolate with two young boys. Clara waved at Jane as she passed, and Jane stopped to ask how she was doing.

"Your sister is so brave," Clara said to Jane. "You make sure to let her know that everything turned out fine."

Jane smiled at the boys, each of them contending with large dollops of whipped cream. Alice had told her all about Clara's adventures with these two young ragamuffins, and though they had given Clara a scare, the whole story still made Jane laugh.

"Where is Daisy now?" Jane asked.

"A neighbor is taking care of her." Clara turned her attention back to the boys. "Now hurry up, Toby and Skeeter. We have to go home and give Daisy her bath."

Jane winked at Barbara as they left the Coffee Shop.

"I have to say, Jane, I'm pleased with how things have gone," Barbara said as they walked back to the inn. "Working on this has given me a real good idea of how to set up a fund-raiser. The most work, the actual play, is already done, and I have some good ideas about how to work the supper."

"I'm glad we could help. I guess the next few days will tell how it will go over."

A passing car honked its horn, and Jane recognized Donna and Patti. The car pulled over, and Patti got out.

"I wanted to say good-bye," Patti said, giving Jane and Barbara a shy smile. "And thanks for the information you gave me, Barbara."

"Now you make sure you stay in touch." Barbara unzipped her briefcase and pulled out a couple of business cards. "This is how you can reach me. Write me and let me know how school is going for you."

Patti nodded as she took them. "Thanks again. I really had a nice time staying at the inn," she said to Jane.

Considering that you broke your engagement while you were with us, that is saying something, Jane thought.

"Please, come again," was all she could say.

"I might." Patti looked around the street as if memorizing Chapel Road. "I really like this town."

"Did you have a chance to say good-bye to Summer?" Jane asked.

"I did. She and Neville came back early this morning, and now she's helping Neville work on Alice's car."

"Pardon me?"

Patti shrugged. "At least that's what it looked like to me. Alice couldn't get her car started this morning, so Neville asked if he could have a look at it."

Jane still had a hard time imagining the well-dressed young man digging in the entrails of a car.

Patti glanced back at her mother, who was motioning for Patti to return to the car. "I'd better go. Thanks again for everything."

Patti smiled warmly and got into the car. Donna gave them both a smile and a wave, and they drove off.

"And so we move from one adventure into the next," Jane said as they walked back to the inn.

"I'm sure you have lots of stories to tell about your guests," Barbara said.

"And here's a new one," Jane said as they ventured up the walk toward Alice's car parked beside the inn.

Its hood was up, and Summer was leaning against the side of the car, holding what looked like a screwdriver and a wrench. Neville was wearing an older pair of pants and a torn T-shirt, and he was bent over the engine. As Jane and Barbara approached, Summer waved the wrench at them. Grease smudged her cheek, and her hands were smeared with something black.

"Hey there," she called out. "It's good to be back. New York is fun, but this is more like home. Neville is performing surgery on Alice's car."

"I see that," Jane said with a laugh. "What's wrong with it?"

Neville straightened and wiped the grease off his hands with an old rag as he turned to her. "The battery cables needed tightening, and I found some wires that were crossed. Nothing too dramatic."

"And you fixed it, honey," Summer said, a note of pride in her voice.

"That's quite a worthwhile hobby you have," Jane said.

"And it saves us a few dollars on mechanic's bills."

"So Friday is the big night?" Neville asked, reaching for the screwdriver Summer held. "Summer has been talking about this since we left. Is everything ready?"

"I'm not the only one who is excited. We're going to figure out this mystery for sure." Summer poked him with the wrench, then the sound of an approaching vehicle made her straighten and look up. She gave Neville another poke, her expression suddenly serious. "Neville. Look who's here."

Jane and Barbara turned to see what had affected Summer so. A large, black luxury car slowed as it approached, the female passenger looking down at something, then back at the inn as if verifying information.

Jane frowned. The Moreaus were their only guests at present, and the sisters weren't expecting anyone new today. The next guests, the ones who were coming specifically for the mystery weekend and one with a long-standing reservation, weren't expected until Friday morning.

She heard Neville's sudden intake of breath. "My parents," he said quietly.

"Finally," said Summer as the vehicle stopped and a couple got out.

In spite of Summer's confident personality, Jane could see that the hands holding the wrench were shaking slightly.

"We'll be inside if you need anything," Jane said to Summer, laying her hand lightly on the newlywed's shoulder.

Summer's lips were pressed together, and she shot Jane an imploring glance. "Please don't go just yet. I'm a little nervous," she whispered. "I was hoping and praying they would come. I told them where we were and that we wanted to see them." Her eyes flitted from Neville to Jane to his parents, who were now coming toward them.

The elder Mr. and Mrs. Moreau were both tall, slender people elegantly dressed. From the cut of Mr. Moreau's gray suit, Jane guessed it was tailor-made and that the burgundy tie cinching his neck was pure silk.

Mrs. Moreau looked striking in a pale green silk dress. Its uncomplicated cut was deceptive. Jane could see that this dress, too, had been custom-made for her. Diamonds winked from her ears and from the simple necklace she wore. Her hair was expertly feathered around her face, and her well-manicured nails were a subtle shade of coral that was picked up in the soft silk scarf draped around her neck. A picture of good taste.

Mr. Moreau inclined his head politely toward Jane and Barbara, but as he looked at his son and daughter-in-law, both with grease on their hands and faces, Jane saw his expression falter.

"Welcome to Grace Chapel Inn," Jane said, and the Moreaus turned their attention back to her. "My name is Jane Howard. My sisters and I are the owners of the inn, and this is a friend of mine, Barbara Bedreau."

Both the senior Moreaus relaxed somewhat as they shook hands first with her, then with Barbara, who was her usual fashionable self. "I'm Thomas Moreau, and this is my wife, Shantelle."

Neville and Summer stood by the car as if waiting to see what their next move should be.

"Thanks for coming, Dad," Neville said finally. "Mom." He held up his grease-stained hands. "I'd give you a hug, but I'm not very tidy right now. I've been fixing Miss Howard's vehicle. Not this Miss Howard, the other one. Alice." He swallowed, obviously nervous.

Dismay flickered across Shantelle's face. "Why are you working on someone else's vehicle? I thought you were on your honeymoon."

"We're just helping out." Summer gave her a careful smile. "You know how Nevvie likes to fiddle with cars and stuff."

Shantelle glanced pointedly at Summer's hands, also covered with grease. "I can see that," she said.

"Neville is a very good mechanic," Summer said. "He's real handy. Almost as handy as my dad."

"I am guessing that is high praise," Shantelle said.

Awkward silence followed her remark.

"We've really been enjoying Neville and Summer's company," Jane said, hoping to breach the conversational gap. "They're a lovely couple. You can be very proud of them. Of both of them." She put extra emphasis on the last comment.

Thomas glanced from Jane to Summer as if trying to connect Jane's praise with the young woman who married his son.

"Mom, Dad. I'm glad you came. I just want to tell you that I'm sorry you don't want . . ." Summer's voice broke, but she recovered. "I'm just . . . I, well, love your son. And I want to be your daughter."

Thomas Moreau's expression softened at Summer's sincerity. "No. We're the ones who are sorry," he said. "That's why we came. We wanted to tell you that we were wrong."

Shantelle looked down at her handbag, her hands working the handle as if she wasn't quite ready to make the same admission. But then, to Jane's relief, when Shantelle looked back up at Summer and Neville, she was smiling. "Thomas is right," she said quietly. "We are the ones who should be sorry. Neville loves you, and that should be good enough for us."

Summer swiped at her eyes, worsening the smear across her cheek. Jane was about to point it out when Shantelle reached into her handbag. She walked to the girl's side, pulled out a delicately embroidered handkerchief, then gently wiped the streak of grease from her face. Shantelle held Summer's chin in her hand, then quietly leaned forward and kissed her on the forehead.

Jane glanced at Barbara, who nodded. It was time for them to leave this family alone.

Inside, Barbara said, "That was wonderful. I am so pleased for Summer that Neville's parents came. Summer is an interesting person. She makes no apology for who she is nor for her love for Neville. Their love was strong enough to go against what his parents wanted. That, I think, was an inspiration, in a way, to Patti—to marry for love, not for expectations.

"Marriage is a huge, huge step," Barbara said. "And what I also found interesting was that Patti was far more enthusiastic about working with my charity than she was about making wedding plans."

"Which clearly shows where her heart is."

Barbara wore a pensive look, and Jane wondered again about her relationship with Rev. Thompson. She had secretly hoped Barbara might enlighten her regarding her relationship with the pastor, but she was quiet on the subject. And Jane was loathe to bring it up herself.

Jane heard the front door open and close, and Summer's and Neville's hushed voices as they went upstairs. A few moments later they went out, and it sounded as though they had left with Neville's parents.

Two hours later, Barbara was gone, and Jane was busy making row upon row of small meatballs for the mystery weekend, wanting to get as much done in advance as she could.

Jane heard the sounds of Neville and Summer returning. She put on a pot of coffee, and set out some cups and a plate of sugar cookies.

Summer popped her head into the kitchen. "Is it okay if me and Neville come in?" she asked.

"Please do. I'm making coffee. Would you like some?"

Neville shook his head. "I've drunk more coffee in the past half hour than I have in the past week."

"Thanks all the same, but we want to decompress," Summer said. "If you don't mind," she added.

"You are more than welcome to." Jane put out the plate of goodies, which Summer eyed gratefully. "And how are your parents, Neville?"

Neville ran his fingers through his hair, smoothing the neat waves. Jane could still see a faint line of grease on his fingernails. "They are, well, coming around." He looked up at Jane with a faint smile. "The fact that they came here to spend time with us is a huge, huge step for them."

"When was the last time you saw them?" Jane asked, dropping another meatball onto a baking sheet.

"Probably about six months ago, when Summer and I got engaged."

"That meeting was not pretty," Summer said with a sigh, licking her fingertips. "I mean, they were sort of okay with the girlfriend thing. I guess they hoped it would pass, but to have their son marry me? Wrong story."

"And now?"

Neville smiled at Summer. "I guess it will take time for them to see Summer the way I do, but I think she'll grow on them."

Summer squeezed Neville's hand. "I promised them lots and lots of grandbabies." She giggled. "Nothing like bribery to help people see things differently."

Jane had to laugh. Summer was one of a kind. "I'm glad they came. I think it shows that they are at least willing to close the gap."

Summer grew serious as she caught Jane's eye. "I know you were praying for us, because the visit went great. Thanks a bunch."

Jane smiled. "You're welcome. I'm thankful that they realized what they were missing. You are a special person."

To her surprise, the outspoken young girl blushed and ducked her head. "Thank you," she murmured.

Neville covered Summer's hand with his own. "I'm glad you agree with me, Ms. Howard," he said, squeezing his young wife's hand. "I have always thought she was special."

Summer bit her lip and surreptitiously wiped her eyes, sniffed once and looked up. "Okay. Enough with the greeting-card moment." She sniffed again, then gave her husband an affectionate smile. "And thanks, Neville, for believing in me."

"Yoo-hoo!" The back door opened, and with the entrance of Ethel, the tender moment floated away.

"Things are busy at the Coffee Shop," Ethel huffed as she pulled off her coat. "All kinds of comings and goings. I saw some older people with that young couple—" She stopped as she saw Summer and Neville sitting at the table, and Jane suspected that Ethel had hotfooted it here to give Jane the latest about their young guests. "And here you are," she finished lamely, blinking in surprise.

"Here we are," agreed Summer. "I'm guessing you saw us with Neville's mom and dad."

Ethel scooted over to the table and slipped into an empty chair. "Was that who that elegant couple was?" she asked, her gaze zipping from Neville to Summer as if the confirmation could not come fast enough.

"They came to see us," Neville added.

"Some coffee, Aunt Ethel?" Jane asked, hoping to forestall a full cross-examination.

Ethel nodded absently, her attention never wavering from Neville and Summer. "I heard that they didn't want you two to get married."

Jane stifled a groan, but Summer laughed. "How did you know that?" she asked.

Ethel just shrugged. "I hear things."

"Be warned," Jane said as she poured her aunt a cup of steaming coffee. "Ethel Buckley hears everything. So be careful what you tell her." She patted her aunt on the shoulder as if to show dear Ethel that she meant no malice.

"Oh, don't pay a lot of attention to her," Ethel said, pooh-poohing Jane's warning. "I'm interested, that's all."

Which was true. The trouble was, Ethel seemed to think that everyone else in town should be interested in what she was interested in.

"Where are they from?" Ethel continued, taking a sip of her coffee.

"Pittsburgh. I grew up there but moved to Potterston after I graduated from college," Neville said. "And where did you grow up, Mrs. Buckley?" Neville asked, neatly turning the conversation back to something more innocuous.

"On a farm in Englishtown. Daniel Howard was my half brother." And soon Ethel was regaling them with stories about Jane's father, the Reverend Howard, and about his wife Madeleine, as well as about her own adventures on the farm.

Louise joined them for a while, helping Jane to finish making the meatballs, and preparing their own supper while Ethel chatted away. Jane was more than content to keep working with her sister, both listening to their family history as told by her aunt. It was comforting and helped pass the time in a most delightful way.

Eventually, one of Louise's students came for a lesson, so she left, but then Alice joined those in the kitchen, and she was pleased to find out her car had been repaired. That news moved Alice to give Neville a gentle hug along with her thanks.

"It sure smells good in here," Summer said during a lull in Ethel's narrative. "What are you making?"

"I'm making meatballs for the weekend, and Parmesan chicken for tonight," Jane said, dipping an egg-coated chicken breast in a mixture of Parmesan cheese and flour, adding it to the pieces already frying. "The chicken is a secret family recipe."

"Of course it is," Summer said with a grin. "Every family has to have at least one secret recipe."

"Would you like to join us?" Alice asked, adding water to the potatoes and putting them on the stove.

"No, we don't want to put you out," Neville demurred.

"Don't be silly. You've been here so long, you're practically part of the family," Ethel said. "Like me." She frowned as if she just grasped something. "By the way, why did you plan such a long stay here?"

Summer glanced at Neville as if seeking his permission, and he nodded. "I was hoping that Neville's parents would come and visit us before we left for our new place. That's why I was nervous about being away in New York. I thought if we stayed here long enough, they might come around, and sure enough, thank the good Lord, they did."

"That is a blessing," Ethel said, nodding thoughtfully.

"Is there anything I can do to help?" Summer asked, glancing over at Jane and Alice. "I feel funny just sitting here. And if I'm family, I should be helping, right?"

"You can set the table," Alice suggested.

Later, Jane presented her chicken, coated with the Parmesan mixture and covered with a piquant tomato sauce. As she set it on the table next to the mashed potatoes and broccoli salad, Summer looked around with a happy smile. "We can sure be thankful that God gave us family," she said. "And I feel, in a small way, like you let us be a part of yours for a while."

"We are thankful for you," Louise said warmly.

They bowed their heads, and Alice prayed, thanking the Lord for the day and for their work. She added a heartfelt prayer for Neville's parents.

When she looked up, a group of smiling faces was looking back at her.

Chapter Sixteen

he buzz of conversation ebbed and flowed as Jane walked around with a tray of appetizers. Everyone was smiling, chatting and, it seemed, having a good time. Friday evening had finally arrived, and though so far everything was going according to plan, Jane could not stifle a nervous flutter in her stomach.

Fred Humbert had helped set up a small stage at one end of the living room for the various "suspects" to stand on when they spoke. That way everybody could see and hear them, even from the foyer.

As the grandfather clock in the hallway chimed the hour, Barbara took her place on the stage and clapped her hands for attention.

Conversation slowly died down, and all heads turned to her. The overhead light highlighted her blond hair like a halo around her face. Under her ivory suit jacket she wore a bright green silk shirt that brought out the green of her eyes. *She truly does look beautiful*, thought Jane, who could not help glancing at Rev. Thompson to see if he was watching her.

He was. And he was smiling. He had informed the sisters that he had another obligation for the evening, but Jane was pleased to see that he stopped by beforehand.

"I would like to welcome everyone here for this special occasion," Barbara was saying as she looked around at all the people gathered. "Before we go any further, I would like to give a special thank-you to Louise Smith, Alice Howard and Jane Howard, who were more than generous in donating their time and expertise and in allowing us to have this event here." Barbara began applauding as heads turned toward Jane and her sisters.

To her surprise, Jane felt a light flush warm her cheeks. She glanced at her sisters. Alice was smiling, and Louise, with a gracious nod of her head, accepted the guests' applause. It was heartwarming and typical of Barbara's thoughtfulness.

"As many of you know, we hope to accomplish a combination of things this evening," Barbara continued once the applause had died down. "One is your entertainment. The other is using this weekend as a practice run for future benefits for Doctors Without Borders. I believe strongly in this organization, which is composed of doctors who voluntarily give their time to countries where people are in dire need of medical aid."

As Barbara explained what the organization did, once again Jane found herself captivated by Barbara's passion and her deep conviction in the excellence of this charity. Jane hoped that the other audience members would also get caught up in Barbara's enthusiasm.

But as Barbara continued, Jane felt misgivings. She saw in Barbara's eyes a light that never flashed when Barbara spoke about Rev. Thompson.

Jane brushed her thoughts aside. Tonight was the culmination of a lot of hard work, and she meant to enjoy it. She didn't need to be playing matchmaker all the time.

"As you know from the invitations you have been given, we are celebrating something very special this evening," Barbara was saying, her voice taking on a dramatic note as she easily slipped into her role. "Tonight is the official Acorn Hill celebration of a remarkable literary achievement."

Craig Tracy and Zach Colwin, the owner of Zachary's, a supper club, exchanged puzzled frowns. They glanced back at Jane, who just shrugged. She knew what was going on, and in time, they and the other members of the audience would too.

"The author whose work we are celebrating tonight was at one time well known. Each year brought another best seller. Then came the dark years, the lean years. Her muse deserted her. Not only deserted her, but took up residence in the homes of other authors." Barbara looked around the room, her eyes wide. "Her agent, Peter Proxy, almost gave up on her. Her assistant, Gilbert Gopher, was thinking about getting another job. But then, in a sudden reversal of fortune, all this changed. With a blast of inspiration, Tilda Tome has penned a runaway best seller. It has been translated into seventeen different languages. Movie companies have been blitzing her agent with requests to buy the movie rights to the book. Things are definitely looking up for Tilda Tome." Barbara paused as the audience caught on to the fact that the main event had begun.

"Tilda has been so generous as to invite us to be a part of her celebration party. We are so thankful for her generosity. And so, without further ado, I would like to present Tilda Tome," Barbara held out her hand and turned toward the entrance.

Jane saw a flash of red and gold, then suddenly Tilda Tome, aka Ethel Buckley, was on the stage.

Jane could not help gawking. She hardly recognized her aunt underneath the bright rouge, the heavy false eyelashes and the bright pink lipstick. She wore a red turban bound with gold cord, and a flowing red-and-gold dress with broad sleeves. With fake diamonds glittering on her ears, encrusting her neck and decorating her fingers, she was a picture of wretched excess.

Ethel spread her arms wide as if welcoming all the people there. "I'm so very happy that all of you could be here to celebrate my success. I know it has been a long time since I've had a best seller." Here Ethel paused and pressed the back of her hand against her forehead, looking to the ceiling. She lowered her hand and rested it against her bosom, gazing earnestly at the crowd. "However, my muse has returned to me, and I am so thankful and humbled to say that my gifts are being celebrated once again. I am also thankful and humbled that some of the people who were part of this success could be here with me tonight. Miss Bedreau, would you be so kind as to introduce them?"

She snapped her fingers imperiously, then swept to one side as Barbara once again took the stage.

Jane had to laugh. Ethel was in her element.

"Thank you, Tilda Tome," Barbara said, somehow able to keep her expression serious. "We are honored with your presence here this evening." She turned back to the audience. "Another very important person here tonight is Gilbert Gopher, Tilda Tome's capable assistant. I would like to introduce him now."

A tall figure bounded onto the stage and bowed with a flourish. When he straightened Jane had to laugh again. Fred Humbert was wearing a dark wig and a tiny penciled mustache. He wore a flowing white shirt with wide sleeves gathered at the cuffs, and narrow, black pants. He looked like a bohemian poet.

"Would you like to give us a few words about yourself and your relationship to Tilda?" Barbara asked, stepping to one side.

Gilbert glanced at Tilda and gave her an exaggerated wink. Tilda pretended to simper. He turned back to the audience, which was now laughing, caught up in the moment.

"My name, as you know, is Gilbert Gopher. I have worked for dear Tilda for many years. I am thankful to be in this position and to realize that not all rewards of work need to be monetary. Though I know I could make more working for other authors, the respect and admiration of my employer is ample reward. Tilda is a very, very special friend." He glanced at Tilda again, giving her a sappy smile.

"Thank you, Gilbert," Barbara said, motioning for him to step aside. Gilbert joined Tilda and brushed a kiss across her cheek.

Jane burst out laughing, joined by many in the audience. She knew her aunt harbored dramatic tendencies, but she hadn't known that Fred could be such a ham.

Barbara cleared her throat loudly, a stern expression on her face. "Please withhold your applause for now, as we have a number of other people to recognize, and we don't want them to feel slighted." She waited for the laughter to die down and continued.

"Our next guest is Wilma Wannabe." Again Barbara stepped aside as the next guest slipped onto the stage.

This person wore a long wig of curly black hair. She twirled her finger in her hair and kept her eyes down. She wore a dowdy, blue sweater over a threadbare shirt; a long, pleated gray skirt; white socks and sneakers. It took a few moments for Jane to recognize Hope Collins under the pancake makeup and falsely humble air.

"Hello," she whispered, turning her head from side to side as if afraid to meet any person's eye. "My name is Wilma and I am your standard-issue, struggling novelist. Please forgive me for not dressing up as nice as Tilda," Wilma looked up long enough to give Tilda a narrow-eyed glance. "I don't make near as much money as she does. But someday I hope to. Tilda has been helping me with my writing, and she told me that I have promise." She paused, her eyes flicking over the audience as she lifted her raised fist. "Lots of promise. Lots and lots of promise. All I need is one good chance!"

Barbara, staying in character, eyed Wilma with suspicion as she stepped back onto the stage. "Thank you for that, Wilma."

Wilma glared at her and went to stand beside Gilbert, who smiled encouragingly at her.

"Our next guest is Tilda's agent, and we are glad to have him here with us."

Peter Proxy, aka Joseph Holzmann, owner of Acorn Hill Antiques, slinked onto the stage, smoothing his slicked-back hair, grinning at the audience as he tugged on the wide lapels of his shimmering white suit. He wore a black shirt, and white tie with a large rhinestone placed prominently in the center. He was sleaze personified. "I can't tell you how thankful I am to be here. I've been a major part of Tilda's success, and I know she is thankful for all my help. I'm hoping that in the future we will be able to have a more professional association." He leered at the crowd, then spun and joined the others, giving Tilda a meaningful glance, which she ignored. She was too busy adjusting the folds of her dress and shaking out her voluminous sleeves with exaggerated motions.

Jane felt the pressure of the past few weeks slowly slip away. This was going to be fun, and as she glanced around the rest of the group, she could see that they felt the same.

"Next I would like to introduce Tilda's family members. First off, Tex Holdem."

All Jane could see of Tex was a large cowboy hat and an equally large handlebar mustache. And instead of his usual bow tie, Mayor Lloyd Tynan wore a bolo tie, white shirt and leather vest.

"Evenin' all," he drawled in fine Texas style. "My name is Tex Holdem. Once in a better time of my life I was Tilda's beloved husband." He glanced back at Tilda with a loving glance but took a moment to glare at Gilbert. "We shared many happy years, and I'm hoping that we can get back together again. Darlin', I jest want to tell you I love you." He walked to her side and gave her a big hug.

In spite of her aunt's being totally "into" her character, Jane could see a faint blush stain Ethel's cheeks, which made the situation all the more humorous. She slapped him coquettishly, but smiled all the same.

"Thank you for that, Tex," Barbara said, biting back her own smile. "And if my audience will indulge me, I have one more person to introduce. Tilda's only daughter."

A woman stepped onto the stage and looked around the audience, chewing gum with exaggerated motions. She had on a short, blond wig spiked with shiny gel. Dark eyeliner and dark brown lipstick gave her a hard edge. She wore a leather jacket over the top of a glittery orange T-shirt that had "BABE" spelled out in silver sequins. Bright blue nail polish flashed on her fingertips. A pair of torn blue jeans completed the look. Jane heard murmurs of puzzlement move through the people around her. If Jane hadn't been involved, she knew that she would never have recognized Vera Humbert.

"Hey. My name is Marianne Holdem," Vera said, slouching as she spoke and chewed. "That's with two N's, if you want to write me a check. I don't see many of them anymore, though I used to. Signed by my dear mom." Marianne looked back at Tilda, chewed her gum a few more times, then slipped her hands in the pockets of her jeans and turned back to the audience. "I know I've made mistakes in the past, but I really want to get back together with my dear mom again." She shrugged, then slouched off to join her father, Tex.

The audience burst into applause, and when it finally died down, Barbara took center stage again. "These people are honored guests this evening, and I hope you will make them feel welcome. Feel free to mingle and talk. Because our guests are tired from their long journeys, please do not bother them with too many questions.

"Tomorrow you'll have an opportunity to get to know them better. Refreshments will be served after our next segment, featuring Arthur the Amazing. Arthur comes to us all the way from Strasbourg and has many marvels to show us. In addition, if you wish to purchase a copy of Tilda's book, you may—I emphasize *may*—make arrangements with Viola Reed, our local bookseller. Please join me in welcoming Arthur.

Another round of applause and Barbara left the stage, and a young man jumped onto it wearing a loose white blouse, much like the one that Fred donned for his role as Gilbert Gopher.

"I'm glad to be here tonight," Arthur said as he pulled some small balls out of his pocket. "This is my first time performing here in Acorn Hill." He started juggling the balls. "You'll have to forgive me if I don't talk too much. I have to concentrate. In fact, I try not to let my mind wander. Anything that small should stay close to home." He kept up a quick patter of jokes while he juggled first five balls, then six, then, incredibly, seven. The whole time he juggled he joked and made comments about the people in attendance.

Jane enjoyed the performance, but she had some crab puffs baking and had to leave to check on them. Barbara joined her in the kitchen.

"You got off to a great start. I didn't realize we had such a group of actors here in Acorn Hill," Jane said to Barbara as she carefully drew the sheet of puffs from the oven.

"I didn't either. It took a bit of doing to convince some of them to ham it up. Your aunt is a natural, however." Barbara set out a glass tray for the puffs.

"Our dear aunt does have a flair for the dramatic," Jane said with a grin. "But I can't believe the performances you got from the others. I would not have recognized Vera."

"She was the most fun." Barbara laughed. "I hope they don't give out any information tonight. I told them to simply say, 'no comment' if people start asking them too many questions. I don't want to give anyone an advantage."

"Did Kenneth leave already?" Jane asked, trying to sound innocent.

"I think so." Barbara straightened a puff on the plate, then slowly put another one on. She seemed distracted.

"Is something wrong?" Jane asked.

Barbara shook her head. "No. Nothing's wrong. Just have a lot on my mind lately. I feel so torn between my work and my heart. I sometimes think that I need to make a decision, and I'm not sure which one to follow."

Surely she was talking about Rev. Thompson. "I think that it's important to use your head, but it's important to follow your heart as well."

Barbara treated herself to a crab puff, then stepped away from the counter. "I think you're right," she said with a smile. "Thanks for the advice." And with that positive response, she left.

Jane smiled. Perhaps things were going to go well for the pastor and Barbara after all. It was too bad that he wasn't here right now, but that couldn't be helped.

Jane wished she had time to linger with those watching the magician, but she and her sisters stayed busy serving punch, coffee and tea, and filling the trays holding the hors d'oeuvres, pastries and tarts. All she managed to view were a few card tricks and some disappearing acts.

After the magician finished to appreciative applause, many guests lingered. Ned Arnold, the town's pharmacist, chatted with Ethel, who was maintaining her diva persona and in general having a wonderful time. Jane could see from the grin on Ned's face that Ethel's high spirits were infectious.

Jane managed to catch Sylvia at one point. "The costumes were great!" She squeezed her friend's arm. "You did a fantastic job."

"I had a wonderful time doing it," Sylvia said, cradling a mug of tea, her eyes twinkling. "Vera's—I mean Marianne's costume was probably the most fun to do."

"Where did you get that absolutely garish shirt?" Jane asked. "I've never seen that much sparkle and glitter."

"I made it."

Jane laughed aloud. "I didn't know you were working on it."

"I wanted some of it to be a surprise," Sylvia said, her eyes sparkling almost as much as Vera's shirt. "It's bad enough that you already know who committed the murder."

Jane shushed her, pretending to look surprised. "What murder?" she asked in a stage whisper. "We don't have murders here in the inn."

Sylvia looked around, then leaned closer. "Who did it? You can tell me."

"Why, Sylvia Songer," Jane said, placing a hand on her chest. "You amaze me."

"So? Will you tell me?"

"You'll have to wait until tomorrow after supper," Jane said. "Until then, my lips are sealed."

"Okay, keep your secrets. But my team is going to win, I know it already," Sylvia said.

"Why, you are shameful!" Jane said with mock horror. "And here you were trying to use our friendship to gain an advantage."

"I really want to win one of those prizes."

The prizes were prominently displayed in the foyer. Each member of the winning team would choose from a variety of awards. Among them were crystal vases, an array of compact discs and DVDs, boxes of chocolates made by Jane, some books, a small painting, a watch and a compact disc player. Other than the chocolates, all had been donated by nearby businesses, most of which had also given money to the charity.

"Just think how inspired I could be if I had some new music going while I sew or dream up new designs." Sylvia placed a hand on her chest and sighed dramatically.

"I think you've been hanging around Tilda too long," Jane said with a laugh. "But I agree. Music can be inspiring." Jane straightened the lovely arrangement that Craig Tracy had made of bright yellow sunflowers mixed with white and yellow roses.

"Oh, one more thing," Sylvia said, her voice dropping to a whisper. "I read the latest *Nutshell*. Do you really think that Wilhelm would enjoy visiting packs of rats? That's really weird."

Jane winced. "I simply don't know, but when he returns, trust me, I will make it a point to find out."

As per their instructions, the "guests of honor" surreptitiously left one by one after the magician's performance. Tilda Tome was the last to leave, but there was nothing surreptitious about *her* departure. It was done with much fanfare and panache and with kisses blown to her admirers.

Ethel relished every moment of her performance, and when she finally left, Alice, Louise and Jane could hardly stop laughing.

"I always knew she had a flair for the dramatic, but I didn't realize it was so pronounced," Alice said as she closed the front door behind "Tilda."

"She had to milk it for all it was worth," Jane said, returning to the few guests that had remained. "This is the last night Tilda Tome walks the earth."

Louise grimaced. "That borders on the macabre, Jane."

Half an hour later, the last of their local guests departed. Loren and Nina Van Assen, a married couple who had registered specifically to enjoy the mystery weekend, and a single gentleman, Orest Campion, who had come for the same reason, had already retired for the evening. Their other guest, a salesman with a long-standing reservation, was out and had indicated that he would be returning late. The inn was quiet once more.

"I think stage one went well," Barbara said, as she helped Jane and her sisters in the kitchen. They had elected to use paper cups for the punch and napkins for the snacks, so all they had to load into the dishwasher were the mugs and cups from the hot drinks.

"And we don't have much food left," Alice said, putting the few leftovers into containers.

"I didn't realize we had so many virtuosos in our community," Jane said, closing the door on the dishwasher. "I think we could have a community theater in this town."

"Ethel was absolutely perfect for the role of Tilda," Barbara said. "I almost wish she didn't have to die tonight."

"She certainly threw herself into the role." Alice closed the door of the refrigerator. It was filling up with food for Saturday. Once the salads were made and Clarissa and Hope delivered their contributions, it would be full.

"And the magician was just the right touch," Alice said. "He was very good."

"I met him at another fund-raiser. He's just starting out and was very pleased to get the gig here," Barbara said.

A light knock on the back door caught their attention. Jane could not help an irritated glance at the clock. Who was coming at this hour?

But her irritation faded away when Rev. Thompson entered the kitchen. His gaze skimmed over the sisters and came to rest on Barbara, who glanced at him and then down at the tea towel she was folding.

"How did the evening go? I'm sorry I had to duck out. I had to visit with one of my parishioners, who, by the way, wanted to know if I thought Wilhelm's shooting horses was a Christian thing to do."

Louise moaned softly at that news, then there was silence.

Everyone seemed to be waiting for Barbara to say something.

"The evening was great," Jane said, filling in the gap, surprised at Barbara's reticence. "You should have seen Aunt Ethel work the crowd. She was more over the top than she is in real life."

"Is that possible?" he asked with a smile.

"Oh, most definitely," Alice said. She cleared her throat, then looked from Louise to Jane to Barbara. "I'm feeling tired. I will bid you all good night. Thanks again, Barbara, for a wonderful evening. I know this was supposed to be entertainment, but I want to say that the audience also felt your enthusiasm for your cause."

"I'm glad to hear that," Barbara said with a warm smile. "You ladies know how important it is to me, so I'm glad that others do as well."

Jane and Louise also excused themselves, and as they walked upstairs, they heard the back door close. A few moments later, Jane heard the sounds of Barbara's car leaving.

Not much of a good night, she thought, brushing her teeth. Maybe Barbara was tired.

She tucked herself into her bed and pulled her Bible off the end table and read for a while.

Later, as she prayed, Rev. Thompson and Barbara came to mind. So she prayed for them, too, though she wasn't sure exactly what she should pray for. Barbara's words and actions relating to Kenneth didn't seem to connect. Not to mention her feelings.

Chapter Seventeen

"A re you sure that's not too many?" Louise asked as Jane brought yet another tray of Clarissa's buns into the kitchen through the back door. "It seems to me we have an embarrassment of buns."

"I would hate to run short," Jane huffed as she set down the last tray. "I figure it's better to have too many. Where is Barbara?"

Louise shrugged. "She said she would be here by now, but she hasn't come yet."

Jane tried to keep her expression nonchalant. She knew that Barbara wanted to stop by and see Rev. Thompson before she came to the inn. Despite Jane's doubts, it looked as though things were getting more serious between them.

"We must get these bakery trays back to Good Apple promptly when we're done," Louise said. She took a deep appreciative sniff of the kitchen's aromas. "It surely smells good in here. I don't know if I can wait for the dinner."

"Half the trick will be getting it out on time and warm." Jane lifted the lid of a roaster oven she had borrowed for the occasion. Inside, the spiced meatballs she had made in advance cooked in an apricot sauce. Another borrowed roaster oven contained sweet-and-sour chicken wings, and pans of spring rolls, breaded shrimp, and bacon-wrapped scallops ready to heat up filled the inn's oven. The salads were ready to go and waiting in the large refrigerator.

"All you need to do is tell us when we can help, Jane," Louise said, setting out the bright orange paper plates Barbara had ordered for the occasion. They matched the napkins and paper cups nicely and complemented the decorating scheme Jane and Barbara had pulled together.

Jack-o'-lanterns with their flickering candles lined the front steps, Craig Tracy's arrangements topped the table-cloths, and spider webs draped over the front entrance. The inn looked mysterious and festive at the same time. Alice and her ANGELs had worked most of Wednesday evening carving out the pumpkins, nicely finishing off what had not been used of Jane's prodigious pumpkin harvest.

Wendell wandered around the inn, weaving through the pumpkins that were set out, unwittingly adding just the right Halloween touch.

The pantry and the storage room, both adjoining the kitchen, had been rearranged and decorated along with the main rooms so that they could be used for the interrogation segment of the evening ahead.

"Oh, don't worry, Louise," Jane said, looking up from the meatballs she was gently stirring. "I won't pass up an opportunity to boss my older sister around."

"Then I think this is a perfect opportunity for me to do a quick check through the inn," Louise said. She could do nothing more in the kitchen, so she left.

Alice was busy arranging the table for the buffet in the dining room. "Do you need any help?" Louise asked as Alice adjusted one of the arrangements, then returned it to its spot.

"No, I'm doing fine. I think." Alice glanced up at her sister and smiled. "What do you think?"

Louise looked over the table. Orange candles in holders decorated with fall leaves dotted the surface. Craig's flower arrangement stood at the center, and scattered over the cream tablecloth were orange, red and pale yellow leaves. "It looks lovely."

"Thank you. I'm not sure if I should have the centerpiece more to the left or to the right. What is your opinion?" Alice moved it infinitesimally to one side, glanced at Louise as if to gauge her reaction, then moved it the same amount to the other side.

Louise pretended to study the matter, then said with a definite note in her voice, "The first."

"You think so?"

"Oh, absolutely. It enhances the—" Louise struggled to find what it might enhance—"the candles. Just exactly right."

"Great! Wonderful!" She moved it back, glancing over at Louise. Then she laughed. "Okay, I can see that you can't tell the least bit of difference."

"The same people were here yesterday—why the fuss now?'

"Last night was like a miniparty. This is the main event, and frankly, I'm a little nervous." She fiddled with some of the leaves and moved a candle. "Do you think people will be offended by the whole idea of a murder?"

Louise smiled at her younger sister. "I realize, Alice, that staging a murder goes completely against your mandate as a nurse, but trust me, I don't think there is any impropriety involved whatsoever. People are here to have fun. Judging from last night, we are off to a good start."

"Okay. That's good." Alice moved the flower arrangement exactly back to where it started, and Louise knew it was time to leave.

She took a moment to talk to Loren and Nina Van Assen.

"I'm so glad we came," Nina was saying. Her short red hair framed a face sprinkled with freckles. "This mystery weekend is such a good idea."

"I'm glad you're enjoying it," Louise said. "If you need anything, be sure to let us know. We don't want to be neglecting our guests."

"I'm sure we'll be okay," Nina said.

Summer and Neville were sitting on the large couch in the living room chatting with Orest Campion. Summer was gesticulating wildly, laughing loudly and in general full of high spirits. She looked up when she saw Louise, then threw her a bright smile. "Hello, Mrs. Smith. Do you need any help?"

"No, thank you. Things are under control for now." Louise said with a motherly smile at her offer. She patted the girl gently on the shoulder, then was summoned by the sounds of people arriving at the door. They were a bit early, but Louise couldn't fault their eagerness. She, too, wanted to find out what was going to happen tonight.

Jane and Barbara had been remarkably closemouthed about the whole story line, and Louise and Alice gave no indication of knowing who might have "done it."

As people trickled in, Louise directed them to the carafes of coffee on the sideboard or to the punch bowl, and the murmur of conversation grew louder as more and more people arrived.

"I tell you, Florence, those silly boys about scared me half to death," Clara Horn was saying to Florence Simpson as they both bustled into the inn. "Hello, Louise," Clara said, looking around. "This looks so wonderful. You and your sisters did a splendid job."

Louise was delighted to see Clara. "And how is Daisy doing?"

Clara waved her hand in a dismissive gesture. "I don't know why I was so worried. Those two boys were bored. They're taking care of her now, and I know for a fact she is in good hands. They love her to pieces."

"That's wonderful," Louise said. "I'm glad *that* mystery was solved."

"Your sister is so smart," Clara said. "And so brave." Clara turned to Florence. "Did I tell you how brave Alice was, finding that out about those boys?"

"Yes. You did. Many times." Florence glanced past Louise to take stock of the people in attendance, her eyes glittering in anticipation. "My, what a crowd! Oh my, Miss Bedreau is here already. I don't see Rev. Thompson. I shall have to ask Barbara where he is," she said with a determined look on her face.

"I believe he is tied up somewhere else this evening," Louise said, forestalling Florence's headlong rush into gossip.

"Humph," Florence said, obviously disappointed with this news. "Clara, we shall simply have to see what Jane has cooked up for this evening." She paused, glanced at her friend and gave her a poke with her substantial elbow. "Get it? Cooked up? Jane is a cook and she has been planning this evening?"

But Clara only gave her a blank look.

Louise stifled a smile that would have been at Florence's expense and went back to the kitchen to check on progress. Barbara had arrived, as Florence had noted, but now she and Jane were huddled in one corner of the kitchen, deep in conversation.

Sylvia was upstairs in the sisters' rooms, getting the actors ready for their big evening. Everyone else was waiting downstairs.

Finally, the chiming of the grandfather clock announced the hour. If anything, the visitors' noise level increased, and as Barbara made her way through the laughing, smiling crowd, she was greeted warmly by people eager to find out what surprise awaited them.

She took the stage, a somber expression on her face. She waited for the noise to die down completely.

As soon as silence had descended, she looked around the assembled group. "I'm sorry, but I need to make an announcement of a serious nature." She sighed, shook her head and put her hand on her chest. "It is with deep regret that I must inform you that Tilda Tome was found this morning…" Barbara paused, her hand to her mouth as she drew in a long, shaky breath, then composed herself. "Dead. Strangled. Deceased. Gone to join the choir invisible."

She looked so serious that for a moment some people looked concerned. Then she winked and people started laughing.

"As I said, Tilda Tome was found dead in her room, strangled with a silk scarf. All the police are able to tell us is that she had been sitting at her laptop, which was still on. The phone was off the hook, and her address book was lying beside it." Barbara paused a moment to let this information sink in. "Local police are puzzled, dismayed, confounded and discombobulated. They need your assistance. They have suspects in custody but don't have the resources to question them all. If you would be so kind as to help, they would be forever in your debt. Or at least for a little while." Barbara nodded to Louise, who moved to the table they had set out in the foyer. "When you arrived this evening, you were given a name tag of a certain color. That is the color of your team. Mrs. Smith will be handing out packets of information that the teams will use to help local police. We need you to get into your groups and pick a team leader."

There was much jostling and milling about, and finally people had melded into some semblance of groups.

"Wonderful. I can see you people are going to get this solved in record time," Barbara said, looking around. "Now, I want the team leaders to get your information packets from Mrs. Smith in the foyer."

Louise handed out the folders, and people were opening them as they returned to their groups as if hoping that something inside would give them a jump on the other teams.

As participants regrouped, the noise level rose again until Barbara got their attention.

"Because we realize that this evening will create a huge strain, we want to make sure that you are adequately fed, and therefore we will be having a buffet supper that you can visit as needed during the course of your work. I would like, once again, to acknowledge all the work done on this supper by Jane Howard with the help of her sisters." Barbara lifted her hands in applause as she looked to the back of the room. Jane and Alice stood by the entrance to the kitchen, each wearing a black apron trimmed with orange that Jane had made especially for Halloween. Each apron had a large pumpkin appliquéd on the front.

Folding chairs had been borrowed from Grace Chapel and were scattered through the living room, dining room and foyer for the guests to sit on while they ate. At the end of the evening, dessert and coffee would be served.

"We will first hear a few words from our suspects, after which they will be sequestered in various rooms, where you may question them. The locations are listed in your brochure." Barbara held it up so that people could see what she was talking about. "We have five suspects and seven teams—more than we had originally envisioned. Two teams will start out eating, while the other five are questioning. After ten minutes, each team will move to the next room to question the next suspect. The team questioning suspect number five, Marianne Holdem, will move on to eat something from the buffet, and one of the teams sitting here will move on to room number one, where Gilbert Gopher is waiting. After another ten minutes, each team will move on to the next room, and the team questioning Marianne will come to eat, and so on until every team has had a chance to do the questioning. This will give you each ten minutes to question each suspect and twenty minutes to eat."

"Are we allowed to share information with the other teams?" someone called out.

"Only if you want to share the prizes," Barbara said. She waited a moment longer and then nodded to Louise, who went upstairs to escort the suspects down. They were all in Jane's room, laughing and joking and teasing each other about being the killer. None of them knew. All they had been given was a brochure with information about their history and their whereabouts the previous night. Barbara would be giving out additional clues during the course of the evening, but these were known only to her and to Jane. This way the suspects were unable to help even if someone tried to coerce them.

Ethel was helping Sylvia with some last-minute work on Marianne's overly spiked and gelled hair.

"I am so sad to be done with my part," Ethel said as she yanked one particularly long spike straight. "I had so much fun being a literary diva."

"And what a wonderful diva you were," Louise told her aunt. "Though I'm sure Sylvia is glad for your present help."

"That I am," Sylvia said putting some final touches on Fred's mustache. "There. You look as handsome as Clark Gable."

"Oh. Handsomer," his wife said, batting her eyes.

"I was sent up here to notify you all that you need to make an appearance downstairs to defend your innocence," Louise said.

"Oh, that won't be hard," Vera said. "Look at me." She pressed her hands against her sparkly shirt. "Am I not the picture of innocence?"

"You're a picture all right," Lloyd said with a fake swagger. He dropped an arm on her shoulders. "My little girl."

"Okay, you hams. Time to get downstairs and play your parts for a larger audience."

Louise led them down, and they all assembled on one side of the makeshift stage.

Louise could see the audience looking them over carefully as if hoping to see something in their eyes. Not that it would help.

Gilbert Gopher was the first one to go up.

"I need to emphasize the special relationship that Tilda and I had," he said, placing his hand on his heart. "Though I felt she could have paid me more, and she promised me she would, I, more than anyone else, knew the state of her finances. And I knew that in time, the money would come. In fact, she was in the process of transferring a large amount of money to my account, because of all my help to her, of course." He looked at the crowd. "I had no reason to kill her."

Barbara thanked him for the information and asked Wilma Wannabe to come forward.

Wilma was alternately scratching at her fingernails or chewing on them. "Tilda and I would help each other," she said, keeping her eyes down. "I would help her with her stories, and she would help me with mine. In fact, I was going to have a huge best seller with my new idea. She told me. And she was going to help me make it work." She blinked, casting her gaze around crazily, looking quite unlike Hope Collins, the affable waitress. "If Gilbert says he had no reason to kill her, I had even less. Less, you hear me. If anyone had a reason, I would suspect Marianne with her wily ways and strange hair. Saying she loved her momma when she never, ever wrote to her. In fact, her momma even cut her out of her will. So there. You see. There!"

"Thank you, Wilma," Barbara said, pretending to look a bit frightened. "Our next suspect is Peter Proxy. Peter, what do you have to say for yourself?"

Peter gave the crowd an oily smile, winked at Barbara and cleared his throat. "I know this may be speaking out of turn, but I think it's important to let you know the same thing I said to Tilda." He smirked and pointed at Gilbert. "I told her that smooth-talking, bootlicking young man was trouble. With a capital *T*, that rhymes with *G*, and that stands for Gilbert. I told her to fire him and get Wilma to work for her. At least Wilma is compliant. When she isn't crazy." He shot Wilma an uneasy glance, then looked back at the audience, his expression sincere. "Tilda was going to be my pot of gold at the end of the rainbow. I had no reason to kill her."

Without being introduced, Tex Holdem swaggered onto the stage, his thumbs hung up in his vest, chomping on an unlit cigar. "Well, well. People seem a mite eager to prove their innocence. As for me, I have nothing to prove. I loved Tilda. But Peter talks about warning Tilda against Gilbert. Well, I tell you, I didn't trust that Peter either." He chewed furiously on the cigar, moving it from one side of his mouth to the other, his agitation showing. "How do you think he can afford that fancy car? Not on what he made from what Tilda gave him, that's for sure. Now I loved Tilda, but that woman could hang onto a penny so long it would melt. But, hey, I'm not here to talk ill of the dead. Just to let you know not to believe everything you hear, is all." He tipped his hat and stepped off the stage.

Louise found herself growing more and more intrigued as each suspect spoke. It was far too early to guess who could have killed Tilda, but her initial guess of Tex Holdem seemed to be borne out by his behavior. He seemed to protest too much.

Marianne stepped up with the same insouciant attitude she had displayed before. Louise laughed, reminding herself that this woman with the attitude was sweet, kind Vera.

"Daddy is Daddy, what can I say?" she said, switching her weight from one hip to the other. "But Daddy claiming to love Mom?" She gave a bitter laugh and flipped her hand in a way to indicate her thoughts on that subject. "Then why was he foolin' around with another woman, I'd like to know?" She nodded her head as people began to whisper among each other. "Oh, he can come across all cool and all, and hey, he's my daddy, but I owe it to Mom to tell you what I know. Ask him about that woman he's got tucked away and the money he was hoping my mama would give him. You ask him." And with that she slouched off the stage in a perfect imitation of a bored young woman trying to project an attitude of cool.

Louise joined the applause … and the laughter.

Barbara glanced back at the suspects, then at the audience. "Well, there you have them, our suspects. They will be going to their respective rooms, and I can tell by the wonderful smells coming out of the kitchen that supper is ready to be served as well. So groups, please check your itinerary and see where you have to be. Louise and I will be circulating to make sure that you aren't badgering our suspects."

"Can we get something to eat before we start?" one person called out. "I don't want to wait until it's cold."

"Jane will bring out fresh, warm food with each new group, so you don't have to worry about that," Barbara assured the audience. "Before you go, I want to give you some guidance. Ask lots of questions. Sometimes you may hear the suspects say, 'I don't know.' Believe them. They probably don't. Make sure each person in your group takes notes. Sometimes one person will understand things differently from another. At the end of the evening, you will bring your considerable expertise to bear on solving this case."

People nodded and gathered up their brochures in readiness to leave.

"One more thing, I also need to let you know that you will be receiving a couple of clues through the course of the evening, each one giving you a piece of information that the suspects could not know. They will be written on a card that you can put in your folder, but I would recommend each member of the team write it down as well." Barbara glanced at the clock, then at Jane in the back of the room. Barbara nodded her head. "So, go on to your rooms and enjoy the investigation."

With excited chatter, people left the living room and went to their designated areas elsewhere on the main floor.

Those who remained filed into the dining room and oohed and aahed over the spread. In addition to the warm dishes, Jane had made three different salads. One was a broccoli salad that Louise had recommended. It was a sweet salad with grapes, mandarin oranges, sunflower seeds and bacon bits mixed in with a sweet-and-sour cream dressing. The other was a creamy looking pale green mixture that Louise had not seen before. It had a pleasant lime flavor. The third was an elegant layered salad. The tables were full of food, and the people who had to stay behind suddenly did not mind.

"So, what do you think?" Barbara asked Louise. "Will people enjoy the evening?"

Louise smiled at Barbara, realizing that because of her initial hesitation regarding Barbara's project, Barbara might feel she had to gain some assurance from the eldest Howard sister.

"They are enjoying it already. What a lot of work you and Jane have put into this. It is turning out great."

Barbara smoothed her hand over her hair in an uncharacteristically nervous gesture. "I guess we'll find out at the end whether we've made it too hard or too easy. If this goes well, it will help me convince the fund-raising committee to give it a try in other places." She abruptly stopped speaking, pressed her lips together as if smoothing out her lipstick and straightened the sparkling pendant at her throat. As Louise followed her gaze, she saw Rev. Thompson coming into the dining room.

"Excuse me, please," Barbara said, giving Louise a vague smile.

Louise watched Barbara and Rev. Thompson leave the dining room. She glanced over the group of people who were eating, thankful to note that Florence wasn't among them.

She wondered for a moment how the relationship would play out. She knew that Barbara was deeply committed to this group she was working for. Louise wondered if she would be willing to settle down in Acorn Hill.

But her curiosity over the unfolding murder mystery sent her off to listen in on one of the groups.

"How often did you work with Tilda?" someone was quizzing Wilma in the library.

"About once a week."

"Did she ever tell you about her ideas?" Betty Dunkle, the local hairdresser, asked.

"Sometimes."

"Weren't you tempted to steal her ideas?" This came from Nia Komonos, the librarian.

Wilma chewed her nails. Louise heard some muttering as if someone had discovered something, then the leader asked, "Has she ever used any of your ideas?"

"Yes," Wilma said vehemently. "She stole my idea."

"Is that the idea for the current book?"

"Yes."

Betsy Long stared at her a moment, as if trying to figure out if her friend Hope was lying, then she nudged Betty Dunkle, and they quietly conferred.

Louise moved to the sunroom, where Peter was being interviewed.

"I may have loaned Tex some money," Peter was saying.

"Where did that money come from?"

Peter shoved his hands in his pockets. "From Tilda's account."

"Did she know?" Ned Arnold asked.

"She might have. She said something to me about it once."

In the parlor a group was grilling Gilbert.

"I bought the scarf in Paris," Gilbert was saying, dabbing at his eyes. "I could barely afford it, but I wanted Tilda to have it."

"Had you ever approached her about giving you a raise?"

"Oh, many times, but she always put me off."

"Were you happy in your job?"

"Of course. Who wouldn't be?"

"Did she mention you in her will?" Carlene Moss fired off her questions rapidly as if hoping to catch Gilbert off guard.

This group was sharp, Louise thought as she listened to their questions. She would never have thought to ask that.

"She did say she was going to put me in, but I did not push the matter." He smiled and Louise started to change her mind about this man.

Of course what she heard Tex say during his interrogation in the storage room made her change her mind about him too.

"Mama said she was going to cut me clean out. Just clean out." Marianne was in full form, her voice reverberating in the inn's large pantry.

"How did that make you feel?"

"How do you think?" Marianne glared at Dee Butorac, a fellow teacher. "It made me mad."

"Mad enough to kill her?"

Marianne realized she might have gone a bit far, and Louise realized the wisdom of the suspects' not knowing whether they had killed Tilda.

"Of course not," Marianne said. "I love my mama."

As Louise made her way back toward the dining room, she heard Wilma holding forth about her visit to the psychiatrist and how she thought she was getting better. Again Louise was amazed at Hope's acting ability. She made Wilma look like a slightly deranged . . . killer.

Who knew?

Chapter Eighteen

"$\mathcal{H}$ere is the first clue," Barbara announced to the two groups in the dining room a little later on. "I'll be announcing this to the others as well. The police told me they have discovered some possibly incriminating evidence. Dear departed Tilda had a strand of dark, curly hair caught in her rings, and both Gilbert and Tex have reported that they heard sounds of a struggle."

Alice thought of Wilma's dark hair. But Peter Proxy had dark curly hair too. Only one could be the villain.

She turned to Louise, who was standing beside her in the dining room. "What do you think?"

Louise leaned over to whisper, "I was thinking Marianne, but that Wilma seems a little crazy. She could easily have done it."

"My money is on Tex. Apparently he wanted Tilda to give him money to cover some large gambling debts incurred in Las Vegas. But she wouldn't do it." Alice was convinced about Tex. After listening to all the suspects, she had also found out that Tex had connections to the Mob.

"When do we find out?"

Alice had to laugh at Louise's impatience. "I guess when everyone else does."

"I don't suppose Jane would let me know."

"Not a chance."

"I was afraid of that."

As Alice put out some fresh buns, she listened to one group in the dining room exchanging their theories.

"Wilma was named in the will," Florence was saying, looking earnest. "That much we know."

"And you have to admit she's loony." Craig Tracy spun his finger by his temple to make his point. "We know that she wanted to get some money from Tilda."

"But if she was named in the will, why should she kill her?"

"That is exactly the point."

Everyone pondered that for a moment until one person spoke up. "But, remember, Tilda changed her will, putting Marianne in it."

"And taking Gilbert out."

Alice frowned herself. This was truly a puzzle. As she went into the kitchen, her puzzlement must have shown on her face.

"Confused, my dear sister?" Jane teased, putting a fresh batch of spring rolls into the oven. "Who do you think did it?"

Alice set down her tray and leaned on the counter, her hands folded. "I know you won't tell me, but for the record my guess is still Tex."

"What makes you say that?"

"He was jealous of Gilbert, Tilda's boyfriend. He was so angry he even threatened to use his connections to the Mob. He wanted money from Tilda that she wouldn't give him." Alice ticked off the points on her fingers.

"What about the dark curly hair?"

Alice waved her hand. "That's a red herring. People said she had a fight with Wilma. It could easily have happened before she was killed."

"Whatever you say."

Alice glanced at her sister. Though Jane wouldn't tell her, Alice knew her sister well enough to sense she was on the wrong track. "Okay. I can see I'm going to have to start all over again. When does Barbara give the next clue?"

"In about ten minutes." Jane took some bottles of sauce for the spring rolls out of the refrigerator. "When you have a minute, could you refresh the sauce dishes for me?"

"Where is Barbara?" Alice hadn't seen her upstairs, or in the living room or the dining room.

Jane glanced around, looking puzzled, still holding the bottles. "I don't know. Maybe she's talking to Kenneth."

"You seem to know more about them than the rest of us. How serious are they?"

Jane carefully arranged the bottles on the countertop, buy-
ing time. "I know they really care for each other," she said
finally. "But I also know that she really likes working with this
organization, and if she quits her other job and gets a job with
Doctors Without Borders full-time, it would mean leaving
Potterston completely." She shrugged. "Who knows? Maybe
Kenneth will go with her. We know that he has a heart for ministry. And he did mention something about it the other day."

Alice felt a prick of dread. Though she wanted
Rev. Thompson's happiness, she didn't like to think that he
would leave. It had been difficult enough finding a pastor
to replace their father when he passed away, and Kenneth
had been such a good fit for their community. She didn't
like to think of the church board having to go through that
process again.

But more than that, she didn't like the thought of
Rev. Thompson's leaving Acorn Hill . . . and them.

"It's always hard, isn't it, when two people are so dedi-
cated to what they are doing," Alice said.

Jane gave her a melancholy smile, and Alice knew that
her sister agreed.

Alice pushed herself away from the counter. "No sense
in borrowing trouble. As the Bible says, 'Each day has
enough trouble of its own' (Matthew 6:34). So for now, I'm
going to see if I can discover anything more about our trou-
blesome murderer."

But as Alice left, she said a short prayer for Kenneth and Barbara . . . and for Grace Chapel.

$\backsim$

"It was the daughter," Summer said with confidence as she addressed her group, mostly younger people from the town. "Marianne."

A young man laughed. "And how do you figure that?" he said. Jane recognized Trevor Walker, a young man who helped Craig Tracy at Wild Things.

Summer raised her eyebrows. "Not hard to tell. I mean, deal with her outfit for a moment."

"You're going to base a decision on her taste in clothes?"

"Or lack thereof," Summer said with a grimace. "I mean sequins are so yesterday. And there was that big fight she had with her mother that night. Can't imagine fighting with my mother, then killing her. My sister, maybe."

Jane had to laugh at Summer's conclusions. She obviously had her own methodology. And sense of humor.

"A hint, Jane?" Summer said, catching her eye. "For us poor youngsters who are struggling without the wisdom of many years to help us along."

Jane saw the hopeful faces turned to her but laughed and shook her head. "Sorry. You're on your own until Barbara gets to you." Little did they know how tempted she was to give them the tiniest clue, but she resisted. It wouldn't be fair to the rest.

"Everyone had a fight with Tilda that night," someone huffed, sounding frustrated. "They all had a motive of sorts."

Barbara came by and handed Neville, the spokesperson for the group, the next clue.

He held it up and read it aloud.

"And who was seen coming out of Marianne's room at eleven o'clock last night?" He put it down and frowned. "Since when is a question a clue?"

"Using questions to get people thinking is what teachers do all the time," Summer said, her eyes sparkling. She looked down at her notes. "I'm sure we have the answer to that somewhere. All we need to do is review."

"According to Tex, he was in Marianne's room at nine o'clock, so it couldn't be him."

"And Peter Proxy said he was downstairs talking to Wilma at ten."

"That would leave Gilbert."

"I thought we were trying to figure out who killed Tilda, who, incidentally, was killed at twelve o'clock when everyone claimed to be in their rooms," one of the younger girls said, her elbows on her knees, rocking back and forth as she added, "So why do we need to know this? Or guess this?"

They talked the issue back and forth for a while, and Jane left them, curious to learn what the other groups had discovered. She had a few moments before she was to serve dessert.

"So what about your dead cat?" someone was asking Wilma. "How did it die?"

Wilma twirled a lock of dark hair around her finger and frowned. "I was mad at it because it wouldn't do what I wanted. So I, well, put some poison in its food, and when that didn't work, I, well, strangled it."

Jane glanced through the room to see people's reactions to this piece of news, but most people were simply writing down the information as if Wilma's were a normal reaction to a cat's disobedience.

In another room, Tex was discussing his gambling habits and demonstrating some of the martial arts he had learned in the self-defense course he took after the Mob started making noises about some unpaid gambling debts.

Gilbert was waxing eloquent about his loving relationship with Tilda, who, though older than he was, was a person he respected and adored. He wished that she and her daughter got along better, and he had convinced Tilda to put her back in her will.

Peter was fuming about the letter that Tilda had sent to him, telling him that he was fired. He described how angry it made him.

Of course, Jane knew what had happened and how, and as she heard the suspects talk, the truth seemed so obvious to her, but so far no one seemed to be on the right track.

She went back to the kitchen to get the desserts out just as Barbara came into the kitchen from the dining room. She was smiling.

"This is going very well," she said as she helped Jane take the cheesecakes out of the now-empty refrigerator. "I can't believe how people are so taken with this whole puzzle."

"They sure seem to be enjoying themselves. I think you could easily do this again and with a few more people per team," Jane said. "Provided you have a large enough facility."

"It's going better than I had dreamed. In fact, I did some rough estimates on the event and it looks as though it will make some money."

"And we didn't charge that much. I'm sure people would be willing to pay more for something this good."

Barbara looked at Jane. "And I have you and your sisters to thank for helping me with this. I have to confess that initially I was concerned about the success of the evening and how the work would affect you and the running of the inn."

"We have been delighted to help." Jane set another wedge of cheesecake on a plate and lined it up with the others she had already done. "The hardest part was coming up with the story. I wouldn't want to face that again any time soon."

"But now we have it, and I can use it elsewhere." Barbara wiped her hands. "So what else do you need me to do?"

"You don't need to help," Jane protested.

"I'm not wanted for a few moments yet, and I feel bad making you do all of this work."

"Trust me, I do enjoy it. But if you really feel a call to help, you can start cutting up that layered dessert I have in those rectangular pans."

"This all looks so yummy. What is it?"

"In keeping with the whole harvest theme, and in an effort to get rid of the last of my darned pumpkins, this is pumpkin cheesecake, and what you are cutting up is layered pumpkin dessert, and, of course, I still have some traditional pumpkin pie."

Barbara shook her head. "I'll pass on the pumpkin pie. Never one of my favorites. As far as I'm concerned, pumpkin pie is an excuse to eat cinnamon and whipped cream."

Jane laughed as she drizzled a caramel sauce over the cheesecakes in an artful swirl. She squirted a dab of whipped cream on each and stood back to examine the effect.

"You always make your food look so attractive," Barbara said.

"I was taught that eating is as much a visual as sensory experience," Jane replied, setting the plates on trays.

Barbara finished slicing up the dessert, then wiped her hands. "And speaking of guests, I better get back to the mystery and see how things are progressing."

"How much more time do we have?"

"I'm going to give a five-minute warning. Then they have to turn in their reports." Barbara glanced at the slender gold watch on her wrist. "In fact, I'd better do that now if we want to stay on schedule. After I deal with the mystery, I'm going to announce that coffee and dessert will be served. Does that give you enough time?"

"Plenty. If you see them, ask Alice and Louise to stop by to help me to set it out."

"I will do that," she said and left.

Jane watched her go, feeling a pinch of frustration. She had hoped that they could talk about things other than food and the mystery weekend. She, like the people in the town that she had teased for being curious, was just as interested to know how things were progressing with Kenneth. In spite of Barbara's seeing him earlier in the evening, she hadn't mentioned his name to Jane once.

Exactly five minutes later, Barbara again stood on the small stage, seeking the audience's attention.

She had it in seconds. Everyone was interested to hear what she had to say next.

"First off, let me congratulate all of you on your amazing sleuthing abilities. I was impressed by the questions you asked the suspects and how quickly some of you got important information from them. Well done. Now we need to know who has solved this mystery." She held up the envelopes the teams had given her. "I asked you to fill out the sheets saying who did it and why. I'm going to read them one by one, then tell you what the real answer is."

The entire room held its collective breath while she opened the first envelope. "This first one is from the green group. It says, 'We believe that Peter Proxy, because he thought he was going to get fired, killed Tilda Tome by choking her.' That is a good answer, but, unfortunately, not the right one. There is a lapse between the time he saw Tilda and the time she died that cannot be reconciled."

The green group groaned.

Barbara read the next two. One of them accused Wilma Wannabe, citing her history of mental problems and her dead pet, as well as her accusation that Tilda stole her best-selling idea.

The other said that the killer was clearly Tex, claiming that his size and the fact that his self-defense course pointed to him as the only true suspect in the murder.

"Here is another accusation against Wilma Wannabe." Barbara glanced at Hope, who stood to one side, still in character, still chewing her fingernails. "You had them convinced, Wilma. Good job."

Wilma flashed Barbara a grin, then dropped a quick curtsy to the crowd at their impromptu applause.

"This group says Colonel Mustard did it in the kitchen with the pipe wrench." Barbara looked up, puzzled. "What is this?"

"We gave up," called out Orest Campion, the spokesperson for his befuddled group. "So we made up our own result."

A burst of laughter greeted this comment.

"I guess it would be unnecessary to tell you that you lost," Barbara said, laughing as well. She opened the next envelope and read it aloud, "Had to be Tex. No doubt."

Barbara shook her head. "Sorry. Tex maybe had a motive to kill Tilda, but if you remember, he and Wilma were together at the time that Tilda died, which rules out Wilma and Tex at the same time." She glanced at Jane, who was feeling a bit nervous. Had they made it too hard? It seemed so easy while they were working on it.

Barbara held up the last envelope. "I hope this one is it," she said. She slit it open, pulled out the paper and started reading. "We believe that Gilbert Gopher choked Tilda Tome and is the guilty one."

Barbara looked up with a smile of relief. "Who is the red group?"

Neville, Summer and their group surged to their feet, cheering with the exuberance of youth and competition. "Way to go, red!" Summer called out.

"I didn't say you won," Barbara said with an indulgent smile.

"But we know we did," Summer called out.

"Actually . . . you are right. Very well done. Here is what the red group surmised. Gilbert Gopher and Marianne Holdem were going to get married. Gilbert knew that Tilda had called the lawyer. After the big fight Marianne had with her mother, Tilda was going to take Marianne out of her will. Before that could happen, Gilbert decided to protect his true love, and to keep suspicion from falling on her, he killed Tilda himself." Barbara turned to Gilbert who stood to one side, looking hangdog. "Shame on you, Gilbert. You have misused your employer's trust, and you must pay the penalty."

Tex and Peter caught him by the arm and pretended to take him away.

"I'm innocent. I was framed," he called out as they led him through the foyer and to the parlor beyond.

"I'll wait for you, Gilbert," Marianne called, running after them. "No matter how long it takes, I'll wait for you."

Everyone laughed at the dramatic departure. By now, most of the participants knew that Vera was Fred's wife, which only added to the humor of the moment.

"Now that justice has been served, red group, you may think about your prizes. After I introduce those brilliant actors who played the suspects, you can come forward to claim your treasures. I'm sure you'll need some time to decide."

As Barbara spoke, the suspects, most of them still in costume, came onto the stage. Ethel was also there, minus the turban but wearing her wide red dress.

"I think we need to give an especially loud round of applause for our victim and suspects, and I would like to introduce them now." Barbara gestured for the group to come forward.

"Ethel Buckley was our ravishing Tilda Tome, and Fred Humbert was our nefarious murderer, Gilbert Gopher. Hope Collins, our friendly Coffee Shop waitress, was Wilma Wannabe. Joseph Holzmann starred as Peter Proxy. Acorn Hill's mayor, Lloyd Tynan, was our Tex Holdem, and Vera Humbert, wife of Fred Humbert, was Marianne Holdem." All bowed as they were introduced, and when the introductions were completed, they held hands and bowed again.

"You all did a marvelous job. Thank you so much for all your time," Barbara said, acknowledging them with her own applause. She turned back to the audience.

"Again, I want to thank you all for participating," Barbara said when the sound of clapping died down enough for her to speak. "As you know, this was a pilot project, and I thought you might be interested to know that we raised over two hundred dollars for the group I represent. Because this evening was such a success, I am hoping to use this play and this format at other venues to raise money for the organization. So thank you again for your generosity and your cooperation. I also want to invite all of you to enjoy some of the bounty of Grace Chapel's Inn's garden in a couple of ways. First, we have dessert for you in the dining room. Please help yourself. And everyone who came tonight is welcome to take a pumpkin home for participating. These jack-o'-lanterns were all carved by the ANGELs, a group of wonderful young girls that Alice Howard works with. We want to thank them also for their work. Have some coffee, enjoy some visiting and comparing notes, and thank you all again for coming."

Barbara left the stage smiling to another round of applause.

She worked her way through the crowd, taking a moment to talk to the people who had come to know her in the past few weeks. Finally she came to stand beside Louise and Jane. She unbuttoned her jacket and smoothed back her hair and sighed lightly. "So. That's done."

"I think the participants enjoyed themselves," Louise said. "You and Jane did a wonderful job. I must confess I had my own suspicions about the villain, but I was wrong."

"Okay, Louie, fess up. Who did you think did it?" Jane asked.

"My eyes were on Tex. Especially after I heard him talk about the self-defense course he took."

"Were you surprised?" Jane pressed.

"A little. Though once I found out who had done it, I could look back at the information I had gleaned and realize that indeed Gilbert was the one who had strangled poor Tilda Tome."

Viola bustled up to them, smiling. "What a wonderful evening. Such fun!"

"Did you guess who did it, Viola?" Jane asked.

Viola adjusted her glasses and shook her head, suddenly all indignation. "I thought for sure that Wilma person. Anyone who could kill a cat . . ." She shuddered, as if thinking about her own numerous cats.

"It was just a story, Viola," Barbara assured her.

"I know. But I tend to get involved in my stories. Did you and Jane really think this all up yourselves?"

"Yes, we did."

Viola nodded. "A little over the top, even for a murder mystery, but the fact that I didn't solve it does add some credibility to the story. I don't know that it's publishable, but it's perfectly adequate for an evening of entertainment like this."

Jane gave Louise a surreptitious sidelong glance and saw her press her lips together, hiding her smile.

"As you said, Viola, it is just for entertainment," Jane said. "I wouldn't hope to compete with any of the mystery authors that Alice likes to read."

Viola frowned as if those books weren't worth much of her attention. "The food was delicious, the company very pleasant, and I must say I enjoyed myself thoroughly," Viola declared. "Is it true that I can help myself to a carved pumpkin?"

"Please," Jane begged, catching Viola's hands. "Take two if you want."

"Why, thank you," she said. "I would like two. They would make a lovely display in the bookstore."

She left with two fierce-looking specimens, one under each arm, well satisfied with herself and the evening.

"One gratified customer," Barbara said.

"Oh, I think there are more," Louise said. "I'll check the punch bowl and fill up the carafes." She left Jane and Barbara alone a moment.

"So, wasn't it worth it?" Jane asked, almost sorry now that the evening was over.

"Yes. I'm really delighted." Barbara glanced at Jane. "You seem to agree."

"I am pleased." She looked around at the subdued activity in the inn. Some guests had left already, saying thank you and good-bye and taking their pumpkins. But most seemed content to sit around and compare deductions and simply talk.

A burst of laughter sounded from one end of the room. *Summer's group*, thought Jane. That girl had boundless enthusiasm and contagious energy. And, of course, having been part of the group that solved the puzzle, she had extra reason to be giddy this evening.

"So what's next for you, Barbara?" Jane asked, trying to make the question sound casual.

Barbara massaged her own neck, looking momentarily uncertain. "I have to take stock. Make some decisions." She gave Jane a cautious look. "Who knows what comes next?"

Jane wanted to be encouraged by her ambiguous remarks, but she sensed an undertone of ambivalence in Barbara's voice. Jane longed to ask more, but sensed that the time wasn't right.

"Do you want to come for an informal lunch after church tomorrow?" she asked.

Barbara pursed her lips, considering the offer. "I don't have to leave until three o'clock, so yes, I'd like to come," she said. Then she patted Jane on the shoulder. "Now I'd better help clean up and get home. I have to confess that I'm truly tired."

She began gathering up discarded paper plates, smiling and chatting with people as she went.

Jane returned to the kitchen to see what she could do with the leftovers. In spite of Clarissa's generosity, there weren't many buns left. And, to Jane's relief, not much of the food either.

Chapter Nineteen

I enjoyed your sermon, Kenneth," Barbara said, looking across the dining room table at Rev. Thompson. "I especially appreciate how you challenge people to recognize that all we have is from God and that we have an obligation to use it for Him. How did you phrase that again? 'What we give God'?"

"Our gifts to God are like giving Him flowers from His own garden," the pastor said with a smile. He sat back in his chair. "And this meal is a wonderful gift to us, Jane. Thank you."

Jane had asked Rev. Thompson to join her and her sisters, and Barbara and Ethel, for leftovers after church. She was pleased when he accepted.

He was looking relaxed now that his sermon had been delivered. At Jane's urging to make himself comfortable, he had hung the jacket of his navy blue suit over the back of his chair, carefully rolled up the sleeves of his white shirt, loosened his navy and pale blue silk tie.

Barbara wore a peach-colored suit today. The color set off the blonde of her hair and complemented her sea green eyes.

Jane wondered if it was the pastor's presence that brought out the rose in Barbara's cheeks and the light in her eyes.

"Considering it's a rerun, I'm glad you like the meal," Jane responded.

"It's still delicious," the pastor said. "I'm sorry I missed the original yesterday."

"We were too. The mystery weekend was quite a success," Jane said, glancing from him to Barbara. To her disappointment, they weren't looking at each other.

Then again, maybe they were simply pretending not to be interested. After all, Ethel was present, and she had already been the cause of enough gossip about the pair.

"Do you plan on doing it again, Barbara?" Rev. Thompson asked.

"Yes. The charity will be excited about our success." She picked at the food on her plate, still avoiding his gaze. "I have learned a few things from this debut that will make it easier for anyone wanting to put it on."

"So what are you going to do after this, Barbara?" Ethel asked, helping herself to another meatball. "Go back to working full-time again?"

"I have to do some follow-up work in regard to my current clients. And then"—she gave a light shrug—"I have to think about what I'm going to do from there in terms of my career."

"I'm sure you have some hard decisions to make," Rev. Thompson said. "But I am also sure that much thought and prayer will guide you."

Barbara glanced at him, then smiled.

But her smile gave Jane a sense of misgiving. Something had subtly shifted between these two in the past few days. It was almost as if they were each finding a way to part company gently.

Jane knew she shouldn't be so nosy, but she had truly grown to care for Barbara. And the pastor was a good friend.

"What about your work with the charity?" Louise asked. "I understood that you hoped to do more in that area."

"I do. I have spoken with the director, and we are trying to figure out where my talents lie," she said, delicately setting her knife and fork across the plate. She wiped her fingers on the napkin and declined Louise's offer of coffee.

Jane caught her surreptitious glance at her watch. Surely she wasn't in a hurry to leave?

Rev. Thompson pushed his chair back, thanking the sisters for their invitation as he did so. He got up and put his coat on. "Barbara, I was wondering if you would be willing to take a short walk with me?"

Finally, thought Jane, sinking back with relief into her chair. Maybe she had been reading them wrong.

"I should help clean up—" Barbara started to offer assistance.

"We'll manage fine without you," Jane said. "There's not much, and we have lots of help."

"Are you sure?"

"Go already!" Jane said, flapping her hands at her in a shooing motion.

Barbara laughed as she stepped away from the table. "Okay, I get the message." She gave the pastor a smile, and together they left the dining room.

As soon as they had left, Ethel was up, heading in the same direction.

"Aunt Ethel, what are you doing?" Louise asked, catching her by the arm.

Ethel blinked in surprise, then looked back in the direction the couple had gone. "Why, I was just...well..."

"Going to check on them?" Jane said with a grin as the front door of the inn clicked shut.

Ethel rotated her shoulder in a vague gesture. "Maybe..."

"I think they might want their privacy, Aunt Ethel," Alice said.

Ethel sighed her frustration, but her displeasure bounced away as quickly as it came.

"I wonder if he's going to propose to her?" she asked, her eyes bright with anticipation.

Though Jane doubted that their relationship had progressed to the marriage-proposal stage, she did have hopes that more than going for walks was in store for these two people who meant so much to her.

"So what do we do with leftover leftovers?" Louise asked, holding up a bowl of about a dozen meatballs.

"I think heating them up twice is more than enough, though I hate throwing them away," Jane said.

"I can package them up and take them to Viola," Louise suggested. "I hope to visit her this afternoon, and I'm sure her cats would love the food."

As if on cue, Wendell slipped out of the pantry.

"I'm sure you're glad all the fuss is over," Alice said, picking him up and stroking his soft head.

His only response was a rich, rumbling purr. After a moment, he jumped from Alice's arms with a muted *thunk* to the middle of the kitchen floor.

"And isn't that the perfect example of how a cat can run a house?" Ethel said as she wiped down the table. "I hate to think what kind of pampering Viola has to do in her home."

"Excuse us."

They all looked up to see Summer and Neville standing at the kitchen entrance.

"We've come to say good-bye," Summer said.

"And to thank you for your amazing hospitality," Neville added.

Louise frowned. "I thought you weren't leaving until tomorrow. You are paid up until then."

"Come on in," Jane said. "Don't stand there like strangers."

With light laughs, Summer and Neville stepped into the kitchen. To Louise's surprise, Summer was wearing a simple bronze-colored turtleneck sweater and a gold chain. Instead of her usual torn blue jeans, she wore a beige corduroy skirt and simple brown pumps.

"You look lovely, my dear," Louise said approvingly.

"Thanks." Summer ran her hand self-consciously over her skirt and blushed. "Nevvie and I went shopping yesterday. I thought maybe I should tone it down a bit. For now."

"My parents are meeting us in Potterston for dinner with Summer's parents." Neville slipped his arm around Summer's shoulders. "Mom and Dad thought it was time they meet."

"That's wonderful," Louise said. "I'm so glad to hear that."

"I hope I don't mess up and use the wrong utensils," Summer replied.

"Don't tell me you're worried about what people will think," Jane said.

"They aren't as uptight about me as before, so I figure if they're gonna try, I should too."

"And that's why we're leaving a day early," Neville said. "They want us to return with them to Pittsburgh tonight.

As for our early departure, please make the extra payment a contribution to Barbara's charity."

"Why, thank you both. She will be most grateful," Alice responded.

"We get to stay in the guest bedroom at 'Moreau Mansion.'" Summer flashed them a mischievous smile. "And I'm going to make sure to use up my share of the guest soap."

"Now, Summer, you know that proper guests leave the guest soap alone," Jane teased.

"Now, Ms. Howard, you know that I'm not a proper guest," Summer returned.

"I think you're proper enough," Louise said. "It has been a real blessing having you stay with us."

Louise's quiet comment made Summer blush. "Thank you, Mrs. Smith," she said, ducking her head and fiddling with her necklace. "That means a lot."

"We'd better get going, hon" Neville said, tightening his arm around Summer's shoulder. He gave each of them a charming smile. "And thanks again. Staying here has given us wonderful memories."

"Hey, we'll be back again, won't we?" Summer asked, glancing up at Neville.

"I hope you will," Louise said.

They said one more good-bye, and they, too, were gone.

As the door closed behind the delightful couple, Louise felt as if the inn had been deflated.

The silence they left in their wake showed her that the others felt the same way.

"I am going to miss that girl," Louise said quietly as she hung her tea towel up on the drying rack by the stove.

"She was definitely a colorful character," Alice agreed.

"So. We have a bit of a breather," Jane said finally, closing the door on the dishwasher. "I don't know about you, but I could use a nap."

"Not yet," Ethel called from the front hall. "Here come Rev. Thompson and Barbara."

"Already?"

"Were you spying, Aunt Ethel?"

"Please come back here," Alice pleaded.

"Yes, no and I'm coming," Ethel said with a huff as she flounced back into the kitchen.

Just in time too. No sooner had she dropped into a kitchen chair than the front door of the inn opened, and the pastor and Barbara entered.

As they came into the kitchen, Ethel and her nieces pretended to look busy.

"So you make sure to keep in touch," the pastor said to Barbara as he held the swinging door open for her. "I would love to hear how things are going for you and about the work you are doing."

"I will. I'll have to write down the address."

Keep in touch? Write? Jane glanced from one to the other, frustrated. This was not what she thought they would be discussing after a leisurely stroll in Acorn Hill.

"What's the matter, Jane? You look puzzled," Barbara said.

"I …uh… it's just that . . ."

"We thought you were going to get married," Ethel put in, blissfully ignoring social niceties.

The minister frowned and Barbara laughed.

"I'm sorry, Ethel, but no," the pastor said. "Barbara and I are simply good friends."

Jane stifled her own small disappointment. The phrase *good friends* was the death knell of romance.

"Besides, we can't possibly get married." Barbara giggled. "Just think of it: We would be known as Ken and Barbie."

Jane blinked, then laughed out loud.

"We both have work that requires a lot of dedication and time," the pastor continued, glancing at Barbara. "And romance would complicate things."

Barbara gave him a smile. "I've enjoyed our times together, though. You've taught me a lot about priorities. I especially appreciate the reminders you've given me about our responsibilities in this world as followers of Christ."

"I know it's something I struggle with every day, so I guess it's a matter of the preacher preaching to himself as well as those around him."

Jane looked at the minister again trying to read his expression. But all she saw was a peaceful smile and the look of a man content with himself and his life.

She had to admit that as long as he was happy, then she should be too.

"Well, then." Ethel looked disappointed. "I guess we won't be decorating the church for a wedding any time soon."

"You could help us out there, Aunt Ethel," Jane said with a wink.

Ethel angled her a puzzled frown. "How?"

"*You* could get married."

"Nonsense," Ethel said with a light snort. "Lloyd and I are simply good friends."

"That seems to be the trend," Jane said.

Monday morning, Barbara made one last stop at the inn to say good-bye. Jane, Alice and Louise all joined her for one last visit around the kitchen table.

"And where are you going tomorrow?" Alice asked over a cup of tea.

"Chicago, to meet with a committee member responsible for fund-raising for Doctors Without Borders. She wants to discuss what we did this weekend and a few other possibilities. She also offered me a full-time position on the board, so we'll see where my life takes me in the next few years." Barbara took a sip of tea and looked around the kitchen. "I'm going to miss this place. I had a lot of fun working here." She looked at the cake on the plate Jane had set in front of her. "And I think I'm going to miss all the great food as well."

"Enjoy that cake, Barbara. It's special," Jane said.

"Why is that?"

Jane dropped a generous dollop of whipped cream on the cake with a flourish. "This cake represents the last of the pumpkin harvest."

"That calls for a celebration for sure," Barbara said, toasting Jane with her teacup. "It doesn't seem that long ago that you were standing in the garden muttering at your pumpkin patch, wondering what your next step should be, and now, here you are. Done."

"One small step for Jane, one giant leap for pumpkinkind."

Louise frowned at her. "That is one of the worst paraphrases I have ever heard."

"I agree, Louise. That pair of phrases was really bad."

Louise shook her head.

"And I'm going to miss how you get along," Barbara said with an affectionate look at Louise. "But, like Summer, I hope to stop by from time to time."

"You make sure you do," Alice said. "We would really like to hear how you are doing in your new job."

They chatted awhile, then, all too soon, it was time for Barbara to leave.

"What can I say that I haven't already said?" Barbara hesitated a moment, then gave each one of them a hug. "Thank you again for all you've done. I've been really blessed by you."

They walked her to her car and waved good-bye as she got in.

As she drove away, Jane, Louise and Alice lingered outside a moment longer, watching the car disappear down Chapel Road.

"That was an interesting episode," Louise said.

"Did you enjoy it after all, Louie?" Jane asked.

Louise gave Jane a wry smile. "You will have your pound of flesh, won't you?"

"You two better not get started," Alice said. "I think we have company again."

A tall, elegant man was walking toward them. He wore a long topcoat and held a cane that he twirled from time to time. He wore a bowler hat, and a narrow mustache graced his upper lip. A bright green, silk ascot at his throat finished off the picture of a dapper gentleman. As he came closer, he saluted them with his cane, and Louise finally recognized him.

"Wilhelm! I'm so glad you're not ..." she stopped herself before she could say "in jail."

"Good afternoon, ladies," he said with a jaunty air. "It's a lovely day."

Indeed it was. The sun had graced them with warmth today, a last gift before winter descended on them.

Louise looked him over carefully. He had changed, but not drastically. Despite all his adventures—not to mention his anglicized clothing and accessories— he looked much the same as the Wilhelm who left Acorn Hill three weeks earlier.

"How lovely to see you," Alice exclaimed. "How was your trip? When did you come home?"

Alice knew exactly how Wilhelm's trip was, for she had read the reports that Louise and Viola painstakingly transcribed, but Louise silently blessed her for acting so blasé about it.

"I came home last night. And in answer to your first question, my trip was a wonder and a delight from beginning to end," he said with a smile. "And the shop was in good hands in my absence."

"Europe seems to have agreed with you," Jane said, brushing her own upper lip with her forefinger. "You look cosmopolitan. Not sinister at all."

Louise shot Jane a warning glance, knowing that she was referring to the "'jail" stint that it seemed Wilhelm had endured.

"Yes, well," Wilhelm looked a bit discomfited. "I think I will be shaving it off. It seems a bit pretentious, but a friend suggested I try it out."

One of the colorful widows? Louise wondered.

"Would you like to come in? We still have some coffee on," Alice said. "It's a quiet day for us, and we would love to hear all about your trip."

"Would we ever," Jane said and winked at Louise, who simply frowned at her.

Once a youngest child, always a youngest child, Louise thought.

"I would like to do that," Wilhelm said, following them into the inn. "I have not had a chance to speak to Carlene Moss yet, though I am assuming you got my letters?" he asked Jane as he settled into a chair in the kitchen.

"I got them, and, I have to confess, I passed them on to Louise." Jane put out clean cups and added more cream to the cream pitcher. "I was involved with the supper we put on this past weekend. I hope that's okay with you."

"Fine, fine," Wilhelm said. He looked expectantly at Louise. "Would you happen to have copies of the papers that my articles were in? I would enjoy seeing the finished products."

"Wilhelm, let me explain something," Louise hesitated. "We had some difficulty transcribing the first letter, so it didn't get to Carlene on time. Consequently, the first article made it in only last Wednesday. Viola has been helping me, and we have finished the second one. You should probably look it over before we deliver it to her."

"I have the *Nutshell* right here," Alice said, handing it to him.

Wilhelm produced a pair of narrow reading glasses, perched them on his nose and paged through the paper, then stopped when he found his article. As he read, Jane, Alice and Louise watched him carefully.

A faint frown appeared between his eyebrows after a few moments. It only deepened as he went along. When he had finished, he tapped his fingers on the paper, then looked up at Louise.

"I never went horse hunting. And what is this about rat kennels?"

Louise lifted her shoulders in a careful shrug. "We were wondering ourselves, but it was what we understood from what you had sent us."

Wilhelm glanced over it again, shaking his head.

"I'll get you the original and maybe you can enlighten us," Louise said, getting up from the table.

She quickly found the letters and the latest article she was going to send to Carlene. If they misinterpreted the first letter, there was a good chance Wilhelm hadn't been in jail at all.

Wilhelm took the letters from her and laid them on the table, smoothing them out. He read through them, pursed his lips and read again, one long finger running down the lines of writing. "I can see that you would have had some difficulty," he murmured. "I wrote this in a hurry. Mostly on the train." He read the article once more, glancing periodically at his letter, comparing the two.

"So what did you really say?" Jane asked.

"As far as I can read and recollect, I wrote to you about the Kasteel Radbout in Northern Holland. They spell castle with a *K* in the Netherlands. A friend of mine took a picture of me in the stocks there. I'm assuming that's where you got the rat's part. From Radbout. I couldn't remember how to spell it."

"I thought the castle was a kettle, which didn't make sense. It seemed best to read it as *kennel*," Louise suggested, settling beside him as they went over the letter and the article.

"And this bit about horse hunting near the Black Forest. I did accompany a friend of mine while he went *house* hunting."

"I'm sure Louise is relieved to know that, never mind Viola," Jane said with a mischievous twinkle in her eye.

"What about the bike part?" Louise asked.

Wilhelm adjusted his glasses and read over his letter again. "That I wrote after I went biking on the dykes. They have three sets of dykes leftover from the time when the Ijselmeer, the enclosed body of water between North Holland and Friesland, was the Zuider Zee. The South Sea. The first dyke was called the Watcher. It was the first line of defense against the water from the sea," he explained, shooting a quick glance over his glasses, as if making sure Louise did, indeed, understand. "The second one was called the Dreamer, and the third was called the Sleeper, because mostly it could rest easy until needed. I thought it was a charming little anecdote and wanted to add it to my letter."

"And what about this part, about almost getting blown up?"

Wilhelm stroked his mustache self-consciously and checked again. "Actually I was referring to the excavating done by the people of Northern Holland when they got rid of many of the canals. During the war, a large resistance group was based there, and they buried munitions in the area. The people excavating had to be careful they did not ignite any explosives. I found the Netherlands, overall, fascinating. Tidy and neat and beautiful. It is like one large garden."

"That certainly makes more sense," Louise said, relieved to have been wrong about some of the things they had transcribed. With some hesitation, she drew out the most recent letter she and Viola had interpreted, along with Wilhelm's original. "And now I want you to look at this one and correct it, because as far as we could understand, you ended up in jail."

"Pardon me?" Wilhelm's shock made Louise glad that they hadn't sent their most recent effort to Carlene.

He read it over and, to Louise's relief, started laughing.

"The widows who were flirting with me? I'm guessing that has to do with a chapel I went to in Paris called Saint Chapelle. It was built by a king to house what he thought was the original crown of thorns that Jesus wore at His Crucifixion. It was the most amazing church I have ever seen. The walls contained stained-glass windows that soared fifty, sixty feet above the chapel floor with narrow stone pillars between them. When I stepped inside, it was a glorious symphony of light and color that simply can't be described adequately." Wilhelm's enthusiasm surprised the women. It must have made a strong impression. "I believe I said that it looked as though they were floating."

And Louise understood what the "flirting widows" really were. She should have gone with her first guess.

"And jail?" Jane asked eagerly.

Wilhelm laughed. "Yes. That part is true."

Louise looked at him, shocked. "How can that be?"

"Attached to Saint Chapelle is the place where Marie Antoinette was imprisoned. You could go into the jail there. I had a friend take a picture of me behind the bars." He looked over his letter again, shaking his head. "I was overwhelmed by all the history of the place. Paris was simply awe-inspiring. I would love to go again."

"Speaking of love?" Louise pointed out the passage in question.

"*Ahh*, the Louvre." Wilhelm sighed again. "I could not begin to describe the wonders of that place. So much art and culture all housed in one building. It defies description. I got some pictures of my trip developed while we were in France and brought them along." He pulled an envelope of pictures out of the pocket of his coat, resting on a nearby chair, and quickly flipped through them.

Louise caught glimpses of famous landmarks and wanted to ask him about each, but Wilhelm obviously had other things to show them.

He laid a series of pictures out on the table, overlapping them. "Here I am," he pointed to a tiny figure standing at the end of the wing of a huge, U-shaped building surrounding a beautiful garden. The building was made of stone, three stories high, and it was crowned with a roof that had other windows tucked in it, and arches of carved friezes running along it. On two floors, windows had niches between them, each one holding a statue. It was a marvel of architecture combined with sculpture and art, and if the outside was so remarkable, one could only guess at the treasures stored within.

"It would take months to see all the wonders stored in the Louvre," Wilhem said, fussing with the photos. "I spent two days inside, and I only saw a small part of all that was there."

"Did you see the Eiffel Tower?" Alice asked.

"Oh yes. And Notre Dame and the Arc de Triomphe and much, much more." Wilhelm shook his head, as if still overwhelmed by what he had seen. "Say what you want about the French, they do have some of the most beautiful architecture in the world. At least in my opinion. There are bridges that themselves are works of art. And the history. I even saw some Roman ruins being restored." It wasn't hard to hear the wonder in his voice.

"Did you find any good French bakeries?" Jane asked.

Wilhelm looked up and placed his hand on his heart. "The *pâtissiers* there . . ." his voice trailed off.

"That good, huh?" Jane said.

"You have to put your pictures in an album," Alice said. "I'm sure more people would like to see them."

"I hope to. I also need to choose some to give to Carlene to put in the paper." Wilhelm went through the pictures he had and explained more of the things he had seen, and he had seen a lot in the short time he had been gone.

After they had chatted awhile, Louise went over his letters and made notes for an article for the *Nutshell* that made far more sense.

"I'm glad you managed to catch us before we had you sitting in jail in Paris," Louise joked as she folded up his last letter.

"Can you imagine the fuss that would have caused?" Alice said. "I'm glad you could clear this up first."

"I am as well. I don't imagine it would enhance my standing in the town," Wilhelm said.

"At any rate, you will still have some explaining to do about the first article," Louise said. "And I'm sorry about that."

Wilhelm waved away her apology. "That doesn't matter. This last column should explain things adequately." He rose and gathered up his letters and pictures. "In a town like Acorn Hill, people have few secrets."

They said good-bye, and when the sisters had gathered in the kitchen again, Jane turned to Alice and Louise.

"Do you ever have an urge to go traveling?" she asked. "To go to interesting places and meet interesting people?"

"You mean that after a weekend of murder and mayhem and Tilda Tome and Tex Holdem, you would want to go somewhere else?" Alice pretended to look shocked.

Jane laughed. "I guess we have more than enough happening here to keep us entertained."

"And if there isn't enough, why, we can embellish on what we are told," Louise said.

"I don't think you need to worry about Wilhelm's story," Jane said. "I think he was a little bit pleased to discover that you thought he had a dangerous, horse-hunting streak in him."

"If anyone has a dangerous streak, I suspect it would be you," Louise retorted. "After your mystery play, I am wondering what dark and sinister tendencies you have."

"Make sure to keep me in your will and everything will be just peachy," Jane said, winking at her sister.

"I guess I'll have to make a visit to my lawyer," Louise said. "Just so I can sleep well at night."

"You don't have to worry about your pretty neck," Jane said. "I love you too much to off you just for some money. I know where my treasure is." She looked at Alice, then back at Louise. "I believe it's right here."

"And I believe you are right," Louise said.

About the Author

*C*arolyne Aarsen is the author of more than twenty books, including *The Only Best Place* and *All in One Place*. She and her husband have raised four children and numerous foster children, and live on a farm in Alberta, Canada.

Tales from Grace Chapel Inn

Once you visit the charming village of Acorn Hill, you'll never want to leave. Here, the three Howard sisters reunite after their father's death and turn the family home into a bed and breakfast. They rekindle old memories, rediscover the bonds of sisterhood, revel in the blessings of friendship and meet many fascinating guests along the way.